REST
IN PEACE

by Bill Crider
Writing as Jack McClane

PROLOGUE

There was no church. As far as anyone knew, there had never been a church. But there was a graveyard.

No one was exactly sure why it was there. It had been there even before there was a town, and by the time people came to live nearby the tops of the earliest graves were already sunken and overgrown, and the words scratched on the rough stones had already become almost indistinguishable.

There were some who thought that it would not be a good idea to build a town there, that the graveyard was a bad omen, but the soil was good and the climate was pleasant. What did a few graves matter?

The graveyard did little to spoil the beauty of the countryside, with its tall pecan trees, its rustling oaks, its whispering elms. In fact, the graves were practically hidden by the trees and the weeds which grew all around in such profusion that it was as if they drew a special sustenance from the soil there.

Perhaps the first grave had been that of a Spanish explorer, for those were the men who had first wandered through the region. He might have been killed by a vengeful Indian, or he might have died from a fever brought on by exposure and hardship. He might have been killed by one of his own companions, who was brought to justice by the others and buried beside the man he had murdered.

It didn't really matter. The first grave was dug and the first stone was set, and after that there were others buried nearby.

The others might have been placed there because one grave had already been dug. Whoever buried the others might have thought that they were using consecrated ground, though there was not church to be seen.

And so the graveyard grew.

One old stone said that the person who rested beneath it had been "killed by Mexican bandits," though it gave no name.

Another said that in the ground there rested a man "who read the Bible."

And another told of a man who was shot by an Indian arrow.

Those were the stones that could still be read when the town was settled by the members of a group trying to escape the effects of the Civil War in Georgia. They had come to Texas looking for a new start, a start they hoped to make with little to sustain them except the willingness to work hard and the hope that what was past would someday cease to haunt them.

They brought with them some broken sticks of furniture, some worn farm tools, their Bibles, and a few bags of cotton seed. Money was in short supply, and some of them had none at all.

There was plenty of land in Texas, though, and this place where they stopped to rest had a spring that ran sweet and clear from the side of a little hill, collecting water in a shallow pool where they could scoop it up in their hands and drink.

They stayed the night there, and when they woke up the next morning someone suggested that they stay.

"The land looks right fertile," he said. "We could clear the land and plant cotton here, build our homes. Why wear ourselves out travelin'? This here's as good a spot as we could wish for."

Someone else had found the graveyard by then.

It was a good way down the hill from the spring, but some of the children had been playing hide and seek and run across the stones in a clearing in the trees.

"It's graves, sure enough," a man said after the children had come running back and told the adults what they had seen. "I don't know as I like the idea of buildin' a town by a graveyard."

The adults trooped through the trees and looked at the graves, tried to make out the inscriptions on the stones.

"Maybe we should just move on," a woman said. "It don't

She was a hell of a lot faster than he thought she had any right to be. It was like shedding the blankets had given her wings.

Or maybe she was just scared.

Gideon guessed he would have been scared too if some fella was chasin' him up the road and wavin' a knife drippin' blood from some man's throat.

Whatever it was, she could run like hell, and Gideon thought for a while there he wasn't going to be able to catch her. His breath was coming hard and there was a burning in his chest. His side felt like somebody was sticking him with a hot poker.

But the woman fell down.

She had gotten back on the road, where the going should have been easier, but she stepped on a rock or maybe just got her feet tangled. Whatever it was, she fell right there in the road, and that gave Gideon all the time he needed to catch up with her.

She started screaming again before he got to her.

She hadn't screamed while she was running, saving her wind for the chase, but she was screaming as she tried to get up, screaming as Gideon grabbed her by the arm, screaming as he brought the knife down on her throat and sliced it left to right, the sharp slivery blade moving so fast that it was no more than a blur.

The scream became gurgling and then died away as Gideon felt the hot blood gush out over his hand.

seem right, there bein' graves here and not even a church around."

"We'll build a church," a man said. "And we'll be needin' a graveyard soon enough."

There was no arguing with that, and before long everyone was in agreement. This was the place they would stay.

They built their homes, and they cleared the land. They planted their cotton, and the fields were green and thick with it by the next summer.

The church was built, too, and they gathered there on Sundays to give thanks to the Lord for their good fortune.

The people prospered, and soon there was a town, with a school and stores and a graveyard of its own.

They named the town Springville, for the water that still flowed pure and sweet from the stones in the side of the hill.

But for some reason they did not disturb the graveyard they had found there. When the first of their number died, the buried him in a new plot not far from the church; somehow they did not want to disturb the old graves with newly dug earth.

It wasn't as if they were frightened. It wasn't that, or so they told themselves.

Oh, there were stories about the old graves, stories that were told late at night around a crackling fire in the winter or in the lazy summer evenings to pass the time. Stories that things had been there at night—the white, moving glow that might have been a ghost, though everyone dismissed it as a will o' the wisp; the unaccountable movement of the trees in the stillest of nights; the animals that approached the trees on a dead run only to stop in their tracks and back away, the hair on their backs bristling stiffly.

So that part of the land was never cleared. The trees there were left to grow thick and tall and throw their black shadows over the land, and if there were noises in the woods—and there were—no one ever went to investigate them.

No one was ever curious enough to wonder what the sounds might be; no one was ever curious enough to see if they were made by man or animal or something that was neither one.

There were places down by the graveyard that would have

made fine home sites, but no one built there.

"We just like it better up the hill," everyone said. "More sunshine, and you can see better from up here. See all around. You can see the cotton growin' in the summer. We like that."

Finally, though, there was a house down there, right in the shadows of the trees, right where whoever lived in it could look out his windows and practically see the graves that moldered in the woods.

It was a strange house, and it was hardly right to say that it was built. More like it was thrown together of ill-fitting boards and whatever came to hand. It looked like it was going to be cold in the winter and wet when it rained.

The people who lived there were a ragged-looking bunch, too, fit for the house they inhabited.

Their name was Harp, but everybody who saw them knew these Harps were not the kind the angels played.

The old man was tall, well over six feet, and burly as a bear. He had a thick black beard and thick, black, greasy hair that hung down from beneath his greasy hat and brushed the shoulders of his coat.

His two sons looked the same, and their slatternly wives were unkempt and plumply white, harried by both their husbands and the swarm of squalling brats that surrounded them.

The Harps had no desire to become farmers.

They did no work as far as anyone could tell, yet they always seemed to have enough to get by on and they always paid their bills at the general store.

They did a lot of hunting in the woods, and people figured they ate pretty well on squirrel and possum and the occasional raccoon. Whatever else they got, and where they got it, they didn't talk about. And no one asked.

The people of Springville knew the Harps were no good, and were up to no good, but as long as they didn't bother the folks who lived nearby no one was willing to say anything.

No one wanted to cause trouble.

No one wanted to stir them up. The Harps looked like they could be mighty dangerous if they got stirred up.

So people left them alone. If they came to town, no one spoke to them except the storekeepers, and they spoke only if they could not avoid it.

There was an unspoken truce between the Harps and the people of Springville that lasted for a good many years.

And then things began to happen.

PART I

"The number of the dead long exceedeth all that shall live."

—Sir Thomas Browne, "Hydriotaphia, Urn-Burial"

CHAPTER ONE

First it was chickens.

Nearly everyone had some around the house and yard. They spent most of the day scratching and clucking, but now and then they would go into the hen house, if there was one, or into the grass nearby, and lay an egg to pay for their keep. Sometimes on Sunday, a good fat hen would be killed and baked or fried for dinner, along with potatoes or dumplings and giblet gravy.

The Harps had chickens, too, but they were a scrawny breed, not much given to laying eggs and hardly fit for the table. But apparently the Harps liked to eat chicken as much as anyone, and if they couldn't eat their own they would eat someone else's.

That didn't seem so bad to most folks. If the Harps needed a hen, well, let them have it. It was better than having them break in the house and steal something really valuable; chickens were easily replaced, and there was almost always some old hen setting on her eggs, ready to bring a new brood into the yard.

There was something a little scary about watching the elder Harp stand in his front yard and wring the chicken's neck. He would grasp the squawking bird in his big hand and cut off the sound in mid squawk as he tightened his grip.

Then he would begin to whirl the bird around and around in front of him, going faster and faster until the bird was almost nothing but a blur of feathers.

Suddenly the neck would tear and the body of the hen would fly across the yard, streaking the grass with drops of its blood. When the body hit it would somehow leap to its feet and run horribly around the yard, now and then bumping into a tree or the wash pot and staggering to the side, only to get up and run again until like a child's toy top its energy was depleted and it flopped over on its side.

Harp would stand there holding the neck in his hand, the head drooping down, its beady eyes half open, as if it might be staring in wonder at the curious gyrations of its former body and puzzling over how the body could do such things without the insignificant brain that had once guided it.

Harp would look up the hill to see if anyone might be watching him, and if anyone was he might hold up the head and neck and let a little of the blood drip down on his tongue. Then he would toss the head aside casually and retrieve the body. Later, when they were singeing the pinfeathers off over a low wood fire, the smell of the burning would carry all the way up to the top of the hill.

There were other things, much worse things, but those didn't affect the people on the hill.

At least they *told* themselves they weren't affected.

What did it matter to them, after all, if a stranger who came through the town didn't make it to his destination? They couldn't be held responsible for every pilgrim who lost his way. Travel in Texas was dangerous; everyone knew that, and if a man couldn't look out for himself he ought not to be a traveler. He ought to stay at home where he belonged.

That was what they told themselves.

Some of them might even have believed it.

But some of them knew better. Some of them knew that the Harps were more than chicken thieves. Some of them knew that the Harps had to be getting their money from somewhere. They bought things at the store—flour and sugar and salt and coffee and now and then a bit of cloth for a dress for one of the women—but they raised no crops and they did not work for anyone.

Some of the people knew or suspected where the money came from, all right.

They kept their mouths shut, though, when relatives of missing men came to the town asking about their kin, or if they talked they said no more than "Yep, that sounds like the fella that was through here a few weeks back. I talked to him while he was buying a can of tomatoes over to the store. Seemed like a nice enough fella, but kinda quiet. He never said where he was goin' to. You say he never made it to your place? I wonder what could've happened to him, now?"

No one ever said what everyone was thinking, and that was that the Harps had killed the man and taken what he had. The first few times, people might have thought it was outlaws on the trail, or maybe wild animals. Or maybe even that the fella had got himself lost and just starved to death before he came to another trail. They even told themselves that the traveler might've found himself some place on the trail that he liked better than the place he was headed and just put down roots right there.

But they knew better.

They knew that the Harps were the cause of the disappearances.

No one said it aloud. No one said how they knew. But everyone knew that it was so.

There was a river not far off, and some people thought that if you could see to the bottom of it, which you couldn't, since it was sort of silty green most of the time, you could see the bodies of those travelers, probably with their stomachs slit open and rocks stuffed inside to weight them down.

The rocks would hold them there until the fish ate them, the gars and the catfish getting fat on waterlogged human flesh.

And there were some whose private thoughts went to the graveyard in the trees. They wondered if there weren't some new graves there, some that were not marked by stones, dug hurriedly and shallow in the depths of the night, the bodies stripped and rolled in and covered over before the dawn.

No one mentioned such a thing, however. No one said a word.

They knew the Harps too well by then, had seen the light of madness in their eyes, had seen the utter contempt with which the Harps regarded others, had seen the complete indifference those eyes held toward human life.

No one wanted to mess with the Harps, and no one did.

Until the day that Jeremiah West came to Springville.

CHAPTER TWO

Jeremiah West was a man who believed in all the things the Harps detested: hard work, honesty, and community.

He came to Springville long after the Harps appeared on the scene, after the elder Harp begun to look more like a biblical patriarch than an outlaw. His long hair and beard were thickly streaked with white now, and he walked bent over and used a cane.

He still killed chickens in the yard, however, and any number of people who passed through town still failed of reaching their ultimate destinations. His sons had become middle-aged and their children were grown.

The old man's grandsons had found wives of their own from somewhere, wives that looked much like the sluttish women their fathers had married. The daughters had gone off, no doubt to be sluttish wives of men like their brothers.

A couple of new houses had appeared down by the graveyard, looking exactly like the original home of the Harps. They looked dilapidated and ancient the first day they were seen, leaky and drafty and entirely unhealthy, though no matter how they looked the Harps seemed to thrive in them.

For his first few years in Springville, Jeremiah West ignored the Harps. They might not have existed for all he seemed to care. He was interested in his wife with the shining blonde hair and in starting a family of his own to carry on his name after he was gone.

And he was interested in his work. He plowed and planted and picked the cotton alongside the men he had hired to help him. He worked harder than any other man in Springville; it was as if he were driven to earn both money and the respect of others.

His final interest was in the town itself. He wanted it to have everything, to be the best town because it was his town.

The money that he wanted came to him, and with it came ideas.

Why should he and the others have to haul their cotton to a neighboring town to have it ginned? Why shouldn't they have a gin of their own?

He used his own money and his land as collateral and got a loan. He built a gin.

With the gin came more money, and West began to believe that the town should have a bank. It was a big enough town, he said. Why shouldn't it have a bank?

Soon it did, and Jeremiah West was its owner. He no longer had to go to the fields and work from daylight till dark.

He did his business in the town now, but he still held onto the land, still saw that it was worked each year, that its cotton crop was planted and picked.

He still owned the gin, too, and the respect he had looked for was fully his. He was looked up to by everyone in Springville as a hard worker, a shrewd businessman, an honest banker, and a devoted family man.

For he had his family now, too, a little girl with hair as fair and blonde as her mother's, and two strong sons who were often seen running and playing in the dusty streets around their home.

Not a day passed that Jeremiah West did not take his children into his arms and hug them to him, thanking God for his good fortune.

He began to think about a new home for them and for his wife, a place more in keeping with his new status in the community, something larger, more spacious, more comfortable.

He could afford it now, certainly, and his wife deserved a reward for her own hard work. She had been beside him in the cotton fields every day, working as hard as he did. She had dragged a sack and picked cotton until her fingers bled. He wanted her to have the benefits of their success, and a new home would be just the thing to please her.

There was a prime spot down by the bottom of the hill, not far from where the spring flowed out of the rocks. No one held title to the land; no one even seemed to want it, though it seemed to West to be a fine place for a house.

"I don't understand it," West said one day to Harmon Giles, one of his tellers and a man West had come to confide in. "That's a perfect spot for a house. You can see the trees from there, and the way the land sweeps on down to the river bottom. Why doesn't anyone want to build there?"

"They like it up here on the hill," Giles said. He was a big man, with a comfortable stomach that strained his shirt front and stretched his suspenders. He took life easy whenever he could and didn't go out of his way to look for difficulties. "Folks say they can see their crops from up here, and they like the feelin' of bein' up high, just in case that river ever floods."

West shook his head. He was tall, with an impressive shock of black hair that fell over his forehead. "That can't be it," he said. That land down there's just as fertile as anything up the hill. Maybe better. They could grow their corps down there just was well as up on the hill. There must be something else."

"Well," Giles said, "there's the Harps."

"The Harps?" West said.

"Them and the graveyard," Giles said.

"What graveyard?" West said. He had come to Springville so long after the founding of the town that he had never seen the graveyard, nor even heard of it. It wasn't something that people talked much about, and most of them had probably forgotten it was even there.

Giles hadn't forgotten. He had been in Springville for a long time, having worked his own farm before taking on the less taxing work of being a teller, a job more in keeping with his desire to keep his hands clean and to work somewhere out of the hot sun.

"There's a graveyard down there in that woods," Giles said. They were sitting in West's office. It was late spring, and the weather was hot and humid. The windows in the office were open, and there was even a slight breeze, but Giles was beginning to sweat in his high-collared shirt, and he could feel the sleeve garters cutting into his arms.

"There's nothing wrong with a graveyard," West said, but he found himself wondering about it. "Who's buried there?"

"Nobody I know," Giles said. "Way I heard it, that graveyard was already here when the town got settled. But you know how some folks are; nobody wanted to build down there close to it. A graveyard is the kind of thing that spooks some folks."

"The Harps didn't mind building near it," West pointed out.

He knew about the family, but only vaguely. He had seen their ramshackle house, now nearly overgrown by the very woods that sheltered the graveyard.

"Well, you know the Harps," Giles said, clearly not comfortable with the subject. He ran his finger around and beneath the top of the shirt collar.

"No," West said. "I don't know the Harps. Why don't you tell me about them."

Giles did not want to talk about the Harps, but once West set his mind on something there was nothing to do but go along with him. He wasn't the sort of a man to give up just because you didn't want to talk to him about a thing.

At the same time, knowing that he was going to tell West what he wanted to know, Giles did not want to talk too much. He had the uneasy feeling that the Harps knew everything that went on in Springville, though they never seemed to have anything to do with the life of the town. He didn't know what the Harps might do to someone who told all their secrets, real or imagined, and he didn't want to find out.

"They kind of keep to themselves," Giles said, squirming on the leather seat of the chair he was sitting in. "There's not much to say about them because nobody really knows that much about them."

"Tell me what you do know, then," West said. It wasn't an order, but his voice was firm.

"I don't really *know* all that much," Giles said. "You've been livin' here a few years now. You probably know as much as I do."

"I don't know a thing," West said. "I just know they live

down there at the edge of the woods and that they aren't customers of the bank."

"I don't expect they'd put much stock in a bank," Giles said. "They don't have many dealin's with people here in town."

"How do they make a living?" West asked. "And how many of them are there, anyway?"

"There's a whole nest of 'em," Giles said. "Nobody knows for sure just how many. There's the old man, of course, and the sons, and their wives, and *their* sons and wives. "Lots of young'uns, too, I'd guess."

"Sounds like quite a family to keep up for a bunch that doesn't ever seem to do any work," West said.

"They don't need much," Giles said. He ran his finger under his collar again, wondering how West could sit there and look so cool on a day like this. Didn't the man ever sweat? "I guess they live off the land, eat a lot of possum, things like that."

"A man gets tired of possum," West said. "I believe I've see some of them in town, too, at the store now and then. They must get money from somewhere."

"Well, I don't know where," Giles told him. "Like you said, they don't appear to do much work."

"But you have an idea of where they get it," West said. "Don't you?"

Giles did, of course, but he didn't want to say. "It's just gossip. Nobody knows, not for sure."

"What's the gossip, then? Those are the people I might be having for my neighbors, after all."

"You wouldn't want to do that, Mr. West," Giles said. "You wouldn't really like livin' down there."

"Why not? You don't seem to know of anything against them."

"Well …" Giles said.

"Out with it, man," West said. "I want to know."

Giles sighed. "They steal chickens," he said, and then he realized how weak that sounded. He had to go on and tell the rest now. "And some folks think they're robbers. They think maybe they're highwaymen."

"Tell me about the chickens."

"It's just chickens. Nothin' unusual. Nobody's ever caught 'em at it, but we all know where those chickens come from."

"Where's that?"

"Somebody else's chicken house, that's where. Old man kills them right in his front yard. Wrings their necks out where ever'body can see. It's like he just dares anybody do something about it."

"And nobody ever does?"

"Nope. Nobody does a damn thing."

West shook his head in disgust. It was the first he'd heard about the chicken stealing; he began to think that he'd spent too much time wrapped up in his own concerns. He needed to devote more time to the town and what went on in it.

"And people think the Harps do even worse things? That they're highwaymen? I didn't think that kind of thing went on around here anymore, if it ever did," West said.

"You'd be surprised at the kind of things that can happen," Giles said. "Now and then somebody comes to town lookin' for a lost relative, someone who was supposed to pass by this way. Sometimes they did pass by here, but they never got no further."

"Is that true?" West said.

Giles was already sorry he'd said it. It wouldn't mean anything but trouble if West got on some kind of crusade about the Harps.

"I don't know that it's true," he said. "I told you it was just gossip." He wished he could get up and leave the office, but he knew better than to try that.

"The part about the chickens … was that just gossip, too?"

"No," Giles admitted. "That part was true, all right. I've seen the old man wring those chicken necks with my own eyes."

"So the other part might be just as true," West said.

"I guess it might be," Giles said. "Nobody's ever proved it, though."

"Has anybody ever tried?" West asked.

It was exactly the question Giles had been afraid of. It would be just like West to go out and try to prove the Harps were outlaws and killers. Nothing good would come out of that. It would just stir things up.

Giles didn't like for things to get stirred up.

"Mr. West," Giles said. "You don't want to live down there by that graveyard. You got a nice place where you are. You could just tear down that house of yours and build a new one right there on the same spot. You'd have you a real good view of the town from there, see what goes on. Down at the bottom of that hill, you won't be able to see any people but the Harps."

"That's what's sort of bothering me," West said. "If I'm going to live by them, I want to know about them. I don't like the idea of living next door to criminals."

"They might not be criminals," Giles said, but his voice lacked conviction.

"That's just something I'll have to find out about," West said.

Giles left the office feeling slightly sick to his stomach. He told himself that it was just something he had eaten earlier that day for lunch, but he knew that it wasn't. He knew that it was what had been said in West's office. Nothing good would come of messing around with the Harps. He was as sure of that as he was of anything in this world.

CHAPTER THREE

It was getting dark sooner than Tom Chandler thought it would. He wished now that he had stopped for the night in Springville, but he had pushed on, hoping to make it to the county seat before dark.

There weren't any real accommodations for travelers in Springville, and Chandler had been hoping to spend the night in a real bed for the first time in weeks. He was getting tired of sleeping in the back of the wagon, covered with a thin blanket, going to sleep to the sound of buzzing insects and night birds.

As the twilight gathered, however, he began to think that he would have been wiser just to stop in Springville. There was something about the woods he was driving by that seemed wrong, somehow.

The trees weren't any different from any other trees, he thought, but there was something sinister in the way the wind whispered through them and stirred their leaves.

"It's just the wind," he said aloud, but saying it didn't make him feel any better.

He listened to the creaking of the wagon traces, and he heard the call of an owl from somewhere in the woods. He flicked the reins to encourage his horses to move a little faster.

Just ahead the road passed beneath a particularly tall tree. Its branches stretched out over the path and joined the branches of another tree on the other side. Beneath the canopy of their limbs the thick shadows were as dark as night.

The horses hesitated slightly, and Chandler flicked the reins again. "Giddy up, you lazy sacks of bones," he said. "There ain't nothin' to be afraid of."

The horses passed under the branches of the trees. Chandler could see the swiftly fading sunlight on the other side.

It was the last thing he ever saw.

Gideon Harp nudged his brother. "Here he comes."

"I see 'im," Gabriel said.

They were crouched on the thick limb that hung over the road, their bare feet clinging to the rough tree bark as they waited for the man to pass beneath them.

They were twins, old Michael Harp's grandsons. They were stringy and tall, with long hair that hung in front of their eyes. They wore ragged clothing that had not been washed in a long time. Maybe it had never been washed. It was stained with grime and grease and other things that were not so easy to identify.

"Get ready," Gideon said.

"Hush your goddamn mouth," Gabriel told him. "You want him to hear you?"

"I just don't want you to make no mistakes," Gideon said. He was the older of the two by five minutes, or so he had always been told. He liked to think that being older gave him the advantage over his brother, made him the leader. He always wanted to be the one to give the orders.

"I know what to do as well as you do," Gabriel said. "Prob'ly better. Who's the one nearly let that bitch get away last winter?"

Gideon didn't like to think about that. He knew he had been at fault, and the whole family knew what it would mean if someone got away from them. The Old Man had told them often enough.

"They'd hunt us down like a pack o' dogs," the Old Man said. "Kill us like we was animals. People like that"—he would always point up the hill when he talked about 'people like that'—"they don't live like us. They think they're better than we are, and it wouldn't be nothin' to them to come down here and kill us all, burn the houses, and take this place for theirselves."

"It ain't nothin' to us to kill them, neither," Gideon said.

"That's different," the old man told him. "We ain't like them. We can kill 'cause that's what God put us on this earth to do. Like a hawk kills a rabbit. It's right for us, but people like that"—he pointed up the hill again—"they don't understand that. They're soft, someway. They think killin's wrong, and they wouldn't do it less they thought there was nothin' else left for them to do."

Gideon didn't quite understand that. He didn't see anything wrong with killin' a man if that man had something you wanted or needed. It was what his family had always done, and when he got old enough, he did it too.

It seemed to him to be the most natural thing in the world, and he said so.

"You're right, sonny," the Old Man said. "Right as goddamn rain. But they wouldn't see it like that. That's why we have to be careful. That's why we don't kill any of them up there. Just the ones passin' by, the ones that we can take care of in our own way. Nobody'll bother us if we stick to doin' that."

Nobody would bother them, that is, as long as no one found out, and no one would find out unless someone told.

And who was to tell? Not the victims, that was for damn sure.

Not unless one of them got away.

Which is exactly what had almost happened one dark winter night.

Gideon and Gabriel had been in the very same tree where they waited now, and they were waiting on another wagon to pass under the limb.

Gideon thought the mistake was as much Gabriel's as anybody's, but it didn't do any good to say that. Nobody would listen to him.

The problem was that there was one more person in the wagon than they thought there was. They were always careful not to take on more than one person at a time.

It wasn't that they were afraid of more than one, or that they doubted that they could take care of them. It was just that they didn't want to take chances.

But the woman had been in the wagon bed, wrapped up in blankets against the cold. The man had been in the seat, and it looked to the twins like he was alone.

They had been watching him since he left town, making

sure that there was no one else traveling with him, no one else coming along the trail after him, and they had seen nobody.

The woman had been there all the time, of course, but they had never noticed her. The bitch had been too quiet, too still.

Hell, Gideon thought, it was like she was half-dead already.

So when they dropped down from the limb, they had taken the man by complete surprise. They had his arms pinned and his throat slit before he even knew what was happening to him.

It was quiet and fast, but the woman heard them.

She rose up and scared the piss out of them, to tell the truth of it. It was like she was some kind of goddamn ghost, rising up out of the back of the wagon.

They dropped the man, who fell out of the wagon and bounced on the road, his cut throat spilling blood all around.

By then, the woman was screaming, and they knew she wasn't any ghost. Gideon made a jump for her, but she moved back and he landed hard in the wagon bed. She threw the blankets off and jumped out before he could get up and started running through the woods.

Since he was the one who had made the move, he was the one who had to go after her. He chased her through the trees, the dead branches scratching at his face and the dry vines trying to clutch at his legs and bring him down.

She was a hell of a lot faster than he thought she had any right to be. It was like shedding the blankets had given her wings.

Or maybe she was just scared.

Gideon guessed he would have been scared too if some fella was chasin' him up the road and wavin' a knife drippin' blood from some man's throat.

Whatever it was, she could run like hell, and Gideon thought for a while there he wasn't going to be able to catch her. His breath was coming hard and there was a burning in his chest. His side felt like somebody was sticking him with a hot poker.

But the woman fell down.

She had gotten back on the road, where the going should have been easier, but she stepped on a rock or maybe just got her feet tangled. Whatever it was, she fell right there in the road, and that gave Gideon all the time he needed to catch up with her.

She started screaming again before he got to her.

She hadn't screamed while she was running, saving her wind for the chase, but she was screaming as she tried to get up, screaming as Gideon grabbed her by the arm, screaming as he brought the knife down on her throat and sliced it left to right, the sharp slivery blade moving so fast that it was no more than a blur.

The scream became gurgling and then died away as Gideon felt the hot blood gush out over his hand.

He dropped the woman in the road and looked down at her. He couldn't tell much about her because she was wearing a coat and heavy clothing. He cut the buttons off the coat and pulled it open; then he began cutting off her clothes.

Blood always excited him.

The woman's breasts spilled out of her dress and Gideon got even more excited. They were large and firm, with a light sprinkling of freckles.

He began tugging at his belt. He was about to lie down on the woman when Gabriel kicked him hard in the side, throwing him off the woman and onto the road.

"Goddamn you, Gideon! You let the bitch get away, and now you're all over her like a fuckin' dog! Get her off the road before somebody else comes along and sees you."

Gideon was immediately sorry for what he had done. He knew that he had put the whole family in danger. Like the Old Man said, folks wouldn't understand that he was just doing what he had to do, what he had ever' right to do.

He dragged the woman off the road and went with Gabriel to get the man and the wagon. They threw the man in the wagon, then drove back for the woman and threw her in, too. Kicked dirt over the blood stains in the road.

"You wanna fuck somebody, fuck Hester," Gabriel said. Hester was Gideon's wife.

"Goddamn it, Gideon, sometimes I think you don't have a lick of sense."

Gideon could tell that although Gabriel appeared to be mad

as hell, he was secretly pleased with what had happened. The younger twin was always gleeful when his brother got into trouble, and he probably just couldn't wait to tell the old man and the others all about what had happened.

They drove the wagon through the trees. The Old Man would take it off and sell it and the horses, coming back in a few days with the money. They never asked where he took the wagons to sell, and he never said.

They would dump the bodies in the river, or maybe bury them in the old graveyard after going through the clothes for valuables. And of course they would take anything of value from the wagon.

That was the way they always did it, and that was what they planned to do with the man coming down the trail right now.

When Chandler passed under the tree branch, the two men dropped straight down upon him.

Gideon took the reins as Gabriel, his knife already in hand, bore the man down in the wagon bed.

They had been careful this time. They knew that there was no one else there.

The man struck a few feeble blows at Gabriel's head and cried out for help, but there was no help coming.

"Don't kill him in the fuckin' wagon," Gideon yelled. "You know the Old Man don't like blood on the wagon."

It was too late.

Chandler's throat was slit and the wagon bed was already slick with blood.

"Shit," Gideon said. "Now we're gonna have to clean the damn thing up."

"You just drive on home," Gabriel said. "Least I didn't let him get away."

Gideon was getting plenty tired of hearin' that, but he clamped his lips together and didn't say anything. He wasn't goin' to let Gabriel goad him into a fight.

"I'm drivin'," he said. In the back of his mind was the idea that one of these days he was goin' to do something about his twin, something that would not be pleasant—at least for Gabriel.

As for himself, he planned to enjoy it very much.

Chapter Four

It was a week later that the man came to Springville looking for Tom Chandler.

He wasn't like other men that had come; the others usually took it for granted that the townspeople were telling the truth when they said no such person had ever turned up in town, or if he had, well, no one really remembered him.

Maybe he'd passed through on his way to somewhere else, but no one could remember having seen him. That was the story they always told, at least.

This man wasn't buying any of that.

"I tell you, I know he was through here. And I know he didn't make the county seat. Now I by God want to know what happened to him, and I'm for goddamn sure gonna find out."

That was the way he talked to people, like he didn't believe a word they said, and he was the kind of man who could say it and make you like it, even if down deep inside you didn't like it at all.

He said his name was Rance Chandler and that Tom Chandler was his brother. He was nearly six feet tall, and so wide it looked like he might have to turn himself sideways to get through a door. He looked like he might could pick up a man with one hand and throw him halfway across the street.

Maybe all the way across.

He wasn't the kind of man that people wanted around town asking the kind of questions he was asking.

Questions like, "If he went out of here on that road, where did he wind up? It damn sure wasn't where he was headin', I can tell you that."

Or, "If didn't any of you people see him, how come folks in the last town down the road remember him? If you're saying he never got here, where in hell did he get to?"

And worst of all, "If he did get here, he sure as to God didn't leave here. So where the hell is he?"

Rance Chandler went all over Springville asking things like that. He went to the dry goods store, to the saloon, and to both of the churches. He didn't moderate his language a bit for the preachers, either.

He was about as mad as a man could get without letting things get completely out of hand.

But that didn't mean anyone would tell him anything, though everyone was thinking the same thing. Even the preachers.

No one said it, though. No one even breathed the name of the Harps, not even when they were safe at home with the doors closed and bolted.

It was as if they believed they could make it all go away if they didn't say the name.

If they didn't say the name, it wouldn't have happened and the Harps wouldn't have done anything and the town could be left alone to go on the way it had been going on for years.

It might have worked out that way, too, if Chandler hadn't gone to the bank.

West heard him questioning the teller, Giles. There were no customers in the bank at the time, so Chandler started in on the only one who was there to ask. Chandler's voice was as big as the rest of him, and carried right through West's office door.

West came out of his office to see what was going on.

"Nothin', Mr. West. This fella was just askin' some questions," Giles said. He was sweating freely, though the day was unseasonably cool.

"What questions?" West said.

"Oh, nothin' much," Giles said, wishing that Chandler would just go away, that Mr. West would just go on back in his office.

"Nothin' much!" Chandler boomed. "You call my brother bein' missin' on the road nothin'? You must be one sorry human bein' to feel that way."

"Why don't you come on back to my office," West said. "Tell me about your brother."

Chandler glared at Giles. He had a good face for glaring, weathered and hard, and red now because he was so mad.

"All right," he said. He followed West to the office.

West offered Chandler a chair and sat behind his desk. "Now tell me your story," he said.

Chandler didn't waste any time. "My brother was comin' to live with me in Waco. I got a little blacksmith shop there, do all right. We were going to be partners. He never got there."

"And what does that have to do with Springville?" West asked. He reached into a wooden humidor and got out a cigar, offered one to Chandler.

Chandler refused. "Don't use 'em."

West didn't either, except rarely. He put the one he had taken out back in the humidor. "About your brother and Springville," he said.

"He had to pass through here on his way," Chandler said. "He either never made it here, or he never left. I want to know which one it was. And I want to know why."

West thought about what Giles had told him not so long ago about relatives who came to Springville looking for people who seemed to have disappeared.

He thought about the Harps.

"I may be able to help you," he said.

Chandler gave him a hard look. He seemed to like what he saw. "All right," he said. "How?"

West would most likely not have been able to do a thing had the Harps not made a mistake.

It could have been overconfidence. They had lived for years with complete immunity from harm, and they had no reason to think that anything had changed.

Or maybe it was simply laziness.

For whatever reason, however, the Old Man had put off selling the wagon Gideon and Gabriel had taken from Tom Chandler.

"That's it, by God. That's Tom's wagon," Rance Chandler said. "Let's go in there and get the bastards."

He and West, along with three other men, all of them armed with either rifles or shotguns, were standing in the woods and looking at the wagon that stood in the back yard of Gideon and Gabriel's house.

"We can't just go in there," West said.

"That's his goddamn horses, too," Chandler said. "Look at 'em. Tied right there in the yard."

The horses stood there calmly. They were not tied as Chandler said. Rather, they were hobbled. The effect was the same. They stood where they were, cropping the grass.

"Why can't we just bust in and get those bastards?" Chandler demanded.

"We're not the law," West said. "We can't pretend that we are."

Springville didn't have a law officer. The town was so small that there had never seemed to be a need for one. The worst crime that anyone knew of was chicken stealing, or at least that was the worst crime that anyone was willing to talk about.

"We're as close to the law as there is around here," Chandler said. "Now we're gonna go in there and get 'em, or I'm gonna do it by myself."

There was no doubt that he meant it.

West stood there looking at the house. It looked like it might fall down at any minute, its weathered sides full of cracks, the windows lacking glass, the roof practically nonexistent. The yard was filled with weeds that came up almost to the horse's bellies.

West wondered how people could live like that.

He also wondered why he was so hesitant. He was convinced that what they were doing was right. The evidence was right there in front of them. In a case like that, he was usually ready to take action.

But something seemed to be holding him back now, and he couldn't figure out what it was.

The other men were even less eager to go after the Harps than West was.

"We ain't the law," Giles said. "Mr. West is right. We ain't got no business here at all."

He spoke in low tones so that his voice wouldn't carry beyond the edge of the trees, but he was still scared that somehow the Harps would hear him. He thought they probably had extra-sharp ears, like animals, being as they were about half animal anyhow, to his way of thinking. He didn't want to have anything to do with them.

He wouldn't have been there himself if West hadn't practically forced him to come along, and neither would the other two men, Harve Preston and Curly Nelson, who now worked the land that West owned. They owed him, just like Giles did, so they were there.

But that didn't mean they liked it.

Rance Chandler didn't give a damn whether they liked it or not. He was going to find out about his brother, come hell or high water. He leveled his twelve-gauge and stepped out of the trees.

West stepped out behind him.

He felt like he had to. He was the one who had suggested they look down there in the first place. He didn't want the others to think he was a coward. But he felt still that something wasn't right, that they were making a mistake by taking action.
He just didn't know what it was.

"Son of a bitch," Gideon said. "They're gonna come after us."

He was looking out of a crack in the wall of the house. Behind him, on the floor, four small children were playing. Their hair was so long and matted it was impossible to determine their sex. The two women in the room, for there was really only one room, sat quietly in cobbled together stools that were even more rickety than the house itself. Their hands were clasped in their laps, and they watched the children with grave eyes.

"Fuckers," Gabriel said, looking over his brother's shoulder. "I knew the Old Man should've sold that rig before now."

"What I wanta know is, should we call him?" Gideon said.

Because West and the other men had approached the house through the woods and come up from behind it, they were out of sight of the other house, the one where Michael and his sons lived, but it was still within easy shouting distance.

"Hell, no," Gabriel said. "We ain't callin' nobody. We can handle those bastards by ourself."

Gideon wasn't so sure. "The Old Man won't like it. He says we oughtn't do any killin' of them folks up the hill."

Gabriel gave a short, harsh laugh. "He didn't know they was gonna come after us when he said that. Look at them guns. What're we supposed to do? Ain't no way him or any other Harp'd let those bastards just come and take 'em."

Gideon still wasn't convinced. "Once the shootin' starts, he's gonna know about it. We might as well give him a holler right now."

"We do that and we'll just give those fuckers a warnin'," Gabriel said. "You want to do that?"

Gideon didn't want to warn anybody, but he didn't want to go against the Old Man, either. He didn't know what to do.

Gabriel knew.

"Here," he said. "Take your shotgun and get ready. We can get ever' damn one of 'em before they know what's happenin'."

He thrust a double barrel into his brother's hand and Gideon took it. He knew it was loaded, but he broke it and checked it anyhow. Then he snapped it back together.

Gabriel handed him some shells. "Try not to hit the horses," he said.

CHAPTER FIVE

Chandler saw them first, as soon as they stepped out of the door, but even then it was too late.

Too late for Chandler, anyway.

Both the twins fired at once, and the first blast from Gideon's double barrel practically took Chandler's head off.

One minute he was walking purposefully across the yard, and then the explosion of the gun sounded. Blood and brains flew everywhere, it seemed to West, who was standing behind him and felt something wet strike his cheek.

The horses whinnied shrilly and tried to run, but there was nowhere they could go, hobbled as they were.

Chandler's headless trunk, like something in a bad dream, took one more step forward and then fell into the weeds.

Giles had already turned to run, but Gabriel's first shot tore out all the meat between his shoulder blades. Took the backbone apart, too. Giles made one step more than Chandler had before he crashed to the ground.

Harve Preston made it almost back to the trees, but Gideon got him with the second barrel. The shot had spread pretty good by the time it hit Harve; he wasn't as messed up as the other two.

Neither was Curly, in a way, because Gabriel nearly missed him. Shot low and blasted his left leg off, just below the knee. Curly fell down and started screaming, clutching his knee and wondering where the rest of his leg had gone. Blood was pumping out of the stump and onto the grass; it didn't take long before all the blood Curly had was drained away, leaving him white and dead.

Gabriel and Gideon broke the guns in two and started shoving in more shells.

That was when West stood up and leveled his Winchester on the two of them.

"That's enough," he said. "Drop the guns."

His voice was shakier than he could ever remember it being. The only reason he was alive was that as soon as the first shot was fired he had dropped to the ground, shielding himself behind Chandler's body, seeing the blood coming out of what was left of Chandler's neck.

He was scared. Flat scared, and he'd never been scared before in his life, not that he could remember. He'd seen men die before, women too, but peaceful, in their beds.

Never anything like this.

It was all he could do to keep his hands from trembling.

Gabriel and Gideon could see that the man was barely in control. They looked at one another and snapped the guns together. The clicking noise they made sounded as loud as thunder in the awful silence that had descended after the shooting.

"I'm telling you," West said. "Drop the guns."

"Fuck you," Gabriel said, bringing up the shotgun.

West acted almost by reflex, pulling the trigger of the rifle. It bucked in his hands and Gabriel staggered backward, a look of terrible surprise on his face. His finger jerked the trigger of the shotgun, but the barrel was pointing down and the blast merely tore a chunk of dirt from the ground, scattering weeds, grass, and clods of earth.

A red stain was spreading across the front of Gabriel's shirt as he fell.

"You son of a bitch," Gideon said.

"Drop the gun, like I said," West told him. His voice was steadier now, and he was no longer afraid. He had discovered in an instant that he was just as deadly as the two men facing him.

Gideon recognized something in the man's face, and he dropped the gun. He had never wanted to kill anyone so much in his life, but he knew he didn't stand a chance.

The fucker had killed Gabriel!

Gideon forgot that he had often thought of killing Gabriel himself, most recently on the very day they had killed the man who owned the wagon. That was different, anyway. Gabriel was his brother, and if anyone killed him, it should have been Gideon.

"Walk over here," West said.

Gideon obeyed sullenly.

"Turn around," West said when Gideon reached him. He put the rifle barrel against the base of Gideon's skull.

The rest of the Harp men, four of them, arrived on the scene then, armed with rifles, pistols, and knives. They stopped short when they saw what was happening, saw that West had Gideon cold.

West had never seen them before, but he was immediately impressed with the Old Man.

Michael peered at him from beneath his craggy brows, his eyes burning with hatred. His white hair swirled around his head like a cloud.

"You let my grandboy go," he said.

"I'm not letting anyone go," West said. "This man's guilty of murder, just like the other one there."

Michael saw the body of Gabriel then, and the eyes burned with an even deeper intensity. The men with him, his sons, muttered to one another.

"You let him go," Michael said. "Now."

"I'm not letting him go. He and the other one killed four men! He's going to be punished for that."

"We Harps do our own punishin'," Michael said. "You let the boy go." He drew a pistol from his belt and pointed it menacingly.

"You point that thing at me and I'll kill him here and now," West said. "I'll blow the back of his head right off. I mean it."

Michael could tell the man was speaking the truth.

"All right, boys, ease off," he said.

The other men lowered their weapons, but they didn't look happy about it.

"We can't let him take Gideon," one of them whined.

"Shut your mouth, Uriel," Michael said. "The man's gonna

kill Gideon if we don't do what he says."

"Gonna kill him anyways, one way or the other," one of the other sons said. "I say we don't let him."

"You can't never tell what might happen later on," Michael said. "Let 'em go, for now."

West began backing toward the woods, careful to keep the rifle pressed into the back of Gideon's head. He did not enter the trees, however, but skirted the edge of the woods. He knew that if he got off into the trees the Harps would come right after him.

Somehow he got Gideon up the hill, and the townspeople came running. They had heard the shots, though they had done nothing. For the first time, West wondered if the town was worth fighting for. Then he put that thought out of his mind.

They tied Gideon up, listening in horror to West's story of what had happened down the hill.

"Good God," Tobe Gregory said. "We got to go down there and get those men's bodies. No tellin' what might happen to 'em if we don't."

Gregory was the owner of the dry goods store and a deacon in the church. His words carried a lot of weight, and the men began to arm themselves. They weren't going to face the Harps with less than enough artillery for an army troop, and they weren't going to face them with fewer than twenty men.

They stashed Gideon, bound and yelling obscenities, in the bank vault and locked the heavy door. Even if he got free of his bonds, he wouldn't be going anywhere.

"What if he can't get no air in there?" someone asked.

"It wouldn't be no big loss, now would it," another man answered, and everyone else agreed.

For the first time they had faced up to what the Harps really were, and they were all filled with the righteousness of the Godly. Had the Harps put up any resistance at all, they would have wiped them out. Everyone in the town knew as well as they knew anything that the Harps were all guilty of the murder of Tom Chandler, no matter whose house the wagon had been standing behind.

But the Harps didn't fight.

The Harps weren't even there.

The houses were completely deserted, though the bodies still lay in the weeds and the horses still stood watchfully by.

"Jesus!" a man called out, looking down at Rance Chandler's headless corpse.

"Oh, God, look what they've done," Tobe Gregory said. He was standing over the body of Curly Nelson. "They've cut off his head."

Curly's head sat on its neck nearby, looking at Gregory's boots with staring eyes.

They had done the same to Harve and Giles.

No one said much after that.

They loaded the bodies into Tom Chandler's wagon silently, all of them thinking more or less that same thing: that if they had moved against the Harps sooner, none of this would have happened. They had known for years what was going on, or if they hadn't known they had certainly suspected. But it was too late to do anything now, or too late to do anything except take the bodies back up the hill and bury them without letting the men's wives get a look at them. That would be too awful.

There were a few of them, however, who had other thoughts, darker ones.

Those were the men who blamed Jeremiah West for everything.

They said nothing then, but later they whispered it among themselves.

"If Jeremiah West had minded his own business," they said, "not a bit of that would've happened. He should never have gone down that hill, down by that graveyard. He knew what the Harps were like, just as much as the rest of us. He could've told that stranger to move along. But he didn't, and now look what it's got us."

Those men were in the minority, though. Most of the others thought that what West had done was right; they were ashamed only that they had not cleared out the Harps long ago.

But the Harps had not been cleared out.

They were right there, all along, watching as the men came down the hill, watching as they discovered the mutilation of the bodies, smiling at the horrified looks on their faces as they saw the form of the Harps' revenge.

"Teach 'em to fuck with the Harps," Saul, one of the sons, whispered.

"Shut it," Michael said.

Saul shut it.

They all watched as the wagon started back up the hill.

"When we goin' back home?" Uriel asked.

"Soon as those bastards are gone," the Old Man said.

They buried the men the next day. There wasn't much the undertaker could do for them.

Gideon survived in the cell, and after the funeral ten men took him to the county seat and gave him to the sheriff. The jail was strong enough to hold him.

He received a fair trial from a jury of his peers and was hanged a few weeks later.

There was nothing the Harps could do.

Not then.

CHAPTER SIX

There were signs, after the hanging, that the Harps were living down the hill again, but those signs were few and far between.

No one ever saw anyone down there.

No one ever heard them.

No one ever went near the spring anymore. It was too close to the woods, too close to the Harps.

There were sometimes glimmers of a light in the Harps' house at night, a light that looked like it was moving from one room to another, but no more travelers disappeared, so people disregarded the light. Just a will o' the wisp, they said.

No Harps ever came to town to buy any kind of goods at all.

It was as if something down there by the graveyard was holding its breath ... waiting.

Jeremiah West was done with waiting. It was time for him to build the house he wanted. Men were hired and the work began.

"Those Harps," Tobe Gregory said. "They might still be down there, Mr. West. They might still be livin' practically right next door to you if you build a house there."

"I don't think they'll bother me," West said. He felt that he had shown the Harps who was boss. They had lost two of their sons and then turned tail and run. It was pretty clear to him what the Harps were made of.

No one reminded him that if the Harps had lost two men, the town had lost three, not counting Rance Chandler.

No one reminded him of the heads.

What he wanted to do was his business, they all supposed,

and if he wanted to build a house where no one else in town would have built one, they weren't going to stop him. He'd been there, and he knew what had happened as well as they did.

Maybe better.

His wife didn't particularly want to go there, but she had expressed a desire for a bigger house and she didn't want to appear to have changed.

One night as they were eating supper, however, she did admit that she had reservations.

"The children are happy here," she said. "Jerry likes to play in the yard, and Charles likes being near town. Elizabeth does, too."

West looked at his wife, the lamplight creating gleaming highlights in her golden hair. He looked at his children, who were watching him expectantly.

"Is that right, Jerry?" he said. "Charles? Is that right? How about you, Elizabeth?"

The children didn't say anything. They all liked the idea of living in a big new house, but they didn't want to upset either of their parents. They didn't know what to say, so they said nothing.

West laughed. He loved them all, and he knew what they were thinking.

"You'll like it in a new house," he said. "Lots of new hiding places, lots of new things to see in the woods."

"I'd like that," Jerry said. He looked at his mother. "If it's all right, I mean."

His mother smiled. She didn't say anything else about moving or not moving. After all, it would be good to live in a new place, with new furniture and new rooms. She didn't know why she felt hesitant.

It didn't take long for the men to build the house.

The Harps watched with interest as the construction progressed. The Old Man knew who was going to live there. He saw Jeremiah West come down every day to see what had been done since the last visit.

He was glad to know who his new neighbor was going to be.

He cautioned the rest of his family to keep indoors and to keep quiet as long as there was anyone around the new house, anyone at all.

He knew that soon his real revenge would come.

Cutting off the heads of dead men did nothing, nothing at all, to ease the rage that was burning in his belly, a rage that had begun the first moment he saw Gabriel's body and that had increased in intensity every day that Gideon was kept in the jail. A rage that had grown so strong at Gideon's hanging that Michael could barely hold it in.

He was afraid that it would burn right through his gut, come roaring out of his busted belly like wildfire and consume his entire body and everything and everyone around him.

But he held it in, straining against it with an almost superhuman strength, and bided his time. He knew that sooner or later his moment would come, that the town was going to pay, someday, for the deaths of Gideon and Gabriel.

Oh, yes, they were going to pay. He didn't know how just yet, but he knew there would be a time of reckoning.

There always was.

The whole town helped the Wests move into the new house.

It was like a holiday for everyone, with the men carrying the furniture that Mrs. West had decided to keep—her cedar chest, most of the chairs, her kitchen table, the beds—and the women spending the morning in the new kitchen, cooking and baking.

They got started early, to avoid the heat of the day, and by noon everyone was more than ready for the food that had been prepared. They had been smelling it all morning, and now their mouths were watering.

There was roast beef with baked potatoes, fried chicken, snap beans (both green and yellow), black-eyed peas, onions, potato salad, pinto beans, sliced tomatoes, and cornbread. There were coffee and tea to drink, along with fresh lemonade made from the clear water of the spring.

Everyone wanted to taste its cool water now that the Wests were moving down the hill. Everyone thought that it would be a fine idea, now, to begin using that water again. Water from the depths of a well was all right, and probably came from the same place, but there was something about a spring and the way it bubbled out of the rocks that made the water more tempting and even a little bit better tasting than water that came from someplace else.

There were cakes, too, chocolate cakes and angel food, along with pecan pie and peach pie, and everyone had to try a little bit of both.

They ate for more than two hours, sitting around under the trees and in the shade provided by the house or on the wide porch.

Afterward, the children ran and yelled, chasing one another around the house and through the deep grass in back. The adults, their bellies stuffed, sat and talked in quiet voices.

Hardly anyone spared a look off toward the woods a quarter of a mile away or toward the hulking houses of the Harps that were almost a part of the woods.

No one gave a thought to Gideon and Gabriel, or even to the men from town who had died not three months before, gunned down in the yard behind one of the ramshackle houses.

This was a happy time for the town, a time for new beginnings.

If the Wests were happy in their new home, it might mean that others would move down the hill, down in sight of the river bottom where the trees grew tall and thick.

The town of Springville might begin to grow. New families might come in. Soon, Springville might rival the county seat in population.

Who could say what great things lay ahead? And all because the Wests had decided to move down the hill.

And if no one was thinking of the Harps, certainly the graveyard did not enter anyone's thoughts.

It was in the graveyard that Gabriel lay, buried in an unmarked spot near where other Harps had been laid to rest when their time came to depart the world. The graveyard held no fears for the Harps, and they were quick to use it to bury their own.

They also used it as a place to bury others, and it was where Tom Chandler lay, too, though his grave was not as deep as

Gabriel's and was not near the area the Harps considered their own.

Others had been put there by the Harps, too, and some were in the river, the muddy waters hiding them forever, or hiding whatever part of them the fish had not gotten.

Either place seemed to the Old Man to be a good spot for disposing of an inconvenient corpse.

If the townspeople had known about the burials, they might have been apprehensive about the Wests' move, but they did not know. They suspected, but they didn't *know*.

If they had thought that the Harps were back, hiding in their house, watching every move the town made, they would have been more apprehensive still, but they did not even think about that.

The future seemed bright to everyone that day as they ate, drank, and enjoyed life.

The Harps were not having quite so much fun.

They were watching, however, as best they could from within their house, watching through the cracks between the warped boards, peering through the windows when they thought there was no chance of being spotted, sometimes even sneaking outside to get a better look at the goings-on by snatching a glance around the corner of the house.

"I hope them fuckers are happy," the Old Man said. "I hope they're havin' themselves a hell of a time?"

"Why's that?" asked Uriel. "Why is it you want those bastards to be happy? Seems to me you'd want 'em dead."

Michael smiled. It was not a pretty sight. Most of his teeth had long since rotted away, leaving him with only a few yellowed stumps. He had a breath that would peel paint.

"I do," he said. "I do want 'em dead."

Uriel shook his head. He didn't get the joke. "I thought you said you hoped they was happy."

"That's what I said."

Uriel didn't say anything else. The Old Man didn't make a habit of explaining himself. Sooner or later he'd say what he really meant. Uriel had learned to be patient.

"Look at them women," Sarah, Uriel's wife, said. "All them pretty dresses. You'd think they didn't never have to do any real work."

Hester and Jezebel, Gideon and Gabriel's wives, looked. They were fiercely jealous of the women from the town, but not necessarily because of their clothes. They were jealous of the fact that most of them seemed to have husbands.

"I wisht I could have me a man," Hester said. "I ain't had no man between my legs for a goddamn year."

"It ain't been that long," Uriel said. "But if you're wantin' a real man, all you have to do is ask, honey."

"That's a pretty damn good joke," Sarah said. "You ain't a man but about half the time you try."

Uriel turned on her. "Shut your fuckin' mouth. If you looked like a woman 'stead of a hog, it might be different."

"Yeah, if she looked like that one over there," Joseph, the youngest of Michael's sons remarked. He pointed a dirt-encrusted finger, and Uriel strained to look through the crack his brother indicated.

"It's his wife," Joseph said.

"Christ," Uriel breathed. "I ain't never seen no woman that looked that good."

Caroline West did indeed look good that day. Her hair was shining, catching the light and reflecting it like pure gold. She was tall, though not as tall as her husband, and her figure was the kind to make a man's mouth water, even a man who wasn't a Harp.

"I'd give a pretty penny to dip my wick in that stuff," Uriel said.

Sarah grabbed Uriel's arm and jerked him away from the crack. "You won't be dippin' it in anything if you don't watch the way you talk," she said.

"Bitch," Uriel said. "I bet she'd love it. I'd have her beggin' for it before I was through."

"That'd be more'n you've ever been able to make me do," Sarah said. "It's more like you're the one who does the beggin'."

"Goddamn it," Uriel said, drawing back his arm as if to strike her.

"No need for that," Joseph said, taking hold of his brother's arm. "There ain't no likelihood of you ever gettin' close enough to that woman to make her do anything, much less beg."

"That's the truth," Sarah said. "She'd run like hell if she was to get a good look at you. Or smell you for that matter."

Uriel thought that his wife was right, much as he hated to admit it. There wasn't any real chance of him ever gettin' next to a woman like that, worse luck, no matter what he smelled like.

"I expect you're right," he said, shaking his head. "It'd sure be fun to get her down, though. I wonder if her hair's that color all over?"

"You might have a better chance of findin' that out than you think," the Old Man said.

"What?"

"You heard me."

Uriel looked at his father, waiting for an explanation, but none was forthcoming, as usual.

The Old Man just looked back at him and grinned his rotten grin.

CHAPTER SEVEN

I n the late afternoon, the town went home.

The lemonade had all been drunk, the pies and cakes had disappeared except for a few crumbs, and there was nothing left of the roast and the fried chicken but bones. A couple of dogs from the town had come down and carried off most of those, and the women had cleared away the rest.

As the people walked up the hill, West stood beside his wife, his arm around her waist, and waved good-by to his departing friends. The children stood by their parents, waving even more vigorously.

The women had spent most of the afternoon cleaning up the house and yard while the men had talked and smoked their pipes. The house was ready for its new inhabitants.

When the last townsman had disappeared, West slipped his arm from around his wife and turned to the house.

It was solidly built of good, stout planking, cypress wood shipped in from deep East Texas, wood to last a century or more. It was two stories tall, with a broad veranda that went around three sides. The windows were tall and the dying sun reflected redly from the top ones. The lower ones were already in shade.

"It's a fine house," West said.

"It is," Caroline agreed. "It's a house to last a lifetime."

West liked that idea, but he liked another idea even more.

"It's a house to last longer than that," he said. "I imagine that there'll be Wests living here long after we're gone. I'd like to think our grandchildren will live here, and their children, too."

His wife looked fondly at the children, who had already begun to play again in the yard. "That's a fine idea," she said. "I'd like to think that, too."

Later that evening, the Wests had finished the cleaning that remained to be done and the last remnants of the day's festivities were gone. The darkness was settling over the house, and the Wests were settling into their new surroundings.

The children had discovered the attic located above the upstairs bedrooms, and they had played there for a while. The attic was still hot from the sun that had heated the roof all day, and it was not quite dark because one tiny window faced to the west and let in the last rays of the setting sun.

Elizabeth did not like it there.

She was only five, and she thought it was too dark and too stuffy. The little window did not let in enough light, and eventually there was hardly any light at all. She had seen the dust motes dancing in the rays of the sun as they passed through the window, and she thought they were getting in her nose and making her sneeze.

She did not stay in the attic long.

Her brothers stayed a bit longer.

Charles, who was ten and the oldest, liked it there. He liked the low roof that seemed not much farther above his head than the ceilings of ordinary rooms seemed above his father's.

He also liked the stuffiness and the warmth, which seemed to him comforting and secure. It was as if there were some kind of safety in the attic, which he thought would be a good place to come if you were in trouble for getting angry at your little sister and maybe hitting her—though not very hard—and making her cry.

He liked to go to the little window and look out. He could see over the tops of the nearest trees, and he thought he could see the place where the river was as it flowed among them. When it got too dark to see, however, he lost interest.

Jerry, who was eight, liked the attic, too, but he had earlier found a place that he liked even better.

The house sat up on blocks so that the air could circulate

under the floor, and Jerry had found a place where he could get under the porch. It was shady and quiet under there, and he could smell the damp earth, which was cool to his touch. There was latticework around all the sides, and Jerry could look out and see the people as they ate and talked, see the children as they played.

He found that he could go all over the house from underneath. He could hear the women walking and talking in the kitchen, hear the older women rocking in the chairs in the parlor. It was a good feeling to Jerry, like being able to see without being seen, even if he couldn't really *see*.

His mother had scolded him later for getting his clothes so dirty, but she didn't really seem to mind. She and his father were too happy with their new home to mind anything very much. Jerry was glad of that; he had been scolded before for getting his clothes dirty, and he didn't like to make his mother unhappy. Somehow, though, he just seemed to get dirtier than either Charles or Elizabeth.

That night as he drifted off to sleep, he thought about the cool earth, about the darkness under the house, and about the way the sunshine seemed so much brighter when you came back out into it.

The Harps were thinking other things.

Bloody things.

The Old Man had finally made his intentions clear, and his intentions were not good, not for the Wests.

"Shit," Uriel said. "We're gonna kill 'em all?"

"Ever' damn one of 'em," the Old Man said, his eyes red with the thought of it, the fire burning in his belly. "Ever' damn one."

"The kids too?"

Michael looked at his son. His voice was flat and cold. "Ever' damn one."

That was fine with Uriel. "We don't have to kill 'em too quick, do we?" he asked.

His father knew what he meant. "No. You can make it last awhile."

Sarah knew what her husband meant, too. "You bastard," she said.

Uriel smiled. His smile was not much more pleasant than the Old Man's, though he had a few more teeth.

"We won't be usin' the guns, I guess," Joseph said.

The Old Man nodded. "That's right, boy. We don't want to call attention to ourselves."

Uriel looked at him. "You think there's gonna be any doubt about who killed 'em?"

"Doubtin' ain't provin'," Michael said. "Besides, not a one of 'em's got the guts to come after us, not if that bastard West is dead."

"And he's gonna be dead," Uriel said. "We won't waste any time on him."

"We might," Michael said. "It might be a good idea if he got to watch while you had your fun with that woman of his."

Sarah spit on the dirt floor, but she didn't say anything.

"What about me?" Joseph said. "Ain't I gonna get my turn?"

"Sure you are, boy," Michael said, smiling. "Don't worry about it. You'll get your turn." His smile widened to match Uriel's. "We all will."

Joseph smiled, too. He wanted the woman, and he thought of how it would be, with all of them taking her and her husband watching. It made his hands sweat just to imagine it.

"We need to sharpen the knives," he said.

All the Harp men carried knives, and in fact the knife was their weapon of choice. Guns made too much noise, and unless you were confronted by an armed man, as Gideon and Gabriel had been, it was usually a lot better to use something that was quick and quiet.

A knife was like that, and it was a lot more personal, too.

All the Harps liked that aspect of the blade. It was part of the fun to kill a man, or a woman, with something that let you look right in their eyes at the moment they knew they were going to die, to be able to watch as the life and light went away.

You could see looks then that you thought would carry you down to hell, if there was a hell; you could see looks that seemed to mean nothing at all; and there were even times when you could see looks that seemed to be thanking you for what you were doing, as if you were helping someone to accomplish something they had always wanted to do but had never quite known how to achieve for themselves.

All those looks meant something to a Harp. He knew them and understood them, looked forward to them the way other men looked forward to a rainstorm after a drought.

If you were a Harp, they were one of the things that made life worth living.

The men sat in the house and sharpened the knives, the silence broken only by the soothing sound of the blades as they slid down the whetstones. The women and children went next door and sat together, saying nothing. Harp children learned early when to be quiet; they learned early that there was very little to laugh about in this life and almost no time to play. Soon they would be old enough to learn more, but right now the killing was for the men.

Harp women could kill too, when need be, but this was not one of those times. Tonight was for the Old Man and his sons, and if the women did not particularly like it, they knew there was nothing they could do to change it. They knew better than to try.

Jeremiah West and his wife lay in their bed. The children were asleep now, and outside the new house the darkness deepened.

There were sounds that were new to the Wests, the sounds the house made as the heat of the day withdrew from it and the cool of the night settled in, shiftings and creakings and now and then tiny popping noises.

Outside the open windows there were other sounds, the sounds of the night.

Insects buzzed and crickets chirped. Down in the river bottom the frogs croaked and there was the occasional deeper thrumming sound of a giant bullfrog.

There was just the slightest of cool breezes coming across the bed from the night outside.

"It's a wonderful house," Caroline said. "We're going to have a fine life here, Jeremiah."

Her husband agreed.

He knew that under her cotton nightdress she was naked and waiting for his hands to settle on her and for the lovemaking to begin.

He knew that somehow it would be different this night, maybe better than it had ever been, though it had always been good.

He thought of the way her skin changed when he touched her.

At first it would be cool and smooth, but when he ran his hands over it, it would change almost instantly, becoming flushed and hot.

She would lie there, trying to remain calm, but it was impossible for her. She became almost instantly aroused, pushing against his hands with her body, pulling him to her, guiding his fingers to the places she wanted to feel them.

There was an intensity about her that was almost frightening to West. He had heard that women were supposed to be subdued, that they were not even supposed to like sex, much less enjoy it.

Caroline enjoyed it.

A lot.

In the dim light of many evenings he had seen her struggling against her passion, biting down on her lip to keep from screaming out her pleasure.

He had felt the way her body moved against him, straining to lift her farther onto him, straining to make him plunge himself deeper and deeper into her, then shuddering almost uncontrollably at the moment of climax, clasping him and squeezing him, like a hand would squeeze him, pumping him dry and then even drier.

It was a wonder they had only three children.

He wondered if they would start another one that night, the first night in the new house.

He thought it would be fine if they did, a good start to their new life together.

With that thought he took her in his arms and began slowly moving the nightdress upward.

CHAPTER EIGHT

The Harps finished sharpening their knives before it was completely dark, and then they waited.

They were all eager to move, to do what they knew had to be done, but they knew that it would be best to wait until the Wests were in bed and sleeping.

They didn't want to give any warning of their coming.

They wanted it to be a surprise.

Finally all the light had drained from the sky. Thin clouds skidded across the face of the waning moon and the stars shone like distant diamonds.

There was no light at all except for the flicker of an occasional moonbeam in the room where the Harps sat silently around the table.

They did not need the light.

They sat there like carven images, their Bowie knives in their hands, each of them thinking his own thoughts.

The Old Man thought of Gideon and Gabriel, the two sons he had lost. Good sons.

They might not have been as smart as some, but they obeyed him and did what he said. They never tried to back talk him, not more than once. They knew what it meant to be Harps, and they never once shirked their duties, whether it was killing or fighting. Jeremiah West had taken those sons from Michael, who was going to do the only thing he could to repay West.

He was going to take everything from him.

He was going to take his wife first.

Then the children.

Then he was going to take West's life.

Joseph and Uriel's thoughts were on Gabriel and Gideon, too, but the thoughts they were thinking were not like Michael's.

It wasn't that they hadn't cared about their brothers, but the fact was that Gideon and Gabriel had been their father's favorites. Maybe it was because they were twins, but the Old Man always seemed to favor them over the other two.

It wasn't because the twins were smarter, that was for sure. And it couldn't have been because they did better work. Joseph and Uriel both remembered about the woman that almost got away. Gabriel had liked to tell that story fairly often.

It could have been simply that the twins were older. That was probably it, and Uriel and Joseph had tried not to be too jealous. Their time would come, they often told themselves.

Except that it never did, not really.

Now and then the Old Man would relent and send them off to bring someone in, but usually it was an easy one, someone almost as old as Michael himself, or someone so young and inexperienced that there was not any fun involved at all.

The old ones hardly ever put up much of a fight, and the young ones, if they fought, did so with little skill and equally little energy, at least after the first few seconds. They were so stunned to know that they were going to die, all the fight seemed just to run out of them like the blood they were losing.

Tonight, though, it was going to be different.

Tonight, it was Joseph and Uriel who were going out and Gabriel and Gideon who would be staying at home, or in their graves.

That was just fine with Joseph and Uriel, because tonight promised to be the most fun that either of them had ever had, and a lot more fun than even the twins had ever experienced.

For just the barest part of a second, both Joseph and Uriel missed their brothers and wished they could be there and join in the festivities. But when the thought passed, it did not return.

Michael's voice broke the silence. "You boys ready to go?"

"Yes, sir," they answered in unison. They slipped the Bowie knives into their leather scabbards and dropped the boning knives into their boots.

"Let's go, then," the Old Man said.

Jeremiah West would have thought he couldn't hear anything, not in the condition he was in.

The blood was roaring in his ears and his wife's legs were clamped around his waist as she pulled him deeper and deeper into her, rolling her hips and grinding against him, thrusting her pubis into his groin so hard that it was almost painful.

But he did hear something.

There wasn't a thing he could do about it, however. If he had been in the middle of a railroad track and if the train had been heading straight for him, blowing its whistle as shrill as could be, there still would not have been a thing he could have done.

In his situation there was only one thing that he could do, and that was to finish what he was doing.

Even though he knew that he had heard a noise at his back, a noise that sounded like a phlegmy chuckle.

So he finished, his legs tightening and the stream boiling out of him hot as a volcano, his wife whimpering under him and biting her lip.

When it was over, before he had even begun to catch his breath, he felt the knife point sticking into the side of his neck.

"That was a mighty fine sight," the Old Man said. "I swear, you were gruntin' like a stud horse." He gave a little jab with the knife. "Now get offa there. Quick."

Caroline heard the voice and then saw the face in the dimness of the room.

She screamed.

Michael pushed the knife harder and brought the blood from West's neck.

"Now lookee what you made me do," he said. "You better be quiet, woman, or I'm gonna kill this bastard right now."

Caroline bit off her second scream and began pulling up the covers, frantically trying to conceal her nakedness.

Keeping one hand firmly on the knife, Michael slapped her with his free hand. Her head flopped back on the bed.

"Don't be doin' that," he said. "We want to see what you look like."

"What the hell is this?" West said. "I'll have you hanged for this!"

"You had one of my boys hanged," Michael said. "And you killed the other one. But you've killed your last Harp, Mr. Jeremiah West. Now get offa there, like I told you to."

West got awkwardly off the bed and watched in horror as Joseph and Uriel entered the room with the children. Now and then there was the faintest glint of a sliver blade.

"What are you doing with my children?" West demanded.

"We thought they might like to watch, too," Michael said. He laughed, and West twisted away from him.

Michael caught his arm and pulled him back, plunging the knife into his bicep. West groaned and tried to stop the flow of blood with his other hand.

"You can take this easy, or you can take it hard," Michael said. "Either way, you ain't stoppin' it."

"What are you going to make them watch?" West said.

"Now I thought you mighta guessed that one," Michael said. "You let me watch you. Now it's their turn to watch. 'Cept they ain't gonna watch you. They're gonna watch my boys there."

"You're crazy," West said.

His wife lay rigidly on the bed, her eyes closed, her breath coming in short gasps, her arms held stiffly at her sides.

"You ought not to say things like that," Michael told him. "You ready, Uriel?"

"Goddamn right," Uriel said. "You watch those kids, Joseph." He put his knife in its scabbard and tugged at the rope he used to hold up his pants.

They fell to the floor and he kicked out of them, advancing to the bed, his stiff penis standing out in front of him.

His harsh breathing sounded like the panting of a rutting animal.

The children watched with glazed and frightened eyes.

It was as if West were trapped in some sort of horrible nightmare, but it was worse than that because he knew it was really happening, and there did not seem to be a thing that he could do.

Not unless he was willing to die, and he suddenly realized

that he was. They were going to kill him anyway, he knew that, and it was better to die now, trying to stop them, than it was to allow them to humiliate him, violate his wife, and murder his children without even so much as putting up a token resistance.

He suddenly shoved Michael as hard as he could, yelling "Run!" to his children as he threw himself at Uriel.

It was as some kind of spell were broken.

The children began to scream and kick Joseph.

Caroline scrambled from the bed, yelling and whipping the covers around her head, trying to lash Uriel's face.

Uriel spun to meet West, but he had no knife, and West smashed his nose with a blow from his right fist. Uriel felt the cartilage give and the blood gush out over his upper lip as he went down under West's charge.

The Old Man jumped on West's back and in his rage he forgot all his plans about making things last, about making West watch the rape of his wife and the murder of his children, about killing West after all the others had been killed.

All he knew was that West had his hands around Uriel's throat and was strangling the life from him. West had to be stopped.

The Old Man stopped him.

He brought the knife down between West's shoulders once, twice, three times.

One of the wounds, at least one, pierced West's heart from behind and he died there on top of Uriel.

The Old Man jerked the knife out of West's body. The knife handle was slick with blood, as were Michael's hands.

Michael stood and kicked at West, kicking with all his might. "Bastard! Bastard! Bastard!"

Joseph was occupied with Caroline, who had missed Uriel but who had succeeded in partially tangling Joseph in the sheet. She was trying to wrap it around him and tie him up in it, but he was slashing it with the knife and cutting himself free as fast as she tangled him.

She had worked her way to the door, however, and was just about to escape when he shook off the last rags and grabbed her.

He crushed her against him and tried to bury his face in her breasts, but she scratched the side of his face, leaving four tracks of blood down his cheek.

"Goddamn bitch," he said. "You'll be sorry you—"

He was cut off when she put a knee into his balls.

"AGGGGHH!" he said moving away from her and bending to clutch himself.

She was going to run into the hall, but Joseph, even in his pain, knew that he could not allow her to escape.

The Old Man would skin him alive.

He lunged at her from his crouch, his arm extended straight out in front of him, the knife pointed right at her belly.

If she had possessed any experience in fighting at all, she could have avoided the blade. She might even have been able to disarm him.

But she was not a fighter. She had no experience. She didn't even have enough skill to dodge out of the way.

The knife entered her soft belly and Joseph ripped upward.

This time she did not scream.

All her life left her in a sigh.

CHAPTER NINE

The children were sleeping when Joseph and Uriel came for them in their rooms.

They had not known what was the matter or who these strange, bad-smelling men with the large knives and red eyes could be, but they knew that the men were not good men like the other men they knew, the men from town.

These men intended to hurt them.

By the time they were taken to their parents' room, they were mostly awake, and they were shocked by the sight of their mother and father exposed and naked. They had never seen them like that before.

They did not want to see them like that now; somehow, it made them feel ashamed, made their faces hot and flushed.

When their father yelled at them, telling them to run, they acted instinctively, taking their rage and shame and fear out on the men who had brought them to the room.

They kicked Joseph, stomped on his toes, avoided his flailing arms, kicked him some more, and then fled out the door and down the hall as fast as they could.

No one went after them, not then.

The Harps were suddenly otherwise occupied, which gave the children a chance to hide themselves.

They were all three running together, but Jerry fell down in the hall and his sister and brother did not stop for him. They were too afraid to stop; it was doubtful that they even saw him fall. They continued down the hall to the attic stairway, knowing that there was a hiding place there, a place where they would be safe.

Jerry got to his feet and watched them go.

He was not so sure they were doing the right thing. The stairs were right there where anyone could see them. There was no guarantee of safety in the attic.

He turned and went the other way, downstairs. He was going under the porch, under the house, where it would be dark, so dark that no one could see him, not even if they were right under there with him.

He did not mind the dark. He had been under there before. That had been in the daytime, but he was not scared of the deeper darkness of the night; it could never be as bad as what must be happening in his parents' bedroom at the hands of the men with the knives. The darkness would be safe, not frightening the way the men were.

Jerry realized that he was crying as he ran down the stairs. The hot tears were on his cheeks, and he could taste them in the corners of his mouth. He told himself to stop, but he could not.

He kept on running.

"Goddamnit! Goddamnit!" the Old Man yelled. He was almost dancing with rage, his white hair shaking around his face. He had been cheated of the most important parts of his revenge.

West was already dead, his wife had not been raped, and the fuckin' brats were gone.

"You sorry bastards!" he yelled at his sons. "It's all your fault! If Gideon and Gabriel had been here, by God, they'd have done things right."

"That's not fair," Uriel said. His voice was strained and tight because of the strength of West's hands. There were long black marks on his throat where West's thumbs had pressed. He looked down at the body of the woman on the floor. It was too damn bad he would never get the chance to fuck her now. "Uriel's right," Joseph said. "You ain't bein' fair."

His voice was not in such good shape, either, as a result of the knee in the balls. "We done our best. Hell, you're the one was supposed to be holdin' him."

Michael looked balefully at his son. For just a second he

thought about killing the little bastard. How dare he put any of the blame on his father!

But then Michael's mind went on to other, more important things.

The brats.

"We got to find them goddamn kids," he said. "If they get away, they can tell the whole town about us. We got to kill them, too."

They forgot about the bodies on the floor. The man and woman were no use to them now. Later, they would come back for them.

It did not take long for them to locate the attic stairway. They looked in the children's rooms first, under the beds and in the chifforobe, and when they didn't find the children there they knew they were up the stairs. That was the only hiding place left.

Michael waited at the bottom while his boys went up. He was going to give them a chance to redeem themselves.

Uriel opened the door at the top of the stairs. It was freshly hung and oiled, so it did not make a sound as it swung inward. He looked into the darkness.

There was not much that he could see.

There was the one window, and a pale beam from the moon came through it and fell upon the floor. There was no sign of anyone in that tiny bit of light.

Uriel stepped into the attic, with Joseph right behind him. The floor was solid and well fitted. It did not shift or creak. West had been right about the house. It would easily have lasted long enough for his grandchildren to live in.

If he had lived to have any.

Uriel stood patiently in the darkness waiting for anyone in the attic to make a move, a noise. He had his Bowie clutched in his hand.

He could hear nothing except the rasping breath of Joseph, who was standing right beside him.

They waited.

Charles and Elizabeth were afraid, very afraid, but they knew that their only hope was to keep as quiet as the wooden walls of the attic, as quiet as the darkness around them.

They did not know where Jerry had gone, but they suspected that the bad men had gotten him. He must not have been fast enough to outrun them.

The bad men had gotten Mother and Father, too. They didn't like to think that, but they knew it was true. The men had knives, and Mother and Father had nothing to protect themselves with. Charles and his sister did not like to think of their parents dead, killed by knives, but somehow they were sure that was what had happened.

They did not want the bad men to get them. They did not want to be killed by the knives.

There were only a few things stored in the attic, and therefore there were only a few hiding places worth mentioning, but they had found a good one. It was so good that Charles didn't think the bad men could find them there.

There were several boxes stacked on top of three other boxes. The middle box of the three was not as large as the other two, and there was room to squeeze in behind it, room for two. Charles had discovered the place that afternoon, and that was where he had taken Elizabeth now. He had also had the presence of mind to take another box, one that was half empty, and pull it up behind them.

They were practically invisible, especially in the darkness. They were so scared that their breathing was almost inaudible. No one could hear it, even standing nearby.

"Goddamnit, what the hell's takin' so long?" the Old Man called from the bottom of the stairs. "Are they up there, or ain't they?"

"I can't see 'em," Uriel answered.

"It's dark up here," Joseph said unnecessarily.

"I don't give a shit if it's dark or not. You find 'em or come down."

Uriel began to move about the attic, looking as best he could behind the boxes stacked there. He was beginning to think that maybe he was wrong. Maybe the damn kids had gone somewhere else.

"What do you think?" he asked Joseph. They were standing right in front of the stack of boxes where Charles and Elizabeth were hiding. They had looked behind it and seen nothing but another box. To them, it was just another stack like the others there.

"I don't know," Joseph said. "You think they went downstairs and ran for the town? If they got to the town we're fucked."

Charles cringed in the hiding place. He felt as if a belt were being tightened around his chest, making it almost impossible for him to breathe. He closed his eyes and prayed for the men to leave.

If only he had thought to run for the town! If he had, he and Elizabeth might be safe now.

But maybe they were safe anyway.

The men couldn't find them, or they would have done so by now.

No, they were going to be all right, and maybe Jerry had not been hurt after all.

Maybe he was running for the town. Maybe he was on his way to the town and would be back in only a little while with men with guns, good men who would make these bad men with the knives go away.

"Shit," Uriel said, thinking about the consequences if the kids had gone to the town. "Those townies will be here in no time, and they'll have guns. Nothin' they'd rather do that shoot us all like fuckin' dogs. We better get out of here."

"The Old Man ain't gonna like it," Joseph said.

"Fuck the Old Man. He's blamin' us for this, and it's all his fault. We're gonna get our asses hung, just like Gideon, if we don't get outta here."

They turned and headed back to the stairs.

And then Elizabeth sneezed.

CHAPTER TEN

Crouched under the house, Jerry cowered in the darkness, wondering what was happening above him.

He could hear nothing, no sound of feet on the floor, no voices talking, so he knew that whatever was going on must be occurring on the upper floor.

He wondered if the men had found his brother and sister yet. If they had, Charles and Elizabeth would be in real trouble. Jerry knew that the men were killers, and he knew that his mother and father were dead. There was no question in his mind about that.

What he didn't know was why.

Why would anyone want to kill his parents? Why would anyone want to kill him? What had he ever done to them?

He knew what death was like; he had seen a fair share of it though he was only eight years old.

He had gone out hunting rabbits with his father, and he knew how it was when you shot one of them with the rifle. One minute they were living, breathing animals, and then they were lying there, blood staining their fur, and they weren't breathing anymore.

They were never going to get up and run again in that funny way they had. They were just going to lie there, their glassy eyes staring at the sky, and if you picked them up they would be limp and hot in your hand; but they would already be growing cold.

He thought of himself like that, limp, warm, his glassy eyes open and staring at the darkness of the hot and sticky night as the bad men held him in their hands and tried to decide whether to skin him or not.

That's what you did with rabbits.

You skinned them, and you cut them open and got their insides out before you fried them.

The men wouldn't fry him, though. You didn't do that to people. At least he didn't think you did.

But then you didn't go around using knives to kill people with, either.

Jerry realized that he was still crying, his body heaving in silent sobs as the tears continued to stream down his face, though he was not making any sound.

He told himself to stop it, that if he didn't stop it the men would surely find him, and if they found him they would kill him with the knives. And after that they might skin him.

He tried, he really tried, but the tears just would not stop.

Charles put his arm around Elizabeth and pulled her closer.

He was holding his breath now, hoping that the men were too far away to hear the sneeze. There was a box between them, so maybe they hadn't heard.

But they had.

Uriel stopped still and turned around, almost bumping into Joseph who was trailing along behind.

"What the hell," Joseph said.

"Somebody sneezed," Uriel said. "Was it you?"

"Wasn't me. I didn't hear anything."

"Well I sure as hell did. It came from over there." Uriel pointed to the stack of boxes that looked like nothing more than a pile of deeper blackness in the shadows of the attic.

"Let's give it a look-see, then," Joseph said.

They walked over to the boxes and examined them.

"Reckon they're hidin' inside a box?" Uriel said.

Elizabeth had to sneeze again. She knew that she shouldn't, but she just had to. There was something in her nose, and it was tickling so bad that she couldn't help herself.

She knew that Charles would be angry with her, so she tried to stop. She put her hand up and pinched her nose between her thumb and first finger. For a second, she thought she was going to be able to hold it in, but then it burst out of her, louder even then the first one, bringing tears to her eyes, and her hand flew away from her face.

Uriel smiled to himself at the sound.

"Well, well," he said. "I guess there ain't nobody here, Joseph. I guess we'll just have to go downstairs and tell the Old Man there ain't nobody up here, nobody a'tall."

"Hold on there, Uriel, I—"

"Yep," Uriel said, speaking right on top of Joseph's protest, "we're just gonna have to give up. Let's us go on down." He tried clumsily to make the sound of feet walking away from the boxes.

Joseph caught on. That Uriel was a real joker, he was. Makin' those brats think they were safe and sound, when he really knew they were right there. Joseph almost had to laugh out loud it was so funny.

It wasn't funny to Charles. He was only ten, but he wasn't stupid. He knew when he was being toyed with.

He reached behind him and began slowly to push the box out of the way. If he could move it far enough without making any noise, he thought that he and Elizabeth could get out of their hiding place and make a run for it.

But Uriel was listening carefully by then. He heard the slight scraping noise of the box moving on the floor, so he reached out and began tossing the boxes off the top of the stack. They bounced around the attic, thudding hollowly on the floor.

One of them broke open, spilling out some plow harness. West had long ago sold his plow horses, but he had kept the harness in case he ever went back to farming.

Charles pulled Elizabeth to her feet and started to run across the attic floor. There was nowhere to run, really. As soon as Uriel had begun to toss the boxes, Joseph had moved to block the doorway.

The children were trapped.

"What the hell's goin' on up there?" the Old Man yelled from the bottom of the stairway.

"We got 'em!" Joseph answered. "We got 'em now!"

Charles had picked up the end of one of the plowlines and was whirling it around, trying to use it as a whip to fend off Uriel, but it was no use. The man was too big. He brushed the line aside and smacked Charles on the side of the head like he was swatting a fly.

Charles flew five feet across the attic, landing hard against one of the boxes. Something snapped in his back.

The hollow of the man's hand had landed right over Charles' ear, which was ringing like a church bell.

The other man grabbed Elizabeth and swung her up in the air.

"You're a pretty little bitch," he said. "Just like your mama used to be."

Charles tried to get to his feet, but something was wrong with his back Pain shot down his spine and he fell back against the box.

Almost instantly, Uriel was looming over him, his knife in his hand, a smile on his face.

"What about it?" Uriel called out. "You want us to bring 'em down there?"

Michael hardly bothered to think about it. "No," he said. "You can do it up there. Then you can bring 'em down."

Uriel turned to Joseph. "Let's do it, then," he said.

And they did.

"Goddamnit," Michael said when his sons descended the stairs, each one carrying a small bloody corpse in his arms. "Where's the other one?"

"What other one?" Uriel said. His face and hands were bloody, and there was more blood on his clothing.

"You sons of bitches ain't got the sense God gave a goose," Michael said. "The other one of the brats. There was three of 'em, remember?"

"Oh, yeah," Joseph said. "I remember now. Is he up there, you reckon, Uriel?"

Uriel didn't reckon. "If he was up there, he'd've come out while we were doin' the job. He must be somewhere else."

"We better find him, then," Joseph said. "We sure don't want him getting to town."

"You're damn right we don't," Michael said. "Put those two in with their mama and daddy; then we'll go lookin'."

They looked for a long time, searching every nook and cranny of the house. They went back to the attic and looked there, moving every box at least twice and opening them all to look inside.

They looked under the beds again, in the pantry, behind all the chairs; they even moved the house's one bookcase and looked behind it to see if there was some kind of secret door.

There wasn't.

"He just ain't here," Joseph said finally. "He must've gone to the town."

Michael didn't think so. "If he'd done that, they'd be back here by now and we'd be shot to pieces. He's here."

"Maybe he hid in the woods," Uriel said.

"Wouldn't hurt to look outside," Michael said. "I don't think he'd be in the woods, though."

They looked all around the yard and on the fringes of the wood. There was no sign of anyone.

"He just ain't here," Joseph said again.

"He's here," the Old Man said. "I can almost smell him. He's here, all right."

"If you're so damn sure, why don't you tell us where he is, then?" Uriel said. He was getting pretty fucking tired of the way the Old Man was acting.

Michael turned on him. "Listen, boy, you don't get uppity with your daddy, you hear me?"

"I hear you," Uriel said. He knew better than to push it.

"Look here," Joseph said. He was pointing to a corner of the porch where there was an opening that lead under the house. "Reckon he went under there?"

"Mighty dark," Uriel said. "I don't think he could see his way around."

Joseph shook his head. "I guess not. But if he ain't there, where is he?"

"You better crawl under there and see," Michael said.

Shit, Joseph thought. He wished he'd kept his mouth shut. He didn't want to go crawling around under there in the dark. No telling what might be there—snakes, spiders, scorpions. He for damn sure didn't want to get bit or stung. He wished they'd brought a lantern.

He'd heard the Old Man tell once about a man that got bit by a fiddler spider. Just a tiny little bite, one the man hardly noticed at all. But before long that bite began to spread, and the man's arm began to go dead on him. The dead place got bigger and bigger; finally the whole damn arm was dead, and if some doctor hadn't chopped it off for him, the man probably would've died.

Joseph didn't want anything like that to happen to him.

"Why can't Uriel go?" he said.

"Because Uriel's too damn big to go crawlin' around under there. Now get your ass through that openin' before I kick you through it."

Joseph crawled through. It was even darker than he had thought it would be. Outside, there was at least a sliver of moon to give the light, but under the house there was nothing at all. Once you got past the latticework there was absolute blackness.

Joseph realized for the first time in his life that he didn't like the dark. He wondered if there was a lantern in the house they could get for him to use.

"I see your sorry ass!" the Old Man yelled. "Get to lookin' for that brat or I'll skin you."

Far back in the darkness, as far away from the porch as he could get, Jerry heard Michael's threat. He was going to skin one of the bad men.

It was just as Jerry had feared. They would skin him if they caught him. He couldn't let them do that.

He had stopped crying now, and the tears were drying on his face. He did not know what else he could do. There was no place to hide under the house. It was all entirely open, except for the supports that held up the floor. He could get behind one of those, but it would be easy for the man who was looking for him to check all sides of the support.

He could hear the man crawling around.

"Shit!" Joseph yelled.

"What happened?" the Old Man asked.

"I hit my fuckin' head is what happened," Joseph said.

He had been crawling forward and bumped into one of the supports. He felt with his hands and crawled on around it. It was so dark that he couldn't see it even though he was right on it.

Even if the kid was under there, Joseph didn't see how he was supposed to find him without any light. He had to keep on looking, though. The Old Man would give him hell if he didn't look.

He crawled forward.

When the man bumped his head, Jerry got an idea. Obviously the man couldn't see, so if Jerry could just stay out of his way, he wouldn't get caught.

It ought to be easy, since the man was making enough noise for two or three men, his breath coming in harsh panting sounds and his big body scraping over the ground as clumsily as a cow's.

Jerry crouched where he was, but he listened carefully. Sure enough, the man finally got fairly close to him.

Jerry moved quietly to his left about six feet and waited.

The man kept moving forward. Jerry thought he might hit his head on the side wall, but he did not. He had learned to keep his hands in front of him. He muttered something and then started moving toward Jerry.

Jerry moved again, this time heading back in the direction Joseph had come from. He did not go far, again about six feet.

When Joseph had worked his way down the wall far enough, Jerry went back and sat where he had been to start with. He didn't think the man was too smart. He didn't think the man would be coming back this way.

He was right.

All Joseph wanted to do was get out. He promised himself that he would make a half circuit of the house, following the wall until he came to the latticework and then following that until he came to the doorway. Then he was getting out from under there.

He had already put his hand on something that he thought was probably a worm, but it might have been a tiny snake. He wasn't going to take any more chances. It was clear to him that the fucking kid wasn't under there.

When Joseph emerged, Michael said, "Well?"

"I went all over. He ain't there."

"Goddamnit," the Old Man said. "We got to find him."

"We ain't got all that much time," Uriel said. "If he went to town, I mean. Why don't we just finish up here and get out?"

Michael didn't like it, but he didn't see what else they could do. They couldn't afford to stay too long.

"All right," he said.

But he still didn't like it.

CHAPTER ELEVEN

Jerry stayed under the house all night.

It seemed like years before the men left, but they finally did. They made a lot of noise before they left, the sounds filtering down under the house through the thick wood floors, but Jerry was not tempted to sneak back into the house and find out what the noises were.

He really didn't want to know.

He was pretty sure that there was no one left alive up in the house, not his mother, his father, his brother, or his sister.

He started crying again when he thought of that, but sometime near dawn he fell into an exhausted sleep.

He woke up to the sound of someone screaming.

It was a woman, that was all he could tell. It was daylight now; what time it was he did not know, but he could see the light around the porch. He began crawling to the opening to see who was screaming.

He didn't really get a good look at her. All he could see by the time he got to the light was her back as she fled across the field and toward the hill on her way to town.

He knew why she was screaming, all right.

She had seen the inside of the house.

Francine Gregory was screaming because she had never seen anything like it.

It was terrible, worse than anything she had ever experienced, even in her worst dreams, even in the nightmares that sometimes came to her in the hours just before dawn.

There was blood everywhere.

On the floors.

On the walls.

Even on the ceilings.

Everything in the house that could be broken had been destroyed.

The chairs had been battered to kindling.

The dishes had been smashed.

The cast-iron stove had been demolished.

The bedding had been ripped to shreds, and it was all stained with blood.

At first, Francine had thought she was going to faint as she walked through the house looking at the thick streaks of blood on the walls, the floors, but she kept walking, though her knees felt like water.

Then she thought she might vomit, but she did not do that, either.

Instead, she finally started screaming, and then she started running. She didn't even know where she was going. She was just running to get away from what she had seen, to escape the horror of what was in that house.

And to get away from what she *hadn't* seen.

Because despite all the destruction, despite all the blood, there were no bodies in the house.

There was no one there at all.

Jerry crawled out from under the porch and watched her go, her broad back becoming smaller and smaller the farther she got from the house. He could still hear her screaming, though.

He stood blinking his eyes in the bright sunlight and looking at the house.

Yesterday, he had thought the house was one of the most beautiful things he had ever seen. He had thought of it as a place of happiness and security, a place that he would call home.

Everyone had been laughing then, eating the food, talking, smiling with enjoyment. He could almost hear the children yelling in the yard if he closed his eyes and thought about it.

It seemed like a long time ago.

Jerry wasn't sure he wanted to go into the house again, but in a way he knew that he had to do it. He had to know what had been done to his family.

He walked up onto the porch.

There was even blood there, spatters of it anyway. Jerry didn't notice them. He was looking through the open door.

He could see the furniture broken into pieces. That had been the noise he heard, some of it at least. He could see the blood smears on the far wall.

Tears started to his eyes, but he shut them off. This time it was easier than before.

He went through the door, afraid at every second that he would see some horrible sight, but he did not, nothing more horrible than he had already seen.

His mother and father were not there, nor were Charles and Elizabeth.

He went slowly up the stairs. The handrails were smeared with blood. He did not touch them.

When he came to the door to his parents' room, he hesitated. This was where it had started. He did not want to look inside, but after a few minutes' hesitation, he did.

There was nothing there.

That was not strictly true, of course. There *were* things there.

There were bedclothes ripped into shreds, and there were dark streaks of blood on the walls, along with other dark stains on the floor.

The chifforobe had been broken to splinters, as if someone had taken an ax to it, and maybe they had. Jerry didn't know for sure.

But his parents were not there.

He went down to the room he had shared with Charles. There was no one there, either. The furniture was smashed and the bedclothes mangled, but there was no sign of Charles.

There was no sign of Elizabeth in her room, either, though the destruction was equally evident there. At the foot of the bed there was a doll with its china hear torn off.

Jerry did not look long. He went instead to the attic stairs.

Once again he hesitated. He could see the spatters of bright red blood there. Finally he walked up. The door at the top was open and he could see the sunlight coming through the window.

All the boxes were broken, their contents scattered all around. There was blood on the floor there, too, though not nearly so much as in his parents' room.

He wondered what the men had done with his brother, his sister, his mother and father. He wondered what they had done *to* them.

He walked slowly over to the window and sat down in the sunbeam, his back to the attic. The window sill was low, and he could just see over it without craning his neck. He could see the tops of the trees in the woods. They were green and comforting somehow. He decided that he would never turn around again.

That was where they found him when they came down from the town.

Francine Gregory had been almost incoherent when she reached home, but Tobe had managed to get some kind of story out of her. He could hardly believe what she seemed to be saying, but his wife was normally a calm, easy-going person. Something terrible must have happened to get her into such a state, so Tobe decided to go investigate.

He didn't go alone. He took three others with him, and they went through the house with a mounting sensation of horror at the sight of all the blood and destruction. It was almost as if the house had been visited by some kind of supernatural monster that had run rampant.

But where were the bodies of the dead? For Tobe and the men with him knew that there had to be bodies. There was too much blood for it to be any other way.

When they finally found Jerry in the attic, they had given up any hope of finding anyone, dead or alive.

Then Tobe climbed the stairs and saw the boy sitting in the sunlight, staring out the window at the trees.

"Jerry?" he said.

The boy did not look around. He kept on sitting there, unmoving, staring out the window, his eyes never blinking.

Tobe walked over to him, not sure that the boy was even

alive. He might have been killed and left there as some kind of warning.

When he got close, however, he saw that Jerry appeared unharmed. There was no blood on his clothing, no sign of any kind of wound.

"Jerry?" he said again.

The boy still did not look at him or make any move. It was hard for Tobe to tell that Jerry was even breathing, but he was. He continued to stare unblinkingly out the window.

"Jerry, it's me, Tobe Gregory. What happened here? Where is everybody?"

Jerry did not acknowledge Tobe's presence. It was as if he could neither see nor hear the man.

Tobe put his hand on Jerry's shoulder. "It's all right, son," he said. "No one's going to hurt you. It's just old Tobe."

The words had no effect, and Tobe looked out the window to see if there was something out there, something that had riveted the boy's attention.

There was nothing, nothing except for the trees.

In the trees, in the graveyard, out of sight of the house, the Harps had finally finished their work.

The Old Man tamped the dirt down on top of the last new grave. "That takes care of the fuckers," he said with satisfaction.

He looked out over the other graves with their rude markers; then he walked over to the inconspicuous stone that marked the grave of Gabriel.

"Son," he said, "there they are. I wish you could've been there, but since you weren't, we did it for you. You'd be proud of your brothers and me for what we done to them Goddamn Wests. There wasn't a one of 'em we left in one piece, and their new house won't never be the same, neither."

Michael looked around. "I just wish Gideon could be here, but they wouldn't let us have him. Buried him their own damn selves, in Potter's Field, they did. But I think he knows what we done, Gabriel. I think he knows that his daddy and brothers didn't let him down."

"Amen," Uriel said.

"Yeah," Joseph said. "Amen."

Michael took one last look around. "I bet those Goddamn Wests never thought they'd be lyin' here with the Harps in their final rest. They thought they were so high and mighty, but we brought 'em down, boys. We brought 'em down."

"Amen," Uriel said again.

"Let's go on back to the house," the Old Man said.

They turned and left the graveyard.

The other men came up to the attic with Tobe, but Jerry did not respond to any of them. They finally had to pick him up and carry him out of the house.

It was an eerie feeling just to look at him, his staring eyes, his rigid body. It was like he was in come kind of a coma, but not any coma that the men had ever heard of.

His eyes wouldn't close. What kind of a coma was that? And he was stiff as a board. If he was in a coma, wouldn't his body relax a little?

There wasn't a doctor in Springville, but they would send for one from the county seat. Maybe he would know what to do. In the meantime, Tobe Gregory would keep the boy with him until they decided what to do about whatever had happened to the Wests.

The first thing was to figure out what had gone on in the house. Tobe Gregory thought he knew already.

"It was the Harps," he told Thad Neal, a blacksmith and one of the men who had been with him. They were sitting in the shade of a tree near Neal's shop, out of the sooty air and the ashes.

Neal was a thin, wiry man with long arms and legs. His trade had given him muscles in his arms, but not big ones. He had a red face that some thought was made redder by looking in the fire all the time.

"You don't know it was the Harps," Neal told Gregory. "It looked to me like it coulda been some kind of animal."

"You ever see an animal that could do that to a house?" Harry Thompson asked. He had been there, too. He was short and fat, and people often thought he was supposed to be jolly.

He wasn't, however. He was generally quite gloomy and morose.

"Harry's right," Claude Morrow said. He was the third man who had gone with Gregory to the house. He was a farmer, with hard, calloused hands and a strong back. "Ain't no animal ever born would do somethin' like that. It was people done it, and we know what people. Like Tobe said, it was the Harps."

Neal shook his head. "Maybe. Maybe not. We won't know for sure unless that kid can tell us."

"It might be a while before he does, if he ever does," Gregory said. I sent Whit Masters for the doctor. Maybe he can help the boy. Then maybe he can tell us what happened."

"What if he does?" Neal said. "What're we gonna do about it?"

"Maybe what we should've done a long time ago," Morrow said. "Go down there and clean those Harps out."

Neal didn't want any part of that. "You want your family to wind up like Jeremiah's? You saw that house."

"If we took care of the Harps," Morrow said, "we wouldn't wind up like that."

"That's what Jeremiah thought," Neal said. "And where is he now?"

"That's what spooks me," Thompson said. "Where's the whole family? You think the Harps just carried them off?"

"I don't know," Gregory said. "But I got to agree with Claude. If we'd taken care of the Harps long ago, none of this would've happened."

"Wouldn't've happened if West had minded his own damn business, either," Neal said. "If he hadn't stuck his nose in where it didn't belong, he'd be down there in his big new house, happy as a pig in shit. But he ain't there, is he? I don't reckon we'll ever be seein' him again."

"You don't really mean that you think we should have let the Harps go on killing strangers and selling their belongings, do you?" Gregory asked.

"Didn't say that. Just said that meddlin' don't never do nobody much good. All it got West was dead."

"You reckon they didn't kill 'em?" Morrow said. "That they just cut on 'em and took 'em somewhere?"

The men all shook their heads. There wasn't anyone who believed that.

"So what're we gonna do?" Morrow said. "Just let 'em get away with it? Let 'em kill the best family in town and not say a damn thing about it? Or are we gonna go get 'em?"

The men sat in silence for a while. There breeze stirred in the leaves of the tree where they sat, and they could see people walking in the streets of the little community. Most of them hadn't yet been told of the horrors at the West house.

"I say we do somethin'," Thompson said. "How about you, Claude?"

"I said it already," Claude told him. "Tobe?"

Gregory didn't want to be hasty. He was thinking not only of the Wests but of the other three men who had died when they walked up on the Harps. He wasn't in any hurry to die.

At the same time, he knew that something had to be done.

"All right," he said at last. "We'll take care of it."

Neal didn't say anything. He didn't want any part of it.

"When?" Morrow said. "When are we gonna do it?

"We'll wait for the doctor to see the boy," Gregory said. "Then we'll see. Maybe the boy can tell us something later."

"If he can't, what do we do?" Thompson said.

"If he can't, then we'll do it anyhow," Claude said. "Ain't that right, Tobe.

Tobe thought about it for a minute. "That's right," he said. "We'll do it anyhow."

CHAPTER TWELVE

It was easier than they thought it would be.

There were some who said that catching the Harps off guard would be impossible, and there were others who wanted no part of it, no matter what, but mostly everyone was simply afraid that the Harps would be the victors in any encounter between them and the townspeople.

Thad Neal was the one most opposed to doing anything.

"Hell," he told anyone who would listen, "that kid can't even say for sure who it was that was in the house that night. We might be goin' after the wrong men."

Tobe Gregory wasn't having any of that. "How many old white-haired men do you know around here? Ones with hair that long and a beard like that? Can you think of two. Or even one?"

Neal didn't have much to say about that, but there were those who took his side. Generally they were the ones who also agreed with his theory that Jeremiah West had been asking for trouble and that leaving the Harps alone was the best policy. They were also the ones who were thinking about what had happened to the men who followed Jeremiah West down the hill the first time and how they had not come back.

"If we let them get away with this, what kind of people are we?" Tobe Gregory said. He had thought about those men, too, but this was not the same. This was a test of the whole community.

And then he answered his own question. "If we let 'em get away with it, we're the kind of people who'll let killers run free just to save our own skins, that's what we are. Long as they don't kill us or ours, we'll give 'em a free hand."

He paused and looked at them. "If that's the kind of people we are, then I don't think we'll always be so lucky. What will we do if the Harps ever decide to come up that hill?"

Nobody had a good answer to that. Most of them had been by Gregory's house to see Jerry West, and many of them had heard the boy tell the story of what happened that night. He remembered it very well, once he decided to recall it.

He remembered the men, the way they looked, the way they smelled, the knives they were carrying.

He remembered his mother and father, naked in their bedroom, but he did not mention that part.

He remembered the man crawling under the house, and he remembered the noises that came from above him later.

The trouble was, at least from the point of view of Neal and his supporters, Jerry had never heard the men call one another by name; or if he had, he could not remember it.

In the end, it didn't matter. Tobe Gregory and several others had made up their minds. They were going after the Harps. They were going to impose justice on them.

"We ain't gonna wait around for no judge and jury, either," Claude Morrow said. "And we ain't sendin' for the marshal. We'll take care of this little business ourselves. That's the way it oughta be."

Harry Thompson, Tobe Gregory, and five other men agreed with him. All they needed was a plan.

"We got to catch 'em off guard," Morrow said. "Like they did the Wests."

"What you reckon ever happened to the Wests?" Thompson said. "What you reckon they did with 'em?"

That was a mystery that had plagued the town. No one was quite sure. There were even those who hinted that it would not be unthinkable that people like the Harps might want a change in their diet from chicken and that "some other kind of meat might seem good to 'em."

No one wanted to believe that, but it was one of the things that was whispered.

"Don't know about the Wests," Gregory said. "All I know is

what needs to happen to the Harps."

"Night'd be the best time," Morrow said. "Catch 'em then, when they're sleepin'."

"Don't know that they sleep at night," Thompson said. "They're like animals, prob'ly sleep durin' the day."

It was hard to decide just when to go for them, but finally the men agreed to go in the depths of night. All of them would be armed, and even if the Harps were roused, the men thought they could prevail.

But the Harps were not roused.

As it turned out, the Harps were not even there.

Except for one.

Old Michael did not really believe that anyone would bother his family. He was almost convinced that the men of Springville were too lily-livered to make a move against him.

His idea was that Jeremiah West was the only man in the whole town with any gumption at all and that the others were sorry excuses for men who wouldn't dare take on someone who might fight back at them.

Hell, they hadn't done a thing for years, and he had been taking their chickens and killing them right in plain sight, wringing their scrawny necks just like he wanted to wring the neck of every man in town, and no one had said a word.

Hadn't he and his sons killed at least thirty men and a few women in the past twenty years or so? Hell, yes, they had, and right there on the road leading out of Springville, to boot.

Had there ever been anyone who dared to say a word to them about it? Hell, no. There wasn't enough guts among the men of that town to fill up the belly of one of the chickens Michael had killed.

So he didn't figure they'd come after him this time, either.

Sure, he'd let the kid get away, and the kid might even have told them who'd come to his house, but that didn't worry Michael. As long as he stayed away from the town itself, he would be safe.

Or that was what he told himself.

He seemed to be right, too. For several days after the

massacre at the West house, the town had been calm. No one had even looked threateningly in his direction.

No guts, he told himself. Not a man in the bunch of 'em with the guts of a gopher.

But somehow the lack of action bothered him. It looked like they ought to be doing *something*, looking for the bodies, getting upset, calling in the marshal.

Something.

But they were doing nothing, and that wasn't right.

The Old Man called the family together. He hadn't survived as long as he had by being stupid.

"I want you boys to take your wives and young 'uns and go on over to the county seat for a while," he told Uriel and Joseph.

"Why?" Joseph said. "You afraid of somethin'?"

The Old Man looked at him with hard black eyes. "I ain't afraid of nothin'. Never have been. But it don't make sense that nobody's lookin' for those Goddamn Wests. Somethin's wrong. It's best you get away from here for a spell."

"How about you?" Uriel said.

"I'll be all right. Those bastards won't dare to bother me. And if they do, they'll be damn sorry."

"Maybe," Uriel said. "But what if somethin' does happen to you?"

"It won't," Michael said. "But if it does, it's that damn West brat's fault, the one that got away. He's the one to take the blame, and I don't want you to forget it. The Wests are sorry as owl shit, and don't you forget that, either. We should've killed that boy, and I won't rest easy till ever' last one of 'em's dead. You hear what I'm sayin'?"

"We hear you," Joseph said.

"Learn it to the young 'uns," the Old Man said.

So when the men came in the night, only Michael was there.

He was so surprised when they smashed in the front door of his house that he didn't even have time to go for his gun, which was right there by his sleeping pallet, not that it would have done him much good against that many men.

"All right, you old bastard," Claude Morrow said as they

stood around him with their guns leveled on him. "Where's the rest of your clan?"

"Fuck you," the Old Man said, baring his teeth.

"Look in the other shack," Gregory said to the men with the guns. He and Morrow stood guard over Michael while Harry Thompson lead the others away.

"Ain't nobody there," Thompson said when he came back. "Looks like this 'uns the only one there is."

"He'll have to do, then," Morrow said, though his disappointment was evident. "Get up you old son of a bitch."

He jabbed Michael with his gun barrel and the Old Man made a lunge at him.

Morrow clubbed him across the jaw. "It ain't gonna be that easy," he said. "First you're gonna tell us what you did to the Wests."

Michael just looked at him.

"We can make you tell," Morrow said, but he knew better. There were probably ways to make men talk, but he would not be able to use them. Old Man Harp would know them all, and he probably wouldn't hesitate to use them, not for a second.

But Morrow and the men from town weren't like that. When it came right down to it, they might not even be able to kill the old bastard.

"Take him outside," Morrow said finally.

Two men went to Michael and grabbed his arms. This time the Old Man did not fight. He knew it would not do any good. They dragged him out of the house.

There was a big elm tree at the edge of the woods.

"Who's got the rope?" Morrow asked.

"I got it," Thompson said. There was a coil of stout rope slung over his shoulder.

"Throw it up over that limb, then," Morrow said, pointing his gun barrel at a thick limb growing out from the tree at a ninety-degree angle.

Thompson threw the rope over the limb and began fashioning one end into a hangman's noose.

"Do you have anything you want to say?" Gregory asked. "You could save that boy a lot of grief if you'd tell us what happened to his family."

Michael just laughed. He wasn't going to say a word. They would just kill him anyhow.

And, hell, he didn't blame them. He'd do the same. *Had* done the same, many times over.

But not blaming them and telling them what they wanted to know were not the same thing.

The Wests were going to lie in that graveyard forever, if the Old Man had anything to do with it.

He knew how the townspeople felt about the graveyard, if they thought of it at all.

They didn't like it, didn't like to think about it, didn't want to think about who might be lying there.

Even if they guessed where the Wests were buried, they would never even go look. Michael was sure of that.

So let them lie there, the sorry fuckers, rotting under the same ground where the Harps' other victims rotted, or many of them.

Let them lie there practically in sight of the homes of the family that had killed them in justifiable revenge.

Putting them there was in fact part of the Old Man's vengeance, and he wasn't about to have them moved.

And so he laughed.

He was still laughing when they put the noose around his neck. It was a good joke on him, he thought, saying they didn't have the guts to do anything. He'd have to admit that.

They had more guts than he'd ever have guessed. More guts than *they'd* ever guessed, probably.

He was even laughing when three of the men began to heave on the rope, his laughter echoing off the trees at the edge of the wood.

The men looked at each other, and they almost slacked off on the rope, but Tobe Gregory, who was standing to the side, grabbed hold of the rope and started pulling along with them, and then Morrow put down his gun and started pulling too.

After that, Old Man Harp didn't laugh for long.

INTERVAL

"Gravestones tell truth scarce forty years."

—Sir Thomas Browne, "Hydriotaphia, Urn-Burial"

Chapter Thirteen

A hundred years is not long when set against the age of the earth, but set against the life of a man or the memory of a man a hundred years can seen an eternity.

In that time span, while the woods down by the graveyard grew thicker and darker, while the leaves fell thickly on the marked—and unmarked graves there—men learned to ride in motor cars instead of wagons. Women received the vote. World Wars were fought and forgotten. Machines flew through the air and through space, and men walked on the moon.

Generations of men and women lived and died, hardly aware of all the wonders coming into being around them.

Towns flourished in some places, even grew into cities.

In other places, they died.

Springville did not exactly die. It just ceased to be a town.

Some said that happened because it was by-passed by the railroad, which went through the county seat instead.

According to others, it died because the young people all went somewhere else when they grew up. Springville really had nothing to offer except for hard work on the farm, and youngsters wanted a different kind of life.

Some traced everything back to that night that Jeremiah West and his family died, saying that the town never recovered. The town's banker, its leading citizen, disappeared; no trace of him or his family was ever found. The bank collapsed, and with it the gin. Farmers took their cotton elsewhere for ginning, and no one came to Springville from the smaller farms around. The stores suffered. That night, then was the beginning of the end.

Or was it?

There were those, few in number, who traced the town's decline to another night, not long after West's murder, the night when eight men went down the hill and lynched old Michael Harp.

There were a lot of stories about that night, none of them related by the participants, but all of them having some kind of dubious authenticity attached to them.

Stories that were told by "someone who knew someone who was there."

Or stories told by someone "who would've gone, but he was too sick with the flu that night."

That kind of thing.

No one really knew what happened, however, except those eight men, and they never told.

What was undoubtedly true was that Tobe Gregory left town less than a year later, moving somewhere "up north" to get a new start. His business was bad and getting worse, and he needed help from his wife's side of the family to make the move.

And Harry Thompson died of a stroke one night while sitting in a rocker on his front porch. He was just sitting there, by all accounts, looking out over the country, when he gave a little cry and pitched straight forward out of the chair onto the porch. A little blood ran out of his mouth, but that was the only sign he was dead. It was just a coincidence, so everyone said, that he happened to be looking at the woods down the hill.

Then there was Claude Morrow. He got dragged to death by his horses the next spring when he was fixing to do a little plowing. No one could really explain how the plowlines got tangled around his neck like that. Claude was a man who knew how to plow. It should never have happened, but it was just one of those accidents like you see sometime on the farm. That was what everybody said, anyway.

In public.

There were other times, however, times when the men of the town got together in the late afternoon, or when the women were sewing in the parlors with the sun streaming through the windows, or when the children were sitting on dark lawns in the deep summer and watching the fireflies blink on and off in the soft air.

At those times, there were other stories told, stories "that a friend of mine heard," or that "my granddaddy told me one time," and those stories did not always match the ones told in public.

Those were the stories of the curse that Old Man Harp put on the men who hanged him, and on the town of Springville itself.

The stories usually went something like this, among the men:

"They say he was laughin' when they hauled him up, and that even when his toes started dancin' on the air he was laughin' still."

"Aw, go on, you know that ain't the truth. You can't laugh with a rope around your neck."

"That's what you'd think, all right. I ain't sayin' it's true. I'm just tellin' you what I heard."

"I still don't believe he was doin' any laughin' while he was hangin' from the end of a rope."

"Maybe he wasn't laughin'. Not all the time, anyway."

"What's that supposed to mean?"

"Just means that he's supposed to have said somethin', too."

"Said somethin'? I thought you were crazy before, but now I know you are. Humph! Tellin' me a man was talkin' with a noose around his neck and him three foot off the ground."

"You don't have to believe it. I'm just sayin' what I heard."

"Well, you might's well go on and tell it all, then. What was it he said?"

"He said somethin' like, 'You sorry bastards can kill me, but you can't kill out the Harps. We'll out-live you and out-hate you, and you'll find out that Death is bigger than all of you.'"

"That don't make a damn bit o' sense, if you ask me. What the hell's that supposed to mean, anyhow?"

"I don't know. Did I say it meant anything? It's just what he said, is all. Course Claude Morrow died, and Tobe Gregory left for good and may have died for all we know. And Harry Thompson, he's sure as to God dead."

"Didn't no Harps have anything to do with it, though."

"Did I say they did? Why'd you want to hear this story, anyhow?"

"Damned if I know.... Say, whatever happened to Old Man Harp's sons. They never did find them, did they?"

"Never looked, far as I know. Nobody knows what happened to 'em, I guess."

"I was just wonderin'...."

"What was you wonderin' about?"

"Well, ever' now and then they say you can see things down there by the graveyard. If you look, I mean."

"What kind of things?"

"You know. Things."

"No, I don't know. And you ought not to talk about that graveyard. It's bad luck."

"I don't believe in that 'luck' crap. But they say you can see lights real late at night, down there where those Harps used to live."

"You believe that?"

"Tell you the truth, I don't know. I never saw 'em myself, of course."

"Must be that they ain't there, then."

"I don't know about that, either. It's damn spooky, when you think about it. That graveyard and all. I heard ...."

"What was it you heard? I thought I was the one tellin' this story."

"Well, you are. But I heard somethin' one time, somethin' that you didn't mention."

"What's that?"

"About that hangin'."

"What about it?"

"I heard ... I heard they just left him there, hangin' from that tree limb. Kinda as a warnin'. In case his boys came back."

"I heard that, too. He hung there a long time, and the birds come and eat his eyes out. Eat a good bit more of him than that, probably. You know what I mean."

"Eat him till there wasn't nothin' left but a skeleton hangin' there, the way I heard it."

"I guess I heard that, too. They say you can hear it late at night, the skeleton I mean. You can't hear the skeleton, exactly, I guess, but you can hear the wind blowin' through the bones."

"You believe that?"

"I don't know. Sometimes I think maybe I do. Sometimes I think I may've even heard it."

"Whatever happened to the skeleton, then?"

"They say it was just gone one day. Those boys of his come got it, is what I think. And I bet ...."

"What? What do you bet?

"I bet it's buried in that graveyard right down there."

Jerry West heard some versions of the stories, but not many. He had continued to live with the Gregorys for a time, but when Tobe had gone north to start again, Jerry was sent to live with a sister of his father's, Aunt Sophie, whom he had never seen before. Aunt Sophie did not like to talk about the events that had occurred in Springville, and she probably had not been told everything. People tried to keep the worst of things from women like Aunt Sophie. So most of the stories Jerry heard from her about his father were of things that had happened years before, when Jeremiah and Sophie were growing up.

In time, because Jerry was young and because his recuperative powers, both mental and physical, were considerable, he got over that terrible night. He did not forget it, but he was able to push it into a part of his mind where he could deal with it and even in a sense understand it.

Aunt Sophie was a widow, and her husband had left her quite well to do. He had not, however, left her with a child, and she lavished all her affection on Jerry. She saw to it that he associated with other children his own age, that he got a good education, and that he got a good start in life when his schooling was done.

He never went back to Springville. After a while, he hardly ever thought of the place.

He remembered his family and what had happened to him, but he did not want to go back to the place where those things had happened. He understood that the man responsible for the crimes had been punished; Tobe Gregory had told him that much, though he had never told him just how. That much, Jerry had gotten from things he heard around the house when the grown-ups thought he wasn't listening.

It didn't really seem to matter to him.

When he left Springville, he didn't look back.

Though a hundred years had destroyed most traces of Old Springville, there were still a few homes in the area and a small community still existed. The place known as "West House" was still there.

Aunt Sophie was a good businesswoman in her way, and she made sure that Jerry's claim to the house would stand up in court should he ever want to live there in the future.

He never did, but the land and house were passed down from generation to generation of Wests, none of whom had much interest in it. They paid the taxes on the land, and occasionally they would even pay the place a visit, sometimes drinking from the spring, which still ran pure and clean from the rocks nearby.

The house was strong, as West had intended, but years of neglect took their toll. There was no glass left in any of the windows, the doors sagged open on their hinges, and the roof leaked badly. The bloodstains were no longer distinguishable from other stains on the floors and walls. The place was nothing more now than a home to spiders and birds and any animals that went inside looking for a refuge.

Thick weeds grew all around and trees had sprung up to hide the house from view; it was as if the woods were going to claim it and cover it.

It was well away from the highway and could be reached only by traveling more than a mile down a graveled road, then turning onto a dirt track for another quarter of a mile. The dirt track was hard to find itself, thickly overgrown with weeds and grass.

But in spite of it all, the house still stood, as if it were waiting for someone, someone to reclaim it from the woods, to make it habitable again. The children of what was left of Springville thought of it as a haunted house, and no one ever went near it, not even on a dare at Hallowe'en.

But there were still people living near West House who had other ideas about it, living in shacks that had been built of the remnants of other shacks, living very much like their ancestors had lived a hundred years before, when the house had been built in the first place.

There were still Harps down by the graveyard.

People knew they were there, but no one bothered them. If anything, people went out of their way to avoid them.

Though there was not much left of Springville, there was a small grocery store that catered to the few people living in the area and in the country near the county seat. There were a few small farms and cattle ranches.

The people living there knew about the Harps, all right. But they did not know much.

How did the Harps earn a living, for example?

The rumors said that there was marijuana growing in the fields, well hidden from the sheriff and his deputies, and any break-in within a ten-mile radius was likely to be blamed on the Harps.

Now and then, though not often, there would be a murder.

Someone living alone and isolated would be brutally killed, the house ransacked, anything of value taken.

The sheriff always tried to pass such crimes off as the work of passing vagrants, "scum from down around Houston," who just happened on the house in the country and decided to take advantage of the situation. It was almost impossible to catch such a criminal, even when the crime was murder, because according to the sheriff the criminal was long gone by the time the body was discovered.

There were some who believed that, and there were some who believed that the criminals were right there nearby. Those who believed the latter were careful to say nothing about it where any Harp might get wind of it, however. There was no need to take chances.

Everyone knew one thing about the Harps. They hunted and fished where they pleased and when they pleased. Fences and seasons didn't mean a thing to them. If they wanted to kill a deer, they killed it, no matter when, no matter where. If they wanted to fish, they went where they thought they could catch a big one, no matter whose land it was on.

Nobody ever tried to stop them.

Nobody ever reported them to the game warden.

Nobody ever messed with the Harps, because if those other rumors were true, the ones about the murders, there was no sense in becoming the next victim.

As for the Harps, they didn't say much to anybody, one way or the other. They just lived out there in their shacks ("worse'n hogs," as one old woman put it) and did whatever it was that they did. Without any interference from anyone.

Now and then they would be disturbed by a visitor to West House, but they kept out of sight and never even let on that they were around. They would watch the man or woman or the children look the old place over, maybe go to the spring for a drink, and then get in their car and leave.

They never stayed for more than an hour or two.

And that was just as well, for if they had stayed any longer they might have been in danger.

Because the Harps had not forgotten what they owed the Wests. The Old Man's last admonition to his sons had been taken seriously, and each new generation of Harps learned the hatred of the last.

Some people have an irrational hatred of those whose skin is a different color, while others hate anyone who worships a different god.

Some people hate the poor; some hate the rich.

The Harps hated the Wests.

The Harps of the present were much like the Harps of a hundred years before.

Uriel and Joseph had returned to the shacks with their wives and children, cut down the Old Man's bones, and moved back into the houses. Every night they told their offspring about the Wests and how they had killed their uncles. How they had caused the death of their grandfather.

The children had passed it along. Over the years the Wests had become monsters of evil, lacking only fangs and claws, and all the Harps hated them with a hate that went beyond understanding.

There were only three adult Harps now living at Springville. Not all Harps stayed around the old home place.

Of those who did, there was Joshua, who was the oldest at sixty-two. He looked much like Michael had so long before, except that his hair had not yet turned white. It was still thick and dark, and he had a moustache that was equally black, though stained by the tobacco that he chewed.

There were Joshua's two sons, Absalom and Jonah, who were twins. The twining seemed to run in the family. They were in their early thirties, with low foreheads and aquiline noses. Their broad, sloping shoulders were powerful, and their arms were corded with muscle.

The women who lived with the twins were Cherry and Nita, sisters from the county seat who had dropped out of high school when they discovered the delights of the cheap beer in the local night clubs, and they had moved on from there to the delights of liquor and hard drugs and sex, all of which were easily supplied by Absalom and Jonah.

There were two children. Cherry had a son, Matthew, who was eleven. She couldn't swear to it, but she was pretty sure he was Jonah's boy. Nita's daughter, Mary, her mother was certain, was Absalom's child, but she would not have wanted to be asked to prove it in court. Mary was eight.

The children did not have any particular responsibilities around the house. They pretty much did what they pleased, living as much like little savages as it was possible to live in twentieth century America.

They slept when they chose, woke when they chose, ate when they chose—if there was anything for them to eat.

They had the run of the countryside, and they spent a lot of time in the woods.

And they liked to play in the graveyard. They felt at home there with the old graves, graves that were now almost a part of the forest floor. The old stones were nearly all worn smooth, and many of them were cracked and toppled.

Of course, many of the graves were not marked at all, but the children knew where some of those graves were and they knew who was buried in them.

They knew which little plot belonged to Gideon and Gabriel, and they knew where the hated Wests lay.

Now and then, when Matthew had to go to the bathroom, he would use the Wests' graves.

"Look at me," he'd tell Mary. "I'm pissin' on the Wests."

Then he would laugh and Mary would laugh with him.

There was another part of the graveyard they knew about, too, the most sacred part of all. That was where the bones of old Michael rested.

Or most of the bones. The skull had been saved from burial. Uriel and Joseph had wanted a reminder of their father, so they had taken the skull home. It had been handed down from one generation to the next along with the story of the Wests.

For a hundred years it had sat on a small table by the front door of one of the shacks. It had been quite white at first, but over the years it had blackened some, with the exception of a smooth space above the nose, right between the eye sockets. The Harps had gotten into the habit of rubbing it there, for luck.

Some of the Harps even talked to the skull. Sometimes there were those who even believed that Old Man could hear that, but there was never anyone so bold as to say that the skull had ever talked back.

Mostly they talked to it about the Wests, and they passed what they said to it along to their children.

"If those fuckers ever come back, it'll be our job to kill 'em," Jonah told the children one day. "That's what we have to do."

"Why?" Matthew asked.

"Because we're supposed to," Absalom said. "The Wests killed Gideon and Gabriel Harp a long time back, two men that hadn't done a thing to them. Then they killed their daddy. Anybody'd do that ain't fit to live."

"Ain't the people who done that dead?" Matthew wanted to know.

"Sure they are, but if they got kids or grandkids, we'll kill them. Any West is the same as any other one."

"Oh," Matthew said. He wasn't sure he understood, but he didn't care. He didn't see anything wrong with killing someone. He knew that his folks did it now and then.

He'd be glad to help.

And then the Wests came back.

PART II

"Some graves will be opened before they are quite closed...."

—Sir Thomas Browne, "Hydriotaphia, Urn-Burial"

CHAPTER FOURTEEN

Sometimes people wondered why Samantha West had ever married her husband.

He was kind, there was that, and he obviously loved her and the children, but she had probably known from the first that he was never going to be what most people looked upon as a success.

He was never going to own a BMW or wear a Rolex. He was never going to be the CEO of some major corporation, or even of a minor one. The only way he was ever going to get close to big money was to win the lottery, and they didn't even live in a state with a lottery.

None of that really mattered to Sam, however.

She hadn't married Riley West for his money or his BMW. She had married him because she loved him.

But now and then he put that love to severe tests, and this was one of those times.

"Springville?" she said. "What's that?"

They were sitting in their aluminum lawn chairs with the green webbing, drinking Cokes in front of their trailer late one Sunday afternoon. The kids were playing next door on the small lawn of the Forrest's trailer with the Forrest's dog. Sam didn't know where the Forrests were.

"I've told you about Springville before," Riley said. He was thirty-nine years old, tall and raw-boned, with brown hair that always looked as if it needed cutting. He had blue eyes and a deep bass voice that still gave Sam a little thrill now and then when it seemed to vibrate at the base of her spine.

"If you did, I don't remember it," she said, taking a sip of the

Coke. The ice had melted, and the drink tasted too watery. She poured it on the grass. She looked at her husband, waiting.

"It's where the House is," he said, taking a swallow of Coke. He didn't mind if the cubes were melted. He liked it that way.

The House, Sam thought.

He always said it with a capital letter like that, and sometimes he called it West House. It was the one thing that connected him with a past that was better than the present, with a time when the name West had meant success, money, leadership.

Sam gathered that it hadn't been that way for a long time, but she didn't care. She loved Riley for what he was, not for some idea of worldly success that she didn't even fully agree with.

"What about the House, then?" she asked.

Riley looked at her speculatively. She was three years younger than he and still looked damn good in her shorts and halter, her long brown legs still slim, her breasts still firm and high, her short blonde hair still alive with highlights and shadows.

"I thought we might go there," he said. He looked away, not wanting to meet her gaze. "Live there."

"Live there?" Sam said. "Is there something you need to tell me, Riley?"

There was something, all right. He'd been waiting for the right moment to bring it up, but the catch was that with things like that there was never really a right moment. Not one that was even close to right.

"It's the job, isn't it?" Sam said. She leaned back in the chair and her shoulders sagged. It wasn't going to be a new story.

"It just wasn't right for me," Riley said. "I wasn't cut out to be a salesman, you know that." His eyes took on a faraway look. "I didn't mind so much showing people the TV sets, you know, the ones that were advertised in the paper. It was just that we were always supposed to 'sell up.' I hated that part, trying to get people to buy a set that cost twice as much as the one they came in to see."

"But your commission was more," Sam said. "And besides, they'd be getting a much better set if they bought the one you suggested."

Riley listened as she repeated the rationalization that he had almost convinced himself was true when he had started his most recent job. But her voice was no more convincing than his own inner voice had been lately. He knew that the low-priced set was a come-on and that his real job, though no one had ever told him that in so many words, was to get the people to buy something more expensive than they had come in for and to sell them a maintenance policy to boot.

He hadn't been doing that lately. He'd been selling far too many of the advertised sets, and he had not been insisting on the maintenance policy at all. And now he was out of a job.

The manager had not been at all sympathetic. "It's your job to sell up, West," he'd said. "If they don't like the deal, they don't like it, and no one's to blame. But if you don't even try, they'll never know about the better set, now will they? And buddy, you don't even try."

It wasn't the first time.

Riley sold furniture once, or tried to. He had driven a delivery truck, waited tables, worked in a full-service gas station (where he got tired of the owner's policy of adding a quart of oil to the crankcase of every car that came in for a fill-up, even if the car was no more than a pint low), tried his hand at TV repair (working as a sort of apprentice to a man whose idea of fixing things was to order as many new parts as he thought the owner would stand for), and as a checker in a supermarket.

Among other things.

Of them all, he'd liked the supermarket job best, but he had a great deal of difficulty dealing with people who got into the express line with forty items instead of fifteen and then insisted on paying by check instead of cash, though the line was clearly marked by a large sign that said, "15 ITEMS OR LESS. CASH ONLY."

And then there were the people who paid for their items and suddenly remembered that they needed a pack of cigarettes, which they wanted to pay for with pennies.

So for one reason or another, he had not been able to hold on to any particular job for any length of time. He liked to work, to do things, to help people, but he'd just never found the job that he was suited for, or the one that was suited for him.

"I just got tired of it," he told Sam about the sales job. "It wasn't right for me."

Sam sighed. "And what does Springville have to do with all this?"

"I thought we could go there, live in the House. It wouldn't cost anything to live there, no rent or anything like that. I could fix the place up, get electricity run to it, put in a septic tank."

"Do we have enough money to do all that?"

"Just about," Riley said. He wasn't really sure. The savings account he had begun with the small sum his parents had left him was now virtually nonexistent. "We can live in the trailer until the house is ready."

Sam looked at him doubtfully. "What about jobs?" She at least still had a job in Houston, though not a very good one. She was a clerk at a convenience store.

"I'll find something. It's close to the county seat, and there's always some kind of work in those little towns."

He didn't really know about that, but he'd heard that people in small towns were always complaining about people on welfare not being willing to work when there were all kinds of jobs available. He was willing to work; he would take one of the jobs that no one else would take, whatever it was.

Just then their daughter, Tammie, all of nine years old, came running up to them. There were tears in her eyes.

"Aldo bit me," she said. Aldo was the Forrest's dog.

"Did not," said Dan, their son, who had followed his sister. He was eleven and regarded himself as infinitely superior to any girl who was younger than he—and to many that were older.

"She's just a big crybaby, is all. She fell down and skinned her knee, and now she's trying to blame it on Aldo. Aldo didn't do anything."

Sam inspected her daughter's leg. There was a red spot on her knee, but the skin had not even been broken.

"You'll be all right," she told Tammie. "I hope Aldo didn't get poisoned by biting you."

"Geeesh, Mom," Dan said, slapping his hand to his forehead.

He was thin and brown from playing outside, and he couldn't abide corniness.

Tammie wiped her eyes with the back of her hand, smudging her face. She was chubby and pink, with the kind of skin that just didn't seem to tan, no matter what, despite her black hair.

"Aldo didn't really bite me," she confessed. "I just said that."

"I know," Sam said. "Why don't you kids go inside and get a Coke. See what's on TV. Your daddy and I are having a little talk."

"Can we listen?" Tammie said, curious.

"C'mon," Dan said, taking her arm and giving a little pull. He liked to think of himself as one of the adults, one who knew when to give the others some privacy. She followed him into the trailer, looking over her shoulder at her parents.

"Who's going to tell them?" Sam asked.

"I will," Riley said. "They'll like it there. There's a spring close to the house, and some woods. We could even have a garden. Grow our own vegetables."

"For a man who likes living in a trailer because you don't have to keep a yard any bigger than a king-size bed, you're sounding a lot like a country boy all of a sudden," Sam said.

"I've been thinking about it a lot," Riley said, realizing that it was true. Without even knowing it, he'd been thinking about the House for the past month or so, not all the time, but every now and then. He'd be standing there on the floor of the Electric Super Store, looking at the front door and waiting for another customer to walk in, and the House would pop into his mind.

He hadn't been there in more than twenty-five years, but he could still see it in his mind's eye, its vacant windows staring at the hill in front and the woods in back, the boards weathered to a flat gray color.

He could remember going to the spring and pushing aside the weeds at the edge to lean down for a drink. His father told him that it was all right to drink, that the water was purified by the limestone it ran through before it came out of the hillside.

The House had looked to be in pretty good shape at that time, and he could recall his father saying that it was built to last, that nothing was going to knock it down short of a hurricane.

"That cypress wood's hard as iron," his father had said. "It just gets stronger and tougher the older it gets. I guess a fire could get it, too, but that's about all."

If it was still there, if it was still that strong, it would be a fine place to live, Riley thought.

Now all he had to do was convince Sam.

It wasn't hard to do.

After all, he was out of a job, and Sam wasn't especially fond of her own job in the convenience store.

Still, she worried about the move.

"What kind of school do you think they'll have there?" she asked that night after the kids were in bed. She and Riley were watching a movie on cable, but it was one they'd seen before and they weren't really watching it, just sort of staring at the screen while thinking of other things.

"They won't have any school right there in Springville," Riley said. "The kids will have to ride a bus into the county seat, probably. Springville's not really even a town; it's more like just a bunch of houses."

"I don't like that much," Sam said.

"Why not?" Riley said. "They have to ride a bus here, don't they? And I bet the chances of an accident around a little place like Springville are a lot less than they are in Houston. There probably won't be any crack dealers hanging around the campus, either."

She couldn't argue with that. He was probably exaggerating about the crack dealers, but not by much, although Tammie and Dan were still in elementary school.

"People in small towns don't like strangers," Sam said. "They might not be very friendly."

For some reason Riley suddenly thought of something else his father had told him. He thought about the Harps.

The Wests, too, had kept the memory of that long-ago night of terror alive within the family, but it wasn't something that Riley had ever mentioned to Sam. She had a thing about violence, so he'd just never brought it up. Well, that didn't matter. It had been a long time ago.

"If the people aren't friendly, we'll still have each other," he said. "After all, how many friends do we have here?"

"Not many," Sam admitted. There were the Forrests next door, but they weren't really friends, just people you spoke to and occasionally shared a drink with or whose dog you looked after when they were gone. There were a couple of other people in the trailer park that they knew to speak to, and a couple more on the job, but that was about it.

"I guess we wouldn't be giving up much when you look at it that way," Sam said.

"That's right. It would be like a fresh start for us. I really think this was something we were meant to do." A note of excitement crept into Riley's deep voice. "It's like the House has just been sitting there all these years, waiting for us."

"Don't you think you ought to check it out first, before you get too worked up about this move?" Sam asked. "That house might have fallen down by now, for all you know about it."

"I'll drive up there tomorrow," Riley said.

"I hope the car will make it," Sam said. They had a '79 Chrysler New Yorker that Riley had bought used in 1983. It had well over a hundred thousand miles on the odometer, needed new tires, and the bands were slipping in the automatic transmission.

"It'll make it. Do you and the kids want to come?"

Sam smiled at his enthusiasm. "I can't speak for the kids, but some of us still have jobs to do. I'll have to go in to work tomorrow, as usual."

"You can give them your notice, then. You won't be going back for long."

"I think I'll wait for the report on the House," Sam said. "It might not even be there."

"It's there," Riley said. "I know it's there."

She wondered why he sounded so certain, but he could not have told her if she had asked him.

CHAPTER FIFTEEN

Riley and the children left at 4:30 the next morning. They had to get an early start because it was the middle of the summer, and Riley wanted to do most of the three-and-a-half-hour drive before it got too hot. Among the Chrysler's problems was a balky air-conditioner whose system leaked Freon, and repairs would have been too costly to consider.

"But the House won't be hot," Riley told Dan and Tammie after they were well on their way. "They knew how to build houses back then, with windows to catch the breezes. And there were high ceilings, too, and floors that sat up off the ground so the air could get under them. And it's not as humid up there as it is here near the coast. It'll be fine. You'll see."

The children were skeptical. It didn't seem possible that a house without air-conditioning could be comfortable.

"I remember one day at school the air-conditioner broke," Dan said. "They had to send us all home at noon because it was so hot."

"That's because they didn't build the school to take advantage of the natural cooling of nature," Riley said.

He had the Chrysler up to sixty, five miles under the speed limit on the interstate, but that was about as fast as the New Yorker could travel without severe vibration problems. The windows were down and the cool early-morning air was blowing in on them.

"Feel that wind?" he said. "That's the way nature cools things off."

"The wind won't feel that way by lunch time," Dan said. He had been on trips on the Texas highways before; he knew what it was like with the sun beating down and reflecting off the paved roadway.

"There'll be trees around the house, though," Riley said. "Shade trees. Grass, too. We'll be cool and comfortable, you just wait. Besides, if we get too hot we can move into the trailer."

The fact that the trailer would be there gave Dan a little hope, even though he knew that the air-conditioner was far from efficient. Cooling a little metal box in the hot Texas sun was not an easy job.

"I need to use the bathroom," Tammie said.

Riley looked at his watch. They had been gone less than an hour. "Wait until we get to Huntsville," he said. "I'll stop and buy you something to eat at McDonald's and you can use the restroom there."

"I need to go now," Tammie said.

"No you don't," Dan said. "I'll tell you a story."

"What story?"

"The one about Hansel and Gretel."

"O. K., but I get to tell the part about when they push the wicked witch in the oven," Tammie said.

"O. K.," Dan agreed. "There were these two kids, see—"

"You didn't say 'Once upon a time,'" Tammie said.

Dan sighed and started over. "Once upon a time," he said.

Well, I sure didn't lie to Sam, Riley thought as the car rolled down the gravel road leading to Springville, stirring up a plume of dust that trailed behind them. It's not really even a town. There's not even a sign anymore.

Springville was, in fact, just a collection of houses. Or not even that, really. The houses were fairly widely spread, and though they were only a short distance from the highway you would never suspect they were there. And you would never turn off on that gravel road unless you were looking for them. But they were all neat, with closely clipped yards and paint that was nowhere near the chipping stage. People in Springville seemed to take pride in their houses, and Riley thought that was a good sign.

Riley drove up to the one store that still remained, a wooden building that looked as if it might be as old as the House. There were two gas pumps in front, however, that looked brand new, and the posted price of gasoline was right up to date, maybe even higher than in Houston.

He parked the car at the side of the building. "You kids want something to drink?" he said.

They did, and they opened the car doors and jumped out eagerly. Riley followed them to the store's front door.

The glass windows on either side of the door were filled with "TODAY'S SPECIALS," canned goods and cereal boxes which all looked a bit dusty and might have been there for quite some time.

Dan opened the screen door and went inside. Riley and Tammie followed him.

There was a modern Coke machine just inside the door, and Riley began feeding change into it. It rumbled and clanked when he pushed the button, and an aluminum can dropped into the proper slot.

When he had bought the drinks, Riley looked around. The walls of the store were lined with canned goods and boxes, but there was not much of any one item. There were no vegetables or meats, but there was a glass candy counter. The store was not air-conditioned, either; it was cooled by a huge fan that was located in the back door and blew straight through the store.

There was a short, fat man behind a counter. He was watching Riley curiously. Riley walked back to talk to him.

"'Mornin'," the man said with a smile. "Something I can do for you?"

"I'm looking for West House," Riley said.

The man's smile changed to something else; it wasn't quite a frown, but it was definitely no longer a smile.

"Why?" he said.

"I own the place," Riley said. "I'm thinking about moving in."

The man was smiling again. "In that case, I ought to introduce myself. I'm Gus Morrow." He put out his hand.

Riley took the hand and shook it. It was soft and fat, like the man. "Riley West," he said. "Those are my kids." He pointed to

Dan and Tammie, who were looking into the candy case.

"Fine looking pair," Morrow said. "You're planning to live here, huh?"

"Thinking about it," Riley said. "I'll have to take a look at the house, see if it can be fixed up. I've got a trailer I can live in while I'm working on it."

"Might not be a good idea to move into a place that old," Morrow said. "Might be dangerous."

"Dangerous in what way?" Riley said.

"Just dangerous," Morrow said. The smile had disappeared again. "You know how those old houses can be."

"We'll be careful," Riley said. "Can you tell me how to get there?"

"Sure enough." Morrow gave him the directions.

Riley gathered up the kids and went back to the car.

The first sight of the House was a disappointment.

Riley turned from the gravel road down onto the dirt track that led downhill and looked as if it were used about once a year. It was hard even to follow the ruts through the weeds.

He looked in his rearview mirror and saw several houses on the top of the hill. They were as neat as the others, well-kept and comfortable, quite a contrast to what was waiting for him at the bottom of the hill.

The House was almost impossible to see. Trees grew thickly around it, and the weeds sprung wild and green in their shade.

The old Chrysler rolled down the hill, crushing weeds under its balding tires. The closer it got to the House, the more apprehensive Riley became. He could see now that the roof was virtually gone, that none of the windows had any glass in them, that the woods had practically claimed the house.

There was a lot more work to be done than he had first thought. He had been too optimistic. After all, the house had been uninhabited for nearly a hundred years. He should not have expected fixing it up to be a weekend project.

"That's it?" Dan said when they reached the bottom of the hill and the car had come to a stop. "It looks like a haunted house to me."

"Has it got a bathroom?" Tammie said.

"I don't think so," Riley said. "We'll have to look it over."

They got out of the car, the doors brushing aside the tall weeds, many of them growing taller than the children's heads.

"I don't like this place," Tammie said. "I can't see, and I need to use the bathroom."

"You'll have to wait," Riley said, taking her hand. "Let's go look at the House."

He led the children through the weeds, thinking about things he had not thought about for years—things like ticks, chiggers, and snakes. At least it was cool, what with all the shade from the trees.

When they got to the House, they stopped to look at it.

It might have been Riley's imagination, but it seemed that Tammie's hand tightened on his own as they stood there.

He had to admit that even in its decay the house was impressive.

It towered among the trees, and there was something imposing about its solidity.

Unfortunately, that was all that was imposing about it. There were birds' nests in the second-floor windows; the porch columns were rotting, as was the latticework around the bottom of the porch; the steps did not look safe; and it was clear even from the outside that the inside was probably going to be worse.

Riley hid his disappointment, but the children did not.

"This place looks worse than a haunted house," Dan said. "It looks like it's about to fall down."

"I don't like it," Tammie said, puffing out her cheeks. "It doesn't look clean. And it doesn't have a bathroom."

Riley was determined not to give up. "Let's go on in," he said. "Be careful on those steps."

They mounted the steps to the porch and went through the doorway, which no longer had a door. It had disappeared long ago, probably taken by someone who wanted it and knew that no one would miss it.

"P.U.," Dan said. "This place smells worse than those ponies we used to ride at PlayLand."

Riley had to admit that the kid was right. The House did

stink. It had probably been home to any number of animals over the years, animals that had decided it might provide some kind of shelter from a severe winter or a howling rainstorm. They had left behind reminders of their presence. Some of them had probably died there.

The floor was covered with leaves and dried excrement, and large piles of leaves had blown into the corners of the rooms. Dirt was thick on the floor, and the leaves had formed a sort of compost heap with most of the unpleasant odor coming from the blackish substance at the bottoms of the largest piles.

But that was the worst of it, to Riley's surprise.

The House had been built to last, and it had lasted. The floor was pegged together, not nailed, and still solid as it had been when new. The walls were solid, too, most of them, and Riley suspected that the frame was as tough as it had ever been. As best he could tell from an inspection of the attic, that was the case.

The upstairs rooms were in a bit worse shape than the downstairs, thanks to the nearly missing roof and a few holes in the attic floor, but that could be taken care of too. The wind and rain had not done too much damage over the years. There was no rot in the walls, or at least not much.

The place was not hopeless. It wouldn't be easy; in fact, it would be downright hard, but he could fix it up. It would take time, but it could be done.

Replace the rotted wood, of which there really wasn't that much, considering the age of the house, put on a new roof, do some painting, put in a septic tank, and you'd have a place where people could live.

They'd need water, but there was what looked like the crumbling structure of a well beside the house. A new well would be necessary, but the water was down there. They could even carry water from the spring if worse came to worst.

They'd need electricity, too, of course, but he'd seen the electric lines along the gravel road, so that wouldn't be a problem.

And they could have the trailer moved there and stay in it for a while, with all the comforts of home. It wouldn't be easy getting it down that hill, but it could be done.

The money was an obstacle, but he didn't have to do everything at once. There was a little in the savings, and surely he could get a job in the county seat, some kind of job. He could work on the House on weekends and in the evenings.

It was possible. Now more than ever, despite the condition of the House, it seemed possible.

"Well, kids, what do you think?" he said.

"I hate it," Tammie said.

"Why?" Riley asked.

"I need to use the bathroom. There isn't one."

"We'll put one in. And you can have your own room, too." They were on the second floor, standing in what had once been the bedroom of Elizabeth West, though they did not know that. "You can have this room, right here."

"I don't like this room," she said, looking up at the clear blue sky that was clearly visible through a hole in the attic floor.

"Why not?" Dan said. "If you don't like it, I'll take it."

He seemed more enthusiastic about the house than his sister. He liked the idea of having all that space. He especially liked the attic, thinking how much fun it would be to play up there on a rainy day with the rain beating down on the roof.

"It's a scary room," Tammie said, looking back down.

"Sissy," Dan said.

"That's enough of that," Riley said. "Let's go look for the spring."

They went down the stairs and out into the yard.

CHAPTER SIXTEEN

Joshua Harp watched the Chrysler as it came slowly down the hill.

He was standing beside his shack, which was well hidden by trees and weeds, so overgrown with vines and brush that it was almost a part of the landscape. He could see, but no one could see him. No one would even know the Harp shacks were there unless he stumbled across them. They were in even worse shape than West House, though the Harps were living in them and found them comfortable enough.

Jonah came out of the other shack, which was equally well concealed, and walked over to stand beside his father. Jonah was holding a bottle of Sunnybrook by the neck, though it was still early in the morning.

"Who's that over there, Daddy?" he said, taking a hefty swig from the bottle.

"Don't know," Joshua said, shaking his head. "Prob'ly just somebody coming down to look at the House." He said it with a capital "H," just the way Riley West did.

"Why you think they want to do a thing like that?" Jonah said.

"People do it ever' now and then," Joshua told him. "I've seen 'em come and go before. They don't ever stay very long."

"What if they do stay?" Jonah said. "What if they're some of them fuckin' Wests come back to live here."

Joshua looked at his son, eyes blazing. He didn't say a word. He didn't have to.

Matthew and Mary did not see the Wests arrive. They were busy at the time, playing in the graveyard. It was one of their favorite places because it was so cool there under the trees, and the game they liked to play there was one they called "Taking Care of the Wests."

It was a simple game, with simple rules.

First, the Wests had to be killed.

Matthew and Mary had made several dolls to serve as the Wests. The dolls were made from old pantyhose that Nita and Cherry had cast off. The hose were full of runners, but Matthew and Mary had cut off the feet and stuffed them with leaves and grass. Then they had put rubber bands around the openings. Mary sewed little pieces of cloth on the dolls for eyes and mouths. The dolls didn't really look much like people, but they were good enough.

Sometimes the dolls would be killed by stabbing. The Harps were still fond of knives, and Matthew had a pocketknife of his own, a pretty good Case knife that he had been given by Joshua.

He didn't use the knife for stabbing the dolls, however. That would have ruined them. Mary had told him that there was too much sewing, and that he shouldn't ruin them by using the knife.

So they stabbed them with sticks instead. The sticks weren't really satisfactory; they didn't penetrate the dolls' skin. But that meant the dolls could be used again and again.

Sometimes the dolls would be killed by pressing. Matthew would lay them on a flat rock and then stack other rocks on top of them. As he added each rock, Mary would give out a realistic cry of pain—"Aaaagggghh," she would groan as Matthew stacked on the rocks.

When she got tired of doing that, she would cry "Uuhh-uh-uuhh-uh-uuhhhhhhhh," gradually trailing off into the strangled moan which was the signal that the doll was dead.

Sometimes they even choked the dolls, with one child making terrible faces and giving out with strangled groans while the other laughed heartily and kept on choking.

They did other things to the dolls, too, but they never hanged them. That was the way old Michael had died, and that was a bad thing to do to anyone, even a West. Or so the children thought.

After the killing came the burying.

Matthew and Mary had no idea about coffins. They just dug graves and put the dolls in them, then covered them over with dirt. The graves were marked with pieces of broken glass, or if the children were feeling especially ambitious they might get a stone and scratch some marks on it with a rusty nail.

They did not know what any of the marks they saw on the other, larger stones meant; neither of them could read or write. The Harps did not hold much with formal education.

The main drawback to the burials was having to uncover the dolls so soon after their interment. They had to use the same dolls over and over, so they did not want to leave them under the earth for too long.

"What we need," Matthew said one day, "is something we can kill and bury for real and just leave there."

Mary agreed. They each gathered up a handful of rocks and went down to the river bottom, looking for something to kill.

All they could find was a turtle, sunning itself on a half-submerged limb a few feet from the shore. It was not easy to catch a turtle, even one that seemed to be sleeping. They were actually quite alert and a lot faster than people thought they were.

But Matthew had learned to move in the woods and even in the water like a shadow, almost entirely without sound. He managed to slip to the limb and grab the turtle, tossing it out on the bank.

Mary immediately began pelting it with rocks, and Matthew splashed to shore to join her.

The rocks thudded into the turtle with a terrible crunching noise, cracking its shell and exposing its vulnerable body. They kept throwing the rocks until they were quite sure the turtle was dead.

It was hard to pick the turtle up then, since its shell was in many pieces and kept falling apart. The turtle wasn't in very good shape, either, but they got it back to the graveyard, put it in the hole they'd dug, and covered it over.

A couple of days later they had returned to the grave and dug it up, just to see what had happened to the turtle.

It was not as pleasant as digging up the dolls.

Mary made a gagging noise. "Do you think people smell like that when they're buried?"

"I guess so," Matthew said. "Probably worse. They're bigger."

"We should've dug a deeper hole," Mary said. "Granddaddy makes our daddies dig real deep."

"Yeah, but they're bigger than us. We don't have any shovels, either. We've just got sticks."

"I don't think I want to bury anything else, then," Mary said.

Matthew agreed. He didn't mind the killing; in fact, he sort of liked that. But he sure didn't like the smell of that dead turtle.

"We'll cover it up," he said, and they did.

It seemed to both of them that they could still smell it, though, even days later.

Today, they were using only the dolls. They had strangled one and stabbed two others.

"Why don't we bury this one alive?" Matthew said, holding the last of the dolls above his head. "We haven't done that before."

"Okay," Mary said. "I wonder how it would sound, with dirt in its mouth and nose and eyes?"

"I'll make the noises," Matthew said. "You cover it up.

He tossed the doll in the tiny grave.

Riley West had found the spring on the side of the hill. It was thickly overgrown with weeds and grass, but there was a small rocky pool of water just as he remembered it.

The spring bubbled out of the side of the hill, running into the pool. The pool overflowed into a narrow stream of water only a few inches wide that flowed down the side of the hill and almost to the bottom before it sank into a wide crack in the earth and disappeared underground.

"It goes all the way to the river," Riley told the children.

"Can we drink it?" Dan asked.

Riley wasn't sure. The water had been all right when he was a child, but a lot had happened to the world since then. When he was growing up, the words "environmental pollution" had never been spoken, at least not by anyone Riley knew. He hadn't even known about the dangers of pollution until he got older and began reading about them in the newspapers and magazines.

Who knew what kind of pesticides, herbicides, and other poisons might be in the spring water? Riley certainly didn't.

Then he recalled what his father had told him about the water being filtered through the limestone for great distances. Maybe it was still all right.

He bent down, cupped his hand, and dipped into the spring. The water was cold, almost icy. He brought his hand up to his face and smelled the water. Some of it dripped through his fingers.

It didn't have any odor that he could detect. The sunlight reflected on it cleanly, and there was no sign of an oily sheen.

What the hell, he thought. He sipped the water from his cupped hand. It tasted sweet and pure.

"You can have a little sip," he told the kids. "Don't drink much, though." He would have the water tested before he started drinking it regularly, just like he would have the well water tested. They could buy bottled water for a while.

As Dan and Tammie tried to drink the water, getting more of it on their faces and necks than in their mouths, Riley looked back down the hill at the House. It looked almost black as it stood gloomily in the shade of the trees, but the top of it was in the sun and looked a bit more cheerful.

This is the place, Riley thought. He could almost feel it in the ground under his feet. This was where he was meant to be, a place where he could belong and settle down.

He decided to drive over to the county seat and begin looking for a job right away.

As they walked back to the car, he was thinking of ways to describe the House to Sam, ways that wouldn't make it sound quite as bad as it was. He knew she would insist on seeing it anyway, but maybe he could convince her before she saw it. Things would be easier that way.

Joshua Harp watched the Chrysler struggle up the hill, black smoke pouring from the exhaust.

Harp didn't think too much of people who had to drive cars. He could drive one, but he didn't own one. If he needed one, he'd steal it and then abandon it later.

He wondered just who the people had been. They had looked at the house a long time, and then they had visited the spring.

Could they have been Wests?

Possibly. He didn't remember the last time there had been anybody looking at the House, though people came down to the spring now and then.

Not the people who lived in the little community at the top of the hill, not them. They would never have walked even that far toward the residence of the Harps.

They knew who was living down there, and Joshua was pretty sure they had an idea that the Harps didn't like them much.

They were right about that, in a way. The truth was that the Harps just didn't think about them very often.

Joshua was smart, just as his ancestors had been. He didn't prey on the people up the hill. If you did that, you might get in some real trouble. Look what had happened to Old Michael.

Of course that was the fucking Wests' fault. If they'd just minded their own business, there would never have been any trouble. Joshua was convinced of that.

Old Michael hadn't done anything wrong, not to Joshua's way of thinking. He had left the townspeople strictly alone, and it was Jeremiah West who had messed in where he wasn't wanted.

The same old things that Michael and his boys had done were still being done today, but Joshua knew that he had to be more careful than his ancestors had been. There were a lot more police now than then, and they were always looking for some way to make themselves look good.

Joshua and his boys were careful, though. They didn't bother anybody nearby, and when they stole they never took very much. Just enough to get by on till the next time. People sometimes weren't even sure they'd been burglarized when the Harps broke into their houses.

And when they killed, they usually killed folks nobody

really gave much of a damn about, old people living alone without any family or friends to speak of. Hell, it was like the Harps were doing them a favor, almost.

Now and then, however, they'd get out of their regular routine, and that was a little dangerous. So far there hadn't been any trouble, but it was something you had to be really cautious about.

It involved people who got in trouble up on the highway. If Joshua or his boys spotted someone with a flat tire or engine trouble or something like that, they would go up and offer to help.

They would strike up a conversation with whoever it was and find out where they were from. If it was someone just passing through on his way to somewhere else, and if the car could be fixed easily, then whoever it was might just wind up dead of a sudden blow to the back of the head with a tire tool.

The Harps would strip the car and its driver of valuables, drive the car off into the river, and bury the unfortunate corpse in the graveyard.

They didn't get to do that much more than once a year, but it was fun when it could be done. Real satisfying, sort of like carrying on the family tradition.

Nobody could say where the car had broken down; it just didn't make it to its destination. Maybe now and then someone would remember seeing it stalled by the highway, but the Harps were careful to pick out nondescript cars, not red Corvettes. No one had ever even questioned them about stalled cars.

Hell, nobody had ever questioned them about anything, not even the coon hunters that got lost down in the river bottoms that time. One of those suckers never made it home, but nobody ever guessed the Harps were to blame. They figured he must've fallen in the river or gotten so lost he starved to death back in the woods.

Joshua smiled thinking about it.

He and the boys had heard the dogs bugling on the trail of the coons, and they had known the hunters were out. It was a crisp fall night with a full moon, the kind of night the hunters liked.

The kind of night the Harps liked, too.

They had left the shacks and trailed along after the hunters. It was easy, especially since the hunters had been drinking a lot and most of them were just barely able to stay on their feet and follow the dogs. They for damn sure weren't thinking about anybody following them.

Once they saw the condition of the hunters, the Harps got in front of them and laid a false trail for the dogs, one that led them and the hunters right through the boggiest, thickest brakes of the river bottom, where the tree limbs grew densely together and blotted out the moon and the vines crawled along the ground like spiky snakes, where fallen trees and broken limbs blocked everything that looked like an easy pathway.

They waited for the hunters to get separated, as would naturally happen under those conditions. Then they sneaked up behind them and without letting themselves be seen tripped them up or tangled them in vines until they were all hopelessly lost, calling out for one another and trying to find the dogs and getting nowhere.

The Harps had settled on one man for their kill, a skinny, balding man that Jonah thought might run the hardware store in the county seat.

They smashed in his temple with the haft of a knife, dragged him back into the trees, and slit his throat.

He didn't make a sound, other than a sort of bubbly sigh.

He wasn't carrying much of value, as the Harps discovered when they went through his jeans, just a five-celled flashlight, along with seventeen dollars in his billfold, and thirty-eight cents in change.

The Harps didn't care.

It wasn't valuables they were after. It was the thrill of the hunt and the kill that excited them, like it was in their blood.

While the skinny man's buddies were still scrambling around in the swamp, getting their faces cut and their clothes ruined by sticker vines, the Harps dragged their victim down to the river, slit him open and filled him with rocks.

"Is this the way old Michael and his boys done it?" Jonah asked.

"Damn right," Absalom said. "Ain't it daddy?"

"Sure is," Joshua agreed. "We'll carry the innards back to the bog." He knew that the gars in the stagnant pools would gobble up the bloody intestines almost as soon as they hit the water.

There weren't many good times like that, Joshua thought now, times when you and your boys were out together like a family ought to be, doing what a family ought to be doing—at least what it ought to be doing if it was a Harp family.

Wouldn't it be something, he thought as the Chrysler topped the hill and turned off down the gravel road. Wouldn't it be something if those people in the car really were some of the Wests, Wests who were doing more than just returning to the old family homestead for just a sight of it.

What if they were looking it over and thinking of living in it again?

Of course, that didn't seem very likely, considering the condition of the House. It hadn't been lived in for a long, long time.

But if it *were* some Wests, and they were coming back, wouldn't it be something.

That coon hunter was nothing compared to what a West would be.

And besides, the Wests and the Harps had a little unfinished business to take care of.

The way Joshua figured it, one West had got clean away from Michael and the boys that night so long ago, so that made one the Wests owed the Harps right there.

And then there was old Michael.

A Harp was worth three or four Wests any day, so that made three or four more the Harps were owed.

Yes, sir, it would really be something if Joshua and his boys were the ones who finally got to collect on that little debt.

It really would.

CHAPTER SEVENTEEN

"It was great, honey," Riley told Sam that night.

The kids were tired and had gone to bed early, too exhausted to wait until their mother got home from work to tell her about their experiences that day.

"I'll just bet it was," Sam said. She was tired, too, since she had been on her feet for eight hours, starting at noon, selling gasoline in dribs and drabs, candy bars, Slushee drinks, beef jerky, beer, milk, loaves of bread, and all the other things people stopped at a convenience store to pick up on their way home or to work.

Not to mention renting out video tapes.

All she wanted to do was sit on the couch and watch TV; she wasn't really interested in talking about some old house which was probably about to fall down anyway.

"I got a job today," Riley said.

That announcement made Sam sit up a little straighter. "You what?"

"I got a job today. I can start tomorrow if I want to."

Things were suddenly moving too fast for Sam. Last night moving to the House had been just a vague idea, something that Riley thought of on the spur of the moment. Now he was talking about getting a job.

"Where?" she said. "What kind of job?"

"Not too far from Springville," he said, answering the first question. "On the way to the county seat. There's a big lumber yard on the highway outside of town, and I saw this sign that said 'Help Wanted' on the fence, so I turned in and applied. They hired me."

Sam wasn't interested in TV anymore. "They hired you."

"What's so surprising about that?" Riley said. "It's a good job, too. People who come to a lumber yard usually know what they want. You don't have to sell them on anything. And the best part is that I can get a discount on the stuff I'll need to fix up the House. Not to mention that I'll get a line on all the best carpenters and people who can help me do the stuff I can't do myself."

"I can't believe this," Sam said. "Are you saying that we're really going ahead and move into that fire trap?"

"It's not a fire trap. It's really in pretty good shape. It'll take some time and hard work, but we can fix it up."

"'Trust me,'" Sam said. "'The check is in the mail.'"

"It's not like that. Trus—Believe me."

"The kids loved the place, I suppose."

"Not loved, exactly. Tammie's concerned with the lack of sanitary facilities."

Sam laughed. "I never heard of a child so worried about her bladder. What did she do about it?"

"She finally had to go off in the bushes," Riley said. "She didn't like it much."

"I can't blame her," Sam said. "You men have it easy, but it's different for us women."

"Look, you can give notice at the store and I'll go up there and start work, get a septic tank put in. By the time it's ready you'll be through here and we can have the trailer moved to Springville. This is what we've been waiting for, a chance to start all over."

Once again Sam had the feeling that events were moving too fast for her. Riley already had a job, he had begun planning what to do about the House, and he was blithely arranging their future as if she would go along without argument.

And she realized that she would.

Riley had never seemed so enthusiastic about anything as he did about the House, and as he had said the night before, what would they be leaving behind?

For her, eight hours a day of sore feet, a couple of acquaintances, and a lot in a mobile home park.

For Riley, less than that.

He was right. It was time for a new beginning, a time to make something happen in their lives.

"What the hell," she said. "Let's do it."

"You really mean that?" Riley said.

Sam laughed. "I said it didn't I? Of course I mean it."

"That's great, just great. You are going to love the House, I guarantee it. Wait until you see it. When's your next day off?"

"Wednesday," she said.

He hadn't been exactly right.

She didn't love the House.

She'd never seen such an accumulation of filth in her life, and she didn't like the lack of sanitary facilities any more than Tammie did.

She also was not fond of the missing roof, the flourishing weeds, the sound of insects humming in the air all around her.

"At least you can breathe the air," Riley said. "And you don't have to worry about inhaling the exhaust fumes from ten thousand cars a minute, either."

"I don't like bugs."

"Those bugs won't hurt you. Dan and Tammie weren't even bothered when they were here the first time."

The children had been bothered more than Riley wanted to admit. They had both gotten chigger bites and had scratched themselves bloody, but he had put some Campho-Phenique on the bites, and that had helped.

"Maybe you can breathe the air outside, but not in here," Sam said. "I never smelled anything like this."

"When we've cleaned up, it won't smell anymore. You'll never know it was like this." Riley hoped he was right. They were going to have to do most of the first cleaning with a shovel.

"It's going to be really hot, too," Sam said.

Riley disagreed. "It's not that hot. Usually there's more of a breeze. You'll see."

"Maybe," Sam said. She didn't sound convinced.

But it wasn't really the lack of a breeze or the smell or the bugs that bothered her.

It was something else, something she couldn't put into words. If Tammie had been able to explain how she had felt on her first visit when she was in the room upstairs, the one that had been Elizabeth's room, Sam would have recognized her own feeling exactly.

But Tammie hadn't said anything to her mother about that. In fact, she and Dan had not even come into the house. They were outside in the yard, playing in the tall weeds beneath the trees. It was cool there in the shade, and they liked the feeling of being able to pretend they were lost in the jungle.

There were places where the weeds were higher than the children's heads, and they pushed through them, trampling some of the taller ones to the ground and clearing a path from the car to the house.

Dan was wondering how much his father would pay him to mow the yard here. He got a dollar for doing the one at the trailer, but that took only a few minutes. It would take a lot longer than that here. He wondered if their lawnmower would even do the job. There was hardly any grass, really, but the weeds were thick, and there were lots of rocks and clods of dirt. Things like that would not be good for the mower blade.

It was Tammie who noticed the opening in the latticework around the base of the porch.

"I wonder if there's anything under there," she said to Dan when she pointed the opening out to him.

Dan got down on his knees and peered into the darkness. "Let's go find out," he said.

"We'll get dirty," Tammie protested, not noticing that it was a little late to be worrying about that. She had green stains from the weeds on her shorts and shirt, and there was sticky residue on her hands and face, to which dirt was already adhering.

Dan didn't look much better, but he didn't care. He wanted to see what was under the house. He crawled through the hole.

It was immediately cooler even than the outside. The earth under the house was rough and hard, but there was a hint of dampness in it that Dan could smell.

"Come on," he called to Tammie. "It's neat."

Tammie was looking through the hole. "I don't want to," she

said. "I'm going to tell Dad on you."

"I don't care," Dan said. He crawled forward, brushing a spider web from in front of his face. There was something he liked about being under the house, something comforting. He knew that when they moved there, this was going to be his secret place.

He crawled to what he thought was about the center of the house and sat there, looking back at where he had come from. He could see the light that marked the hole, but he could not see very far into the yard. Tammie was no longer there.

Then he heard footsteps above his head.

"Dan's under the house." It was Tammie's voice.

"What's he doing under there?" Sam said.

"I don't know. He wanted me to come, but I wouldn't."

"There might be snakes under there, Riley," Sam said.

Dan didn't like the idea of snakes, but somehow he didn't think that he was in any danger from them. He sat where he was.

"You'd better go outside and call him," Sam said.

There were more footsteps, this time moving toward the front door. Dan started for the hole. He didn't want to get in trouble, and by the time his father got to the yard, Dan was already coming out from under the house.

"I don't think it's a good idea to go crawling around under there," Riley said. "You never know what kind of varmint might be hiding out from the world under a porch."

"There wasn't anything there but me," Dan said, brushing the dirt off his pants but not getting much of it removed.

"Look at you," his mother said from the porch.

Tammie was standing beside her looking smug. Dan would get her later for tattling.

"I'm going to have to do three loads of wash a day if we move into this place," Sam said, looking hard at Dan.

Dan looked up at Sam. He thought his mother was the prettiest woman in the world, and she never seemed to get dirty. When he had gone through the house with his father and Tammie, they had all three come out with dust and dirt all over them. But not his mother. There wasn't a smudge on her.

"We'll have plenty of water from the well," Riley said. "You can do as many loads as you want."

Sam looked off in the direction of the Harps' shacks, though from where she stood she could not distinguish them from the woods. For the moment she seemed to forget about Dan.

"What's over there?" she said.

Riley followed her gaze. "Trees," he said.

Dan laughed. He thought his father was funny sometimes.

"You know what I meant," Sam said.

Oddly enough, Riley did know what she meant. It was just a feeling, but he could sense that there was something over in that direction. He vaguely remembered his father telling him something about it.

After a second, it came to him.

"I think there might be a graveyard over there," he said.

"A graveyard?" Sam looked at him disapprovingly.

"A real old one. Some of the graves go back to the time Texas was a republic, I think."

"Is it a historical site?"

"I don't think so. From what I remember, it's never been taken care of. I never saw it, but I got the impression that it was practically overgrown by the woods. You might not even be able to find it anymore."

"I can assure you that I don't want to," Sam said.

"I do," Dan said. "I bet it's neat."

"It is not neat," Sam said. "I'm not sure I like the idea of living down by a graveyard."

"It's not as if the house were built on top of it," Riley said. "You don't have to worry about living in the middle of *Poltergeist IV* or anything."

"I'd better not."

"What's a poster-guys?" Tammie said.

"It's a ghost," Dan said. "A creepy, crawly ghost with big eyes and claws and—"

"That's enough of that," Sam said. Tammie had gotten behind her and wrapped her arms around Sam's legs, hugging herself tightly to her mother. "I don't want to hear anything else about ghosts."

"All right," Dan said.

But he was already making his plans to go looking for the graveyard.

Chapter Eighteen

There was no one in the graveyard.

The only movement was the breeze that softly stirred the leaves of the trees that grew there, and the only sound was the buzzing of insects and the rubbing of the tree branches.

The sunlight filtered through the trees and cast patches of light on the ground, light that played among the shadows as if it were a living thing.

Now it would flicker on a cracked stone, weathered and sunk into the ground; then it would fall on a spot of earth that seemed to be sinking beneath an invisible weight.

Had there been anyone there to see, the person might have thought at first that there was something else moving in the graveyard that day, something that could not be seen distinctly but that moved in and out among the shadows and the light.

Something more like a shadow than not, a thing that danced across the graves, now hardly like graves at all since they were barely distinguishable from the rest of the floor of the woods.

Of course if the person had seen that, or thought he had seen that, it would be immediately dismissed as a trick of the light.

There could be nothing moving there. The graveyard was deserted.

But there seemed to be *something*.

It could not be defined; it was like a wavering of the light, a darkening of the shadow.

If the observer had tried to get closer to the something, he would never have been able to reach it. It would have disappeared like smoke in a storm or rain in a river, and a sensible person would have dismissed it as nothing more than an illusion.

"And yet ..." he might have said later, "and yet there did seem to be something there."

Could it be, he might have wondered, that there are things remarkably like ghosts—not ghosts, certainly, but something like them—that haunt the old deserted graveyards of the earth?

Could it be that the spirits of the dead, though of course having no influence on the living, really did somehow manage an existence after life, an existence that now and then managed to impinge on what we like to call reality?

"No," the sensible person would tell himself. "No such thing is possible. What I saw, if I saw anything, was nothing more than a trick of the sunlight and the breeze."

Telling himself that, he would be able to dismiss it from his mind once again and sleep peacefully at night, unworried.

But every now and then, waking in the middle of the night, staring around him in the darkness, he would seem to see the graveyard, seem to hear the buzzing of the insects, seem to see once more the wavering of the light, the darkening of the shadow.

He would tell himself that it was all a dream, perhaps rising and walking into his kitchen for a drink of water to calm himself.

Then, lying back on his pillow, he would close his eyes and try to rest, but all through the rest of that long night he would hear an echo in his head:

"And yet ... and yet."

But there was no one there to see.

The graveyard was deserted.

CHAPTER NINETEEN

The Harps watched the family's inspection of West House with growing interest.

"It's the same ones that was here before," Absalom said. "The two kids and the man, that is."

"Yeah," Jonah said. "But that woman sure wasn't here with 'em the first time. Would you look at that?" He gave a low whistle.

"You better not let Cherry hear you say that," his brother said.

"Hell, she don't care. Long as I let her smoke a few joints, she don't give a damn who I fuck."

"You two shut up," Joshua said. "You want them to hear us?"

The twins knew that there was no way anyone at the House could hear them, but they shut up. It didn't do to make their daddy angry.

They were all three standing near the corner of one of the shacks, hidden completely by the weeds and trees.

Over at West house, Sam and Tammie were standing on the porch, looking in that direction, and Riley was telling them about the graveyard. If they had lowered their eyes from the tree tops, they would never have seen either the Harps or their shacks there where everything blended into a thick green growth.

The Wests did not stay much longer. Riley and the children showed Sam the spring and got her to take a little drink from it, and then they got into their car and drove away.

"They're Wests, all right," Joshua said to the boys when the car was gone. "Ain't no question about it. They wouldn't be back here this quick if they weren't."

"You think they're gonna move in?" Jonah asked. He smiled, revealing stained yellow teeth. His eyes were yellow, too, like cat eyes.

"Looks like they might be thinking about it," Joshua said. "This time they brought the woman to see the place."

"She's a hell of a woman, too," Absalom said. "I could see those tits even from here. I'd sure like to get my hands around those."

"Your hands ain't that big," Jonah said.

"I'd like to give it a try anyhow. I bet she'd like for me to try."

"Don't get yourself all worked up, boy," Joshua said. "We don't know that they'll ever be back."

"How much you want to bet? They'll be back, you just wait."

Joshua thought the boy had a point. The question was, what were the Harps going to do about it.

First, they had to be sure the people were really Wests and not just someone who had bought the House. The kind of car they drove, they didn't look like they could buy anything, but you couldn't always tell from something like that.

If it was someone who had just bought the House, even that could be trouble. He didn't like the idea of someone living that close to him and his family's base of operations.

There was the little marijuana crop he and the boys cultivated, for one thing. It wasn't much, but it was something that brought in good money when the twins took the notion to sell some of it in the beer joints around the county seat. He'd hate for anybody to stumble across the field, sure enough. The way things were, the sheriff left them pretty much alone, but if somebody turned them in for a marijuana field, he couldn't just ignore the complaint.

So even if those people weren't Wests, they would have to be dealt with. The difference was in *how* they would be dealt with.

Because if the people really were the Wests, the dealing would be hard.

Very hard.

Joshua turned to Absalom. "I want you to go up to the store, see if those people stopped in there. Find out who they are."

"Sure," Absalom said. "I think I'll buy me a Co'cola." He felt around in the pocket of his ragged jeans for change. "You want to come along, Jonah?"

"Nope," his brother said. "No use in showing too much interest in those people. Somebody might get the wrong idea if something happened to 'em."

Absalom laughed. "Somebody might get the *right* idea, is what you mean, don't you?"

"You just go on up there," Joshua said. "Find out what I told you."

Absalom didn't say anything, just wandered off into the woods, still fingering the change in his jeans.

Gus Morrow didn't like it when one of the Harps came in his store, which fortunately for Gus' peace of mind was not often.

Gus would not have admitted it to anyone, but the Harps flat scared the piss out of him.

Literally.

Well, almost literally. When Absalom Harp walked into the little store, Gus felt a sudden hot pressure in his bladder, and it was all he could do to stand there behind the counter. He wanted to go to the little bathroom he had built onto the back of the store and stand over the commode and relieve the pressure before he embarrassed himself. He could almost imagine the hot yellow trickle running down his leg and into his shoe.

He tried not to let the strain of holding it in show in his face, but he knew his smile was crooked and off center.

Absalom didn't seem to notice. He put two quarters in the soft drink machine and punched the button for a Mello Yello. The can clattered down into the trough, and Absalom took it. He popped the tab and drank down a hefty swallow.

"Mighty good on a hot day like this," he said, turning to Gus.

"Sure is," Gus said, his voice quavering only slightly.

He didn't know why he was afraid of this man, a man who had never done anything to him.

Why couldn't he just talk to him like any other customer?

Because of the stories, that's why, the stories that he had heard about the Harps for most of his life.

Absalom walked over to where Gus was standing behind the low counter and plunked the aluminum can down. He was wearing dirty jeans and a denim jacket with the sleeves torn off. The jacket was not buttoned, and Absalom was not wearing a shirt beneath it. His chest was matted with hair, and his stomach looked flat and hard.

"I was just wondering something," he said.

"Wh—what's that?" Gus said. "Wondering what?"

"I was wondering if you've talked to anybody lately about that house down the hill."

"Wh—what house?"

Gus was sweating heavily now, large rings beginning to form on his shirt under his armpits.

"You know which house I mean," Absalom said, picking up the Mello Yello and having another swallow. There was no threat in his voice; there was almost no tone at all. It was simply flat and hard, without inflection.

It had an effect on Gus, however. He backed away from the counter, bumping into the shelf of canned goods behind him.

"You mean West House?" he said, recovering.

Absalom smiled and nodded. "That's the one."

"Well, yes, some people who were going to look at the house stopped in here the other day."

"Did they now. I guess they told you who they were, too, didn't they?"

"Yes, they told me." Gus didn't like the way the conversation was going.

"That's good. Now you can tell me."

"Why—why do you want to know?" Gus wished he hadn't said the words the minute they were out of his mouth. He didn't want to make Absalom get angry.

Absalom smiled slowly, showing his yellow teeth. "If I'm gonna have new neighbors, I'd like to know their names."

"West," Gus said. "Their name is West." He wished that Absalom would quit smiling at him like that, like he was a bird and Absalom was a big fat tabby cat.

"Is that a fact, now. West, huh? Sounds kinda familiar in a way."

"Well, uh, the family's owned that land for a long time."

"Maybe that's why I've heard the name, then," Absalom said. "Yeah, I guess that must be it." He drank down the rest of his soda and set the can on the counter.

"Be seeing you," he said as he left the store.

Gus watched the man go. When the screen door slammed, Gus picked up the can and tossed it into a cardboard barrel that he used to collect aluminum cans and thought about the Harps.

His thoughts were not pleasant ones.

Gus had heard the stories from the time he was very young, as had most of the kids who lived in Springville. Other places might have had the bogeyman, but Springville had the Harps.

The stories were especially scary to Gus because Claude Morrow, Gus' great-grandfather, played such a big part in them. It had never been proved that the Harps had any part in Claude's death, but on the other hand it had never been proved that they didn't.

Not to Gus' satisfaction, at least.

By the time he was grown, Gus was of the firm opinion that Jeremiah West had pretty much deserved what had happened to him. The man had meddled in where he wasn't wanted, and he had gotten killed, along with his whole family. What that proved to Gus was that it was best to mind your own business and leave people like the Harps alone.

If you did that, you would be all right.

And that seemed to be the opinion of most of the people still living in Springville.

Gus knew, and he knew that others knew, about the dope that the Harps grew.

They knew about other things, too.

The people who disappeared along the highway, for one thing.

Nobody ever talked about it to the sheriff, and they hardly ever talked about it among themselves, but they knew, all right.

Every now and then someone would come to Springville

asking about a car that might have passed along the highway, wanting to know if the driver had by any chance wandered off the main road and into Gus' store.

It seemed mysterious as hell to everyone that a car and driver could just disappear.

Not to Gus. He knew about the Harps. He knew what their ancestors had done, and he suspected that the new generation was still doing it. If there were other people in the store, they would look at Gus and he would look at them. There was never a word that passed between them, but you could tell that everyone was thinking the same thing.

Gus figured the Harps were the ones that had gotten Larry Spillers, too, when he disappeared on the coon hunt. The sheriff passed that one off as a drunk falling in the river or maybe getting so lost in the bottoms that he starved to death. He even mentioned quicksand a time or two.

But Gus knew better.

He would have bet good money that the Harps got Spillers, not that he ever mentioned it to anyone. That wasn't the kind of thing you talked about. He was pretty sure others felt the same, too. You could just tell by the way they looked whenever the subject came up, the same looks they got when the strangers came by looking for the missing relatives.

Gus hoped that Absalom Harp was just asking about the Wests out of curiosity, but he couldn't quite bring himself to believe it. He was pretty sure there was another reason.

Well, if there was, Gus didn't want to know about it.

His great-grandfather had wanted to be a hero, and that was fine with Gus.

Gus didn't want to be one, though. No way.

If those Wests wanted to move to Springville, let them. Gus had tried to warn the man that first day, as best he could, anyway, without coming right out and saying anything. If the fella couldn't take a hint, that was his problem, not Gus Morrow's.

The screen door swung open and Gus looked up. Stoney Thompson came in, looking back over his shoulder as he entered.

"Wasn't that Ab Harp?" he said.

Stoney was short and squatty, with big hands that looked like boulders when he clenched his fists. Supposedly that was how he got his nickname.

"Yeah," Gus said. "That was him."

"I don't like those Harps much. They give me the shivers."

That was all that Stoney had to say about the Harps, but the look that passed between him and Gus said much more. It said, "My great-grandfather was in on that Harp mess just like yours was, and I know as well as you do that the best thing for everybody around here is to leave those Harps alone."

"What can I get for you today, Stoney?" Gus asked.

Stoney pulled a piece of paper out of his shirt pocket and handed it to Gus, who began gathering up the few items on the list.

Twenty

Stoney Thompson put the paper bag of groceries in the back of his Chevy S-10 pickup and drove home.

He lived in one of the houses that Riley West had driven past on the gravel road. It was a small house with two bedrooms, a bath, and kitchen/dining area. The yard was clipped close and very green; Thompson fertilized regularly. The house had fresh paint, too, and the roof was only a year old.

Thompson liked working in the yard and taking care of his house. He didn't have much else to do since he had taken early retirement from his job on the railroad. A little gas well on some property that he owned in another county provided him with more income than he needed.

He parked the pickup in the little detached garage and carried the groceries into the house. He set the bag on the kitchen table and looked around.

The house was much neater than most people would expect a bachelor to have, but Stoney liked to have the inside of his house as spiffy as the outside.

He put the milk into the refrigerator and the nonperishables into a metal cabinet in the corner of the kitchen. Then he went into one of the bedrooms, which he had converted into a TV room, and turned on the set.

He didn't really want to watch TV, but he was hoping there would be something on that would distract him from the thoughts that refused to leave his mind, the thoughts that had been brought on by seeing Ab Harp leaving Gus Morrow's store.

Like Gus, Stoney had heard the stories about the Harps from the time he was just a kid. The story of that bloody night of murder at the West House had been told many a time by older kids trying to scare him, and there had been a time or two, because he was known as a daring youngster, when they had taunted him and tried to get him to go down the hill and enter the house.

He had never done it.

He had drunk from the spring, more than once. And he had even walked all the way to the bottom of the hill several times. But that was as far as he had gone. The sight of the house sitting there among the trees, with its decaying roof and vacant windows, was just too much for him.

It was too much for everyone else, too. As far as he knew, no one from Springville had ever gone inside it.

The most recent visitors had, though, and it hadn't seemed to affect them.

From the window of his TV room, Stoney could see every car that went up and down the gravel road running in front of his house. He knew the make and model of every car that used the road with any regularity, and he knew who owned which car. Because people had such regular habits, he could practically tell you where any given car was headed when it passed his house, depending on the time of day and who was driving.

When a strange car came by, Stoney was always curious about what it was doing in the neighborhood, and he usually went to the window to see where it was going. That was how he knew about the people who had gone to the house.

He had seen the old Chrysler the first time it appeared and known at once that it didn't belong, and when it turned off to go down the hill, he stepped out his front door to watch what was going on.

He saw the car parked at the end of the dirt road, and he watched the people get out and look over the house. He saw them go inside.

When the car had returned today, he had watched again. It was the same people, but there was a woman with them this time.

Stoney knew, just as the Harps knew, what all this must mean.

It meant that Wests were coming back to Springville.

Stoney was no more thrilled by that news than Gus Morrow was. He didn't want the Wests coming back. It would mean nothing but trouble, and Stoney didn't like trouble. He liked for everything to go on smoothly, the way it was supposed to. A place for everything, and everything in its place. He had read that somewhere and agreed with it immediately.

Life was meant to be regular and scheduled. Things that upset the schedule were not good.

And Wests moving down by the graveyard would definitely upset things.

Stoney could not say how he knew this was true, but he was convinced that it was. The Harps were not going to like it, that was for sure.

Well, he thought, it's not my trouble. No use for me to worry about it. If somebody wants to move into that old house, it's his own look-out, not mine. Let them do it if they want to. But they better be ready for what comes. They won't be getting any help from old Stoney.

He, by God, was going to stay out of it.

"They're Wests, sure enough," Absalom said when he walked into the shack.

Cherry and Nita were sitting on the front seat of a 1967 Plymouth that served the Harps as a couch, watching Geraldo on a battery-powered TV that sat on an up-ended orange crate.

"I wish you'd be quiet," Nita said. "Geraldo's got on kids whose mamas are in prison. It's real interesting."

"Some of 'em got *both* parents in prison," Cherry said. "Not the same prison, though."

Joshua was sitting in a wooden chair that had only three legs; he seemed able to balance it without difficulty. When he stood up, the chair fell to the floor.

"Let's go outside," he said.

Absalom followed his father out of the shack, Geraldo's voice fading behind them.

"Where's Jonah?" he said.

"Don't know. Went off in the woods, I reckon. You say they're Wests for sure?"

"That's what they told that pussy of a storekeeper. No reason for 'em to lie about it."

"No, I guess not." Joshua walked over to a tall pecan tree and leaned against the trunk. He stood that way for a while, thinking.

Absalom didn't say anything. He knew that his father was puzzling over what to do about the Wests.

Jonah came walking out of the woods. "Those damn kids," he laughed.

"What about 'em?" Absalom asked.

"They're down there in that graveyard playing with those dolls they made. Killing them and burying them."

Absalom grinned wolfishly. "Good practice," he said.

Jonah matched the grin. "Wests, huh?"

"Yeah. That's what I was told."

Jonah licked his lips. "All right! What're we gonna do about 'em, daddy?"

Joshua rubbed his back against the tree, scratching it with the bark. "Kill 'em," he said.

"Hell, I know that. What I mean is, how're we gonna do it?"

"I ain't decided yet. We got to be careful about this."

The twins knew what he meant. Their lifestyle depended on keeping their criminal acts discreetly hidden from the world. As long as they didn't do anything overtly evil, the sheriff didn't bother them. He knew well enough that if he hurt one of the Harps, or put him in jail, the others would be on his ass forever. So he could afford to let some things, like a little dope selling, slide.

But if they just hauled off and killed a whole family there was bound to be trouble. Even the sheriff, lazy and fond of taking it easy as he was, couldn't just sit back in a case like that.

"Kinda hard to be careful about killing people," Absalom

observed. "It does tend to make kind of a mess."

"Maybe they could just disappear, like," Jonah said. "We don't kill 'em in the house. Lure 'em out, maybe. Then kill 'em in the woods." He smiled as an idea came to him. "That's it. We kill 'em in the woods and bury 'em in the graveyard!"

"Bury who?" Matthew said, stepping out of the trees behind Jonah. Mary was right behind him.

The adults looked at the boy.

"Bury who?" he said again. "Didn't you say something about burying somebody in the graveyard?"

"Looks like it's time for a little family conference," Joshua said. He was a great believer in family conferences, an idea that Nita and Cherry had initiated after seeing a show about it on Donahue or Oprah or possibly Geraldo.

"What're we going to talk about?" Matthew asked.

"You'll see," was all Joshua would say.

Matthew didn't mind. He was used to getting answers like that, or no answers at all. He followed the adults into the shack, Mary trailing along right behind.

Nita and Cherry were still watching Geraldo, who was interviewing a sobbing girl of about sixteen, and they turned to the men and put their fingers to their lips to signal them to be quiet.

But when they saw the look on Joshua's face, Cherry got up and turned off the little TV. She could see that the old man was not in any mood to be trifled with.

"What's going on?" Nita said.

"It's Wests," Jonah said. "Moving in next door."

"In that big old house that's about to fall down?" Nita didn't look as if she believed anyone would live in a place like that, which was unusual, considering her own circumstances.

The shacks had been repaired numerous times over the years, and the outside of each one was now at least four layers thick. The original layer of wood was still there on the inside, but that had been covered with another thickness of wood at some time in the past. Then, along about 1950, Joshua, then a very young man, had decided to cover both of them with tin. Some of the tin was galvanized, but some of it was simply metal signs that Joshua had stolen from gas stations and grocery stores. That layer was covered with another one of wood.

In the nearly forty years since the last layer had been added to the shacks, the vines had covered them. Then trees had grown right up to the doors and surrounded the shacks, along with any number of bushes of various kinds, not to mention tall green weeds.

There were trails through all the growth, but even the trails were hidden from a casual glance by the thickness of the greenery.

The insides of the shacks were not in any danger of being featured in *House Beautiful*. Nita and Cherry were homebodies, but by no stretch of the imagination could they be considered interested in housekeeping. And neither was anyone else in the family.

The shacks were furnished with such unfashionable items as the car seat, used as a sofa; the three-legged chair in which Joshua usually sat; army cots, sleeping bags for the kids; an old wood stove; the battery-powered TV; card tables; and very little else.

The walls were not decorated with fine art, or with much of anything else. There was a fold-out from an old issue of *Playboy* tacked up on one wall, and Nita or Cherry had cut out a photo of George Michael from somewhere and stuck it up. That was all.

The floor had not been swept in a long time. It was cleaner than the one in West House, but only because people walked on this one and thus wore through the dirt.

There was however, glass in the windows, and that kept out the birds. There were doors on the hinges, too, and they kept out the larger animals.

"The House ain't likely to fall anytime soon," Joshua said. "It was built right when it was built. This shack we're in has been here longer."

Nita looked around. "Looks like it, too," she said.

"You watch your mouth," Absalom warned her. "I can kick your butt outta here and see how you like it without the comforts of home."

Nita looked around and started to say something about the comforts of home, but she thought better of it. Instead, she said, "How do you know some Wests are moving in on us?"

"We got ways of finding out stuff," Jonah said. "You don't have to worry about that."

"So we're gonna have a little talk about it?" Cherry said. She wished they'd never seen that damn TV show. She hated family conferences.

"That's right," Joshua said. "It's time these kids learned what it means to be a Harp."

"Hey, grandpa, we know all about the Wests," Matthew said. "You've told us before."

"You may know about the Wests," Joshua said, "but you don't know everything you need to know."

"What else is there?" Matthew said.

"That's what I'm about to tell you," Joshua said.

CHAPTER TWENTY

Sheriff Homer Gregory was asleep at his desk, snoring lightly, his chair tilted back, his booted feet up on the scarred desktop, his hands clasped behind his neck, his white Stetson tilted down over his eyes. He liked to take a short nap every afternoon, let his lunch settle before he did anything too strenuous.

Not that he ever did anything that could really be considered too strenuous. He was known around the county as a good old boy, someone you could trust to do the right thing if your nephew had been picked up for DWI or your brother-in-law had been brought in for fighting and busting up the Cosmic Cowboy Club again.

That was why he kept getting elected.

He certainly wasn't elected because of his abilities as a lawman; the county had a very high proportion of unsolved crimes, probably higher than any county its size in the state. But most people didn't care, just as long as they knew that they could go down and bail old Buster out again and be sure that the charge wouldn't stick with hardly more than a good word to Homer.

What the hell, it wasn't like the county was a hotbed of crime like those places you read about Up North. Like that New York City, for example, where a woman couldn't hardly step out the front door without a gang of young bastards jumping her, taking all her money, ripping her clothes off, and raping the shit out of her right in plain sight of half the town and nobody raising a hand to stop 'em. Or where old folks couldn't even go to their mailboxes for fear that they'd be clobbered by some bunch of goddamned ruffians who were there to steal their Old Age Pension check.

If the county ever got like that, then maybe they'd vote in somebody different, somebody who was able to go out and track down criminals just like that fella on TV did, the one in the dirty raincoat. What was his name? Columbus? Colombo? Something like that.

But nobody like that was needed when the worst you had was maybe some schoolkids smoking a little joint now and then or somebody busting heads at the Cowboy or maybe a fella taking a few too many drinks and running the old pickup off the road and into the bar ditch.

Well, sure, there was a thing or two worse than that every now and again, but those old folks out in the country, they were killed by transients, serial killers like that Henry Lee Lucas, who went around the state, or the whole U. S. of A. for that matter, killing pretty much who he damn well pleased and nobody to stop him. If people wanted to live off by themselves like that, they had a right to do it, but they might as well know what they were asking for if they did.

And, yeah, there was a little stealing that went on, but not much, and the insurance companies could cover that. That's why you had insurance, right? To take care of you when something like that happened.

You just didn't see any big-time crime in small-town Texas, and that's why a sheriff like Homer Gregory was just what you needed.

He knew how to take care of his friends.

He knew that he could count on an uninterrupted hour every afternoon after lunch, too, to "rest his eyes," as he put it. The dispatcher and the deputies had strict orders never to disturb him between one and two o'clock when he was in his office, and they never did.

This was one of the days he especially appreciated that.

For one thing, he'd had Mexican food for lunch, and that was the kind of thing that needed a lot of settling, not to mention a couple of Di-Gel tablets and maybe an Alka-Seltzer. The sheriff had an ample belly, and he'd ingested two enchiladas, two tamales, three tacos, a lot of rice and beans, a bowl of cheese dip, a plate of fajitas, and a chimichanga. Not to mention a couple of bowls of salsa that he had eaten with chips. He needed his rest.

Besides, the night before had been a rough one. Not from the law enforcement angle, he had that pretty well knocked. The deputies took care of the patrols and all the sheriff had to do was make sure they didn't arrest anybody of consequence in the county. Most of them knew better, anyway, so that left Gregory time to do pretty much what he wanted to in the evenings, and what he wanted to do was keep company with Estelle Foster.

"Keeping company" was the way he thought of it, but it involved a lot more than that phrase implied, since Estelle was a girl who liked to have a good time, and she was also a girl for whom having a good time usually involved getting out of her clothes.

Sheriff Gregory wasn't sure what a nymphomaniac was, or even if there was such a thing. But if there was, then he was pretty sure that Estelle qualified.

That was just fine with the sheriff, since there were a lot of women who didn't find him attractive.

He was big, two or three inches over six feet, and he was fat, weighing in the neighborhood of three hundred pounds. Besides the belly hanging over his belt, he had thick arms and legs, and he looked a little like a sausage in his tight uniform. He was hairy, too, and when he took the uniform off he resembled King Kong with a barbershop shave. His face was clean, but the skin of his back and chest were not visible; even the backs of his hands were covered with thick, curling black hair.

Estelle didn't seem to mind. He had the equipment that interested her, and it was pretty sizeable equipment, even if he did say so himself, as he often did.

Estelle often said so, too.

"Honey, I've seen horses didn't have dicks that big," she told him once. He didn't ask how well acquainted she was with the horses. He figured it wasn't any of his business.

It was true that many men might not have been attracted to Estelle, no matter how insatiable she was, but Gregory didn't mind how she looked. She was no longer young, probably middle forties, but Gregory was a little past that himself. What the hell. She still had plenty of enthusiasm, and there was no doubt about her expertise. So what if her breasts sagged a little and she had her hair tinted every two months at Natille's Hair Barn and there were a few ripples of cellulite on her thighs and belly? The woman could still practically fuck you to death.

And that was the other reason the sheriff needed the nap that afternoon. She had drained him dry the night before, begging for it time after time. For a guy nearly fifty to get it up and keep it up for hours on end wasn't easy, or at least it wasn't easy for Gregory. He had started taking vitamin E, eating raw eggs for breakfast, and downing raw oysters for supper, but he still wasn't sure how long he was going to be able to keep up the pace with Estelle.

Thank the lord he had a little time for himself in the afternoons and could relax and get a little of his strength back.

Someone knocked on the door and Gregory stirred in his sleep, brushing a hand across his thick lips. The snoring stopped for a second and then resumed.

The knock came again.

Gregory pushed the Stetson up on his forehead and opened his eyes to thin slits. He'd heard something, but he wasn't sure what.

Must've been something out in the street, he thought. Maybe a car backfiring. Something like that. Hell, maybe he was just dreaming. Mexican food made him do that, too.

He pushed the hat back down over his eyes and was just beginning to relax when the knocking sounded for the third time. It wasn't loud, but this time it didn't stop, just kept on.

Thud, thud, thud.

Thud, thud, thud.

It was like someone was hitting the door with the soft part of his fist at the heel of his hand, just loud enough to be aggravating but not loud enough to really do much good unless you were trying to wake a light sleeper, which Gregory was.

The sheriff swung his legs off the desk and the chair crashed to the floor, making a much louder noise than the knocking, which stopped immediately.

Gregory heaved himself out of his chair and slowly crossed the office. His ponderous movements were deceptive. He might be big, but he was quick when he wanted to be, quicker than anyone would ever guess just by looking at him. He could snatch flies out of the air with either hand, and every now and then, when he was actually forced to participate in an arrest, a perp had made the mistake of thinking he could out-quick the sheriff and make good his escape.

Anyone who tried it was usually sore for several days afterward, and more often than not he was the bearer of "a few bruises he got when he fell down," as Sheriff Gregory liked to put it.

Gregory reached out to open the door. The brass knob was lost in his huge paw.

The door swung open and Gus Morrow was standing there looking at Gregory.

A worried deputy with a huge Adam's apple was standing right behind Morrow. "I told him not to bother you, Sheriff," the deputy said. "I told him you were going over some reports and that you said you didn't want to be disturbed, but he wouldn't listen."

"You could've shot him," Gregory said. He wasn't smiling when he said it, either.

"He didn't think it was a shooting offense to knock on a door," Morrow said. "You going to let me come in, or not?"

"Hell, now that you're here, I don't see any way to keep you out. If my deputies won't shoot you, I guess I can't do it, either. But this better be worth the trouble."

"It is," Morrow said. He followed Gregory into the office, closing the door behind him.

When it came right down to it, Morrow couldn't let it go.

He wanted to, but he just couldn't. He had thought about it ever since Stoney Thompson had left the store, and he knew that the best thing to do was to leave things alone.

No one ever got anywhere by meddling in things that didn't concern him, or if he got anywhere it was where Gus' great-grandfather had gotten.

Dead.

And that wasn't anyplace Gus wanted to be.

Those people who had stopped in his store, though, they seemed like nice folks. Those kids were well-behaved and cute as they could be, and the man seemed to be a fine fella, even if he was a West. The Wests had brought trouble to Springville, but this one probably didn't know that. He might not even know the story about what had happened there a long time back. It might not be something the family liked to remember.

Besides, Jeremiah West had at one time been the best thing about the town. Could he really be blamed for his own murder?

He'd just stuck up for what he believed was right, even if it did cause him to get into other folks' business.

So here Gus was, after telling himself he wouldn't get involved, after convincing himself that there was no need to be a hero, after giving himself all the arguments about what had happened to Jeremiah West.

None of it had done any good; in the end, Gus had gone to the law.

Sheriff Gregory sat behind his desk. The chair creaked in protest, accepting his weight reluctantly. He leaned forward, resting his forearms on the desk and lacing his thick fingers together.

"Like I said," he told Gus, looking at him with beady black eyes, "this sure as hell better be good."

Chapter Twenty-One

It was very hot driving back to Houston. Dan and Tammie argued all the way about which of them had found the way under the porch, and Tammie said over and over that she would never live in any place that didn't have a bathroom.

"I like to be clean," she said. "I like to sit in the tub, and I like a place to use the toilet."

Riley pointed out for what seemed to him like the millionth time that they would be living in the trailer for a long time, until there were bathrooms in the house, with showers and glass doors.

"I don't want a shower," Tammie said. "I want a big tub."

"You'll have one, then," Riley assured her, but it didn't seem to help much. As soon as he said it, she started in about not liking the room she was going to have.

Riley explained that the hole in the roof would be fixed and that the room would be very cozy.

"I don't care about no hole," Tammie said.

"*Any* hole," her mother said.

"*Any* hole," Tammie repeated. "I don't care about that."

All the car's windows were down and the hot wind was rushing in. It wasn't doing a very good job of cooling anyone off, and it made conversation difficult. Tammie felt as if she had to yell to make herself heard.

"What do you care about then?" Sam asked.

"I don't know. It just feels creepy."

"Sissy," Dan said. "Sissy, sissy, sissy."

"Hush, Dan," Sam said. "Your sister isn't a sissy."

Riley was glad she was trying to keep them in line; he

didn't feel like coping with them, not while driving down the interstate in a car that felt like a steambath.

"Yeah," Tammie said. "I'm not no sissy."

"*A* sissy," Sam said.

"Yeah," Tammie said.

For the moment, that ended the discussion, and Sam lay back against the old Chrylser's seat cushion and tried to relax. It wasn't the argument that had made her tense up. She was used to arguments. Instead, it was what Tammie had said about the room being "creepy" that worried Sam.

Sam felt the same way, except she felt that way about the whole house. She wondered how she was going to be able to explain that to Riley. Or even *if* she would be able to explain it to him.

She looked over at him as he sat behind the wheel. He had his eyes on the road and was driving with admirable concentration. You had to do that in the Chrysler. It tended to ramble off on a course of its own if you didn't keep a steady hand on the wheel and a watchful eye on the road.

But he looked happy. His lips were curved in a slight smile as he watched the highway unfold before him.

She knew that somehow the House meant more to him than he would be able to explain to her. To him it was as if moving there were something they were meant to do. It was as if the House had just been waiting for him all these years, and now he was going to take possession of it.

But she was wondering if it weren't the other way around.

She was wondering if the House had not already taken possession of him.

Riley had no such thought.

He was thinking instead of how he could fix up the House, what he should do first, what next, what after that.

The roof, he figured, was the top priority. With the roof fixed, there wouldn't be any more water coming in the attic and therefore no more rot in the House, not that there was much of that anyway.

After the roof, he would go through and repair any of the

rotted places, few as there were, and then see about building some closets in the bedrooms. The rooms were fairly large, so putting in closets wouldn't be a problem.

For all that kind of work, he wouldn't even need any help.

Putting in the plumbing was a different story. He didn't know much about that at all, but he could probably find someone easily enough. The septic tank would require some heavy digging, but he could rent the equipment. Running the pipes was where he'd need the help. That, and installing the fixtures.

Air-conditioning was another problem. To air-condition the entire House would be far too expensive. Those old homes weren't built with any insulation, and he didn't want to have to try tearing out the walls to install it. Despite what he'd said to the kids about windows and high ceilings, it could still be plenty hot in an old house. Maybe he could just insulate the bedrooms and put in window units for the cooling.

Getting the electricity run from the road wouldn't be a problem, either, but wiring the House was something else. He thought he could pull the wire, but he'd need an electrician to put in the circuit board.

Thinking about it made getting the House in shape a pretty daunting task, but to tell the truth, Riley wasn't even particularly worried about it. Things would fall into place. He was convinced that they would. He couldn't say why, but he was sure about that.

One good sign was that he'd gotten the job right off, and it was just the right kind of job.

The House was not in nearly as poor a condition as he'd thought it might be, not nearly as poor as he could rightfully expect, and that was another good sign.

The kids seemed to like the place, too, except for Tammie's complaints about her room and about the lack of a bathroom, but he thought those objections would be answered easily.

How could anything go wrong?

Joshua Harp looked at his family.

It wasn't much to work with, he thought. Jonah and Absalom

were all right for some things, but they'd never really been put to the test.

It was one thing to kill an old woman in her bed while she was asleep. Hell, it was almost too easy.

And it wasn't much harder to kill the tourists that they grabbed up by the road. Most of them were so scared that they were pissing their pants by the time you got them into the woods, men and women both. They were shaking and whining and crying and it was a pleasure to cut their throats and shut them the hell up.

But it was something else to kill the Wests. Joshua knew they wouldn't be easy.

He couldn't say how he knew, anymore than Riley West could say why he was convinced things would fall into place when it came to fixing the House, but he knew.

Nita and Cherry were weak links, too. They weren't really Harps, and though they had never given any trouble, Joshua didn't really trust them. All they liked to do was drink, smoke dope, and watch that damn battery-powered TV all the time. It had got to where they didn't even want to go out dancing at night like they used to.

They knew what went on around them, all right, but they'd never taken part in any of it, at least not the killings. They helped harvest the dope and clean out the stems and seeds, but they never went out on the prowl with him and the boys when they were looking for places they could rob, and they sure never went up on the highway and grabbed any of the tourists.

Neither did the kids, and that was the point that bothered Joshua the most. Kids had a way of being soft, and he didn't like that. It was all right to go down to the graveyard and play like you were killing dolls and putting them in the ground, but when it came to doing the real job they might not be up to it.

So that was why he'd called for the family conference. They needed to sit down and discuss what they were going to be doing about the Wests.

It seemed simple enough to Absalom. "We kill 'em. We don't want no more Wests around here. We all know what the Wests did to our family, way back. Even the kids know what we got to do about Wests if they come around here."

"But we got to do it sly-like," Jonah said. "Not let anybody catch on that it was us that done it."

"Make it look like an accident," Absalom said.

"Yeah," Jonah said. "An accident's a good idea."

Joshua was disgusted with them. How could you make murder look like an accident? If you went over there and killed them, what kind of accident could it be? There hadn't been any animals wilder than a possum around Springville for years. Maybe a bobcat, but that still wouldn't do. How could you have a car wreck inside a house, or have a rock fall on somebody who was making up a bed? Even the local law wasn't that dumb.

"Well, we could just make 'em disappear, then," Absalom said, going back to what they had been talking about earlier. "You know. Go over there and take 'em out of the house, kill 'em in the woods, bury 'em in the graveyard, and no one's the wiser."

That made a kind of sense to Joshua. It was something that the sheriff could overlook, just like he overlooked a lot of other things. There were lots of reasons why a family might disappear. Maybe they were running out on their debts, or maybe they just found out they didn't like living down by a graveyard. Lots of reasons.

"It don't sound good to be talking about stuff like this in front of the kids," Cherry said.

"Yeah," Nita agreed. "You ought not to be talking about killing people. It's not right."

That was what Joshua had been afraid of. "Absalom," he said. "Jonah."

The twins stood up, their broad shoulders tensing under the fabric of their shirts. "Yeah, daddy?"

"You take the women over to the other place. I want to talk to the kids, just me and them."

"I ain't goin' over there just 'cause you say so," Cherry said. "You can't push me around."

Jonah reached out an arm and slapped her. His hand didn't seem to travel far, but the *pop* echoed off the walls of the shack and the print of his hand was dusky on Cherry's cheek.

"We don't talk back to Daddy," he said.

Cherry didn't say anything. She was looking at the floor, and tears ran from her eyes.

Matthew and Mary looked at her, their eyes round. They had seen Jonah hit her before, but never like that. Before, it was always more playful; this had been serious. Really serious.

"Come on, now," Absalom said. He took Nita's arm and started for the door. Nita did not resist, and Cherry followed behind. Jonah went out after them.

When they were gone, Joshua looked at the kids.

He was scary-looking, Matthew thought. He always looked a *little* scary, but this was different. His face was halfway hidden by his hair, and his eyes were back in there shining like an animal's eyes at night. Matthew had never seen him like this.

Neither had Mary. She reached out and took Matthew's hand and squeezed it tight.

"I want you kids to understand what we got to do," Joshua said.

"We know," Matthew said. "You've told us about the Wests. We've got to kill 'em."

"That's right," Joshua said. "But I'm not sure you know what killing means."

"We killed a turtle," Mary said. "We buried it, too. And when we dug it up, it smelled bad."

Joshua nodded. "That's part of it, but that ain't all. And killing a turtle ain't like killing a person."

Matthew thought of the turtle, thought about how it sounded when the rocks hit it, how it looked when the rocks broke through the shell. He didn't see how a person could look any worse. He said so.

"They bleed a lot more, for one thing," Joshua told him. "And they fight back. I don't expect that turtle of yours did much fighting, now did he?"

Matthew had to admit that the turtle hadn't done much fighting.

"People do, sometimes. And you can bet your ass the Wests will. They won't go easy. They'll kick and scream and scratch. We got to be ready for that."

Matthew didn't know if he was ready for that.

He didn't like the idea of fighting. He'd been thinking about the turtle, too, about how it smelled when they dug it up and how there were things eating on it.

He didn't know for sure that he could do something like that to a real person. Turtles were different, somehow.

When he told Joshua that, the old man's eyes burned with an even fiercer glow. "That's why you're gonna get some practice," he said.

CHAPTER TWENTY-TWO

Homer Gregory was not impressed by Gus Morrow's story. "I don't see what's got your bowels all in an uproar," he said. "Just somebody looking at an old house, is all I can see's going on. Who's taking care of the store while you do all this running around, anyhow?"

Now that he was actually there in the sheriff's office, Gus' nerve had improved. There was something about being in the headquarters of a law enforcement agency that was comforting to him. It was as if he were safe there from the Harps, and now that he had taken the big step of talking about the Harps to the sheriff, he was going to speak his mind.

"I called my wife. She's at the store, if you just have to know. And you know why I'm upset, even if you don't want to admit it."

Gregory's piggy eyes narrowed. "Maybe I don't. Maybe you'd like to tell me."

"Damn right, I will," Gus said. "You know as well as I do what happened the last time there were Wests living in that house."

"Hell, that was a long time back, a hundred years or more," Gregory said, relaxing slightly. "You can't make anything out of that."

Gus raised his eyebrows. "I can't? Why can't I?"

"'Cause what happened then don't have a damn thing to do with what happens now. Shit, Gus, you know that. It's like saying that if those Wests were blacks, we'd have the Civil War all over again. That's how long it's been."

"It hasn't been quite that long," Gus said. "But it don't make any difference. Things are still the same where those damn Harps are involved. *They* haven't changed any."

Gregory leaned forward slightly. "I'm not getting your drift."

"Yes, you are. You're just playing dumb."

"I never knew you to be so mouthy, Gus. You've always been a quiet sort of a fella."

Gus smiled ruefully. "I still am. I didn't want to come in here."

"But you did, so you might as well go on and tell me what it is that I'm playing dumb about."

Gus took a deep breath and let it out slowly. "You know as well as I do that the Harps we got living here now are just as bad as the Harps were a hundred years ago. That they do things—"

"Wait just a minute, now," Gregory said, holding up a hand the size of a catcher's mitt. "You got any proof of what you're telling me?"

"What kind of proof do you want?" Gus asked. "You got old people getting murdered in their beds, you got people disappearing off the highway, you got—"

"Hang on, hang on. You can't lay any of that on the Harps. We all know that they might not be what you'd call the quality of the county, but there just ain't no proof that they're killers. We got all kinds of trash passing through here these days, people from Houston or Dallas that're out of jobs and looking for some easy pickings. They're probably the ones doing those things you're talking about, not anybody that lives here."

"Maybe so," Gus admitted. "But there might be proof that the Harps were in on things like that if anybody looked for it."

Gregory stood up. He was much bigger than Gus remembered.

"You telling me that I'm not doing my job?" he said. "Is that what you're telling me, Gus?"

"Muh—maybe," Gus said.

Gregory walked over to Gus' chair and leaned down, his hands on the chair arms, his face inches away from Gus' own.

"Just what is it you want me to do, Gus?" he said, his breath hot on Gus' face. "You want me to go down there by the old graveyard and roust the Harps, is that it? You want me to get 'em all stirred up and then see what happens? Huh?"

"Nuh—no," Gus said. "That's not it."

Gregory straightened up and walked back behind the desk.

"My family's got a long history in this county, Gus, just like yours," the sheriff said. "It was old Tobe Gregory that led the gang that got Michael Harp and hung his ass all those years ago."

"I know," Gus said, wondering at the same time how you hung anybody's ass.

"Old Tobe left the country after that, but he couldn't stay away. Came back years later, and found out that your great-granddaddy and Stoney Thompson's were both dead. Natural causes, folks said."

"I've heard the story," Gus said.

"Yeah, I bet you have. And you've heard how old Tobe didn't last more'n a week after that, how he just keeled over one day, dead as a tack hammer."

"Yes," Gus said. "I've heard that."

"Seems like that's what happens to ever'body who messes with the Harps, don't it?" Gregory said. "One way or another."

"I guess you're right," Gus said.

"Hell, Gus, either I'm right or I'm wrong. There ain't no two ways about it."

"All right. You're right. You know you're right."

"And you still want me to go chasing after the Harps, see what I can do to roust 'em? Even knowing what you know?"

Gus wasn't sure anymore. The way Homer sounded, even the sheriff might be a little afraid of the Harps. Gus couldn't imagine that; Homer was big enough and tough enough to handle anybody. And if even he was afraid of the Harps, then Gus didn't think anybody could handle them.

"See, Gus," Homer said, "the problem is that we don't know for sure that the Harps are doing anything wrong. Yeah, they sell a little dope, but so do a lot of other folks that live back down in the woods. They don't sell it to kids, though, and they don't hurt anybody. If they killed people, that would be another story. But we don't know that they do that."

"I guess we don't," Gus said.

"'Course we don't. So we can't go arresting them just for fun. Now if we catch 'em in the act, or get some proof, well, we can do something. But not till then. You can see that, can't you, Gus?"

Gus could see that, all right.

"So you just get me some proof, or you catch 'em in the act. You do that, and we're in business. O.K.?"

It seemed fair to Gus. But for some reason, when he left the sheriff's office he didn't feel any better.

Not a Goddamn bit.

Stoney Thompson was eating a Snickers bar and watching *Name that Tune* when Gus knocked on his door.

Stoney let him in. "You ever notice the way they play the songs on this show?" he said, chewing the Snickers and leading Gus into the TV room. "Hell, you couldn't recognize 'Rock-a-bye Baby' the way they play 'em."

"I never watch it," Gus said. "I'm usually at work."

"Why ain't you there now?" Stoney said.

"I wanted to talk to you about something."

Stoney walked over and clicked off the TV set. He stuck the rest of the Snickers in his mouth and chewed it slowly, which was about the only way you could chew a Snickers. He wasn't in any hurry to let Gus have his say. He figured he knew what it was about. He licked the chocolate off the ends of his fingers.

"You want to sit down?" he said when he'd finished chewing.

There were two chairs in the TV room, both of them rockers with cane backs and bottoms. Stoney sat in the one he liked, not waiting for Gus.

Gus stood there for a minute, then sat down. "I went to see the sheriff," he said.

Stoney had been afraid it would be something like that. "What for?" he said.

"About the Harps. About those people who've been looking at West House."

"I saw 'em when they drove by here," Stoney said.

"They stopped at the store for a drink."

"Yeah. Well, so what?"

"They're Wests," Gus said. "They're thinking about moving into that house."

"Nothing wrong with that," Stoney said, rocking gently in the chair. "It's a pretty good house to be as old as it is."

"I'm not talking about the house."

Stoney frowned. "Then I don't see—"

"Goddamn it," Gus said. "You're as bad as the sheriff. I thought you might have a little more sense."

"No use getting mad," Stoney said. "I got plenty of sense. That's why I don't think I wanta hear what you're gonna say."

"We can't just let it happen," Gus said. "We can't just let those people move in there and let it happen."

Stoney wished he had another Snickers. "Let what happen?" he said.

"What happened before. You saw Ab Harp at the store, and he was there asking about those Wests. He knew they were looking at the house, you can bet on that. He asked me their name."

"And you told him, I guess."

"I wasn't gonna lie to him. You ever looked at one of 'em in the eyes?"

"Not any more than I have to."

"You know what I mean, then."

"You mean you were too scared to do anything but tell him."

Gus thought about saying he hadn't been scared, exactly, but he knew that wasn't true. He had been plenty scared.

Stoney got out of his chair and walked over to the window. The chair kept on rocking for a second or two by itself.

Stoney looked out at the peaceful countryside. It was green and quiet and harmless-looking. Then he turned back to his visitor. "We oughta stay out of it, Gus. It don't have anything to do with us."

"That's what the sheriff said."

"Well, that's it, then. He knows what he's talking about."

"You think the same thing I do, though, don't you. You think the Harps will try something when those folks move in."

"What I think don't matter," Stoney said. "It just ain't any of my business."

"It's not right," Gus said. "Just letting it happen's not right."

"You mess with the Harps, what happens to you might not be right, either. You ever thought about that?"

"I thought about it. Hell, it ain't like I *want* to mess with 'em, Stoney."

"Then drop it," Stoney said. "Forget about it. Sell a few groceries, a few cold drinks, and forget about it. That's what I'm gonna do."

"And if something happens? You just gonna forget that, too?"

"That's right. I'm just gonna forget that, too. A man gets to be my age, he finds out he can forget a lot of things real easy. A lot easier than he used to."

"I don't like it," Gus said. "I wish to hell there was something we could do."

Stoney thought about it for a minute. "There might be one thing," he said.

"What's that?" Gus said.

"Well, next time they stop in your store, tell 'em what a bad place that house is. Tell 'em it's haunted because of the old murders. Or it's dangerous because of being so old and rotten. Tell 'em something that'll make 'em not want to move there."

"You think that'll work?"

"It might. It's better than messing with the Harps. This way, we don't have to deal with them, and if those folks move in, well, you tried to give 'em a warning."

"It won't work," Gus predicted.

"Yeah, probably not. But if it don't, and something happens to 'em, you can at least say you tried."

Gus sighed. "Yeah. I can at least say I tried."

For all the good it'll do, he thought as he drove back to his store. For all the Goddamn good it'll do.

CHAPTER
TWENTY-THREE

R iley had never told Sam the whole story of the House. He had told her about Jeremiah West, about how West had been the biggest man in Springville, going there to farm and then building the cotton gin before becoming the owner of the local bank.

He had told her how West had practically made the place into a town, singlehandedly. "It wasn't much more than a wide spot in the road when he came there, but he made it a real place where people wanted to live and bring up their families. After he died, the town sort of died, too."

He had never told her, however, just how West and the rest of his family had died or what had happened afterward, except to mention that the son had gone to live with the aunt and that the House had never been lived in since that time.

He was going to have to tell her now, though.

He didn't want to. In fact, he had pretty much pushed that part of the story into some unused part of his own mind, a place like a dark closet filled with dust and cobwebs where things he didn't want to look at were kept and mostly forgotten.

But when she started talking about the "creepy" feeling Tammie had and saying that she felt sort of the same way, Riley knew he was going to have to tell her.

It wouldn't be good for either of them if they moved to the House and she heard the story from someone else.

They were lying in their bed in the trailer, the air-conditioner going full blast. Everyone had taken a cold shower as soon as they had gotten out of the car, and that had helped. Then they had eaten some sandwiches and drunk a lot of ice water. That had helped, too.

The kids were tired and had gone to bed early, but Riley was excited and wanted to talk about the House, about his plans for fixing it up. He and Sam lay in the bed, and he told her what he thought would have to be done and how he would go about doing it.

That was when she brought up the "creepy" bit.

"It's just a funny feeling," she said. "I can't explain it, but Tammie feels the same way, so there must be something to it."

So he told her the whole gruesome story, as best he knew it. He really didn't know exactly what had happened that night. No one did. But what he did know was bad enough.

"That's terrible," Sam said when he was finished. "That's— horrible. Why didn't you ever tell me about it before?"

"I don't know," Riley said. "It was something I didn't like to think about. My father told me the story when I was a kid, and it scared the hell out of me, or anyway that part of it did. I guess I just wanted to remember the good part, the part that made the family sound like it meant something, even if it was a long time ago."

Sam could understand that. She had never met Riley's family; his mother and father were both dead before she married him. She knew, however, that the father had been a heavy drinker and that he and his wife had died in a car accident that had been his own fault. No other car had even been involved in the wreck. He had simply run off the road and into a ditch. The car had rolled over five times. He had been drunk when it happened.

So she supposed it was natural for Riley to look for something good to tell about his family and to ignore the disgusting part of the story. But still—

"You should have told me," she said.

Riley shook his head. "I know. I don't know why I didn't. It was almost like I'd forgotten that part. I *hadn't* forgotten it, but I really didn't think about it."

Sam believed him. She knew it was easy to forget things you didn't want to think about.

"Besides," Riley said, "I don't see how that could have anything to do with the way you felt. You don't believe in ghosts or any of that kind of stuff, do you?"

If he had asked her that before she had seen the house, before she had felt whatever it was she had felt, before Tammie had said the room made her feel "creepy"—if he had asked her before that, Sam would have said that of course she didn't believe in ghosts.

Ghosts were something you thought about on Hallowe'en, maybe, or saw in a movie you rented for the VCR; they weren't something you believed in, or even something that you ever thought about.

But she had felt *something* in the House, and it was something that wasn't right. She wouldn't have called it a ghost, though maybe that was what ghosts really were, things that didn't haunt a place but that gave it a feeling of wrongness.

Whatever it was, whether you called it a ghost or not, there was something in the House that bothered her. Knowing that there had been murders committed there, that the bodies of the victims had never been recovered, she was convinced that the old crime, the old evil, was still there.

It wasn't anything she could explain rationally.

It was more powerful than that. It was something that she could feel deep in her inmost being, and she wondered why Riley couldn't feel it, too. It was his house, after all, his ancestors that had been murdered.

"I don't know," he said. "It seems just the opposite to me. When I got the idea to go look at the house, I felt good about it, and things have seemed to work out right everywhere along the line, almost like we were meant to go there."

Sam would have liked to believe that his feeling was the right one and that hers was all wrong, some silly thing that could be attributed to her being a woman and therefore more prone to fear change and at the same time more superstitious than a man.

But she knew that was bullshit.

If anything, she was better able to accept change than Riley and a lot less superstitious.

She wasn't the one who turned off the TV if her team was losing and she thought she was jinxing them by watching; Riley did that.

She wasn't the one who sometimes turned a corner and went miles out of the way to avoid taking a street that a black cat had just crossed; Riley was the one who did that, too.

She didn't do other silly things, either. She didn't lose jobs for the reasons Riley did, and in fact she had never lost a job at all. She had been working at the same store for the past five years.

So it wasn't just some "woman thing" that made her feel the way she had felt at the House. She didn't believe in "woman things" at all, and Riley didn't, either.

That was what made it so hard for her to understand what had happened that day, why she had felt the way she had.

Why her?

Why Tammie?

It didn't make sense, not even now that Riley had told her the story of what had occurred in the House, not unless she accepted the idea of a ghost being something like lingering evil and then went on to believe that she and her daughter had somehow detected that evil.

"Do you think maybe we shouldn't move there?" Riley said.

His voice was hesitant, and she could tell that he was genuinely concerned. He had been so happy earlier that she couldn't bring herself to tell him no. Besides, she *wasn't* superstitious.

"I think it will be all right," she said. She didn't know what else to say. "You're going to have a good job there, one you're happy with, and the town seems so peaceful. It might be a very good place for our children to grow up."

Riley smiled. "It can't be any worse than this city, that's for sure."

She reached for him and pulled him to her, her breasts flattening against his chest. "We've had some pretty good times here, haven't we, sailor?"

He laughed. "Sure we have. But think how much fun we can have in a real house." He lifted an arm and tapped on the thin wall behind him. "Somewhere that the kids aren't a quarter of an inch away."

"You have a dirty mind," she said.

"That's true," he admitted, slipping a hand underneath her pajama top and caressing her breasts. "And you love it."

"Yes," she sighed, lying back. "I do."

Later, Riley was not sure how much later, he was awakened by a cry from Tammie's room. He sat up in the bed, the sheet falling off him.

"What was that?" Sam said, turning over. She was no longer wearing the pajama top.

"Tammie, I think. I'll go see."

He got out of bed, walking barefoot into his daughter's room. He could see her dark silhouette. She was sitting in the bed, sobbing, silently now, her shoulders shaking.

Riley sat down on the bed and put his arm around her. "Daddy's here," he said. "What's the matter, baby?"

Tammie continued to sob, her eyes tightly shut. She did not reply, and it seemed to Riley that she was not really awake, that she was crying in her sleep.

He shook her gently. "You've been having a bad dream," he said. "Wake up, honey."

The sobbing slowed and Tammie seemed to become aware of his presence. "Daddy?" she said. "Daddy?"

"Yep, it's me. You need a drink of water?"

"I'm scared, Daddy. I don't want a drink."

"Bad dream?"

"Yes," Tammie said. She started sobbing again.

"It's all right," Riley said. "It wasn't real. Daddy's right here."

After a while, Tammie stopped crying. She hugged Riley and lay back on the bed.

"Will you sit in here with me, Daddy?" she said.

"Sure," Riley said. "As long as you want."

"All night?"

"Well," Riley said, laughing, "maybe not that long." He put his hand on Tammie's forehead. "But long enough."

"Good night, Daddy," she said. "I love you."

"I love you, too," he said. He wondered what she had been dreaming about, but she never said.

In a few minutes she was asleep.

CHAPTER TWENTY-FOUR

S heriff Homer Gregory was not sleeping.
He was in a bed, true, but he was wide awake. He hadn't been quite so awake in a long, long time.

"I just don't understand it," Estelle was saying, running her hand up and down the shaft of his limp penis. She was lying beside Homer in the king-sized bed in his bedroom. "I've never seen you like this, honey." She cupped his balls and hefted them, squeezed them none too gently. "You been seeing some other woman?"

"Jesus, don't do that," Homer said. "No, I haven't been seeing anybody else. Hell, when would I have the time."

He didn't understand it, either. He'd eaten oysters for super, and that was supposed to be sure-fire. Besides that, he'd never failed to get it up, not with some woman crouched over him licking up and down the shaft with her muff right in his face.

Then it came to him. It was that damn Gus Morrow's fault, him and his story about somebody moving into the West House out in Springville. It was bad enough for Gus to start talking about that, but then he had to start up about the Harps and what they might be up to.

Homer didn't like to think about the Harps. He figured that as long as they didn't do anything too obviously bad, he could safely ignore them, and that was exactly what he wanted to do.

He wanted to ignore them for lots of reasons, not the least of which was one that he would never have discussed with

Gus or with anybody else, not realizing that Gus had already gotten an inkling of it.

Homer Gregory was afraid of the Harps.

It was as simple as that, and as complicated. He couldn't explain why he was afraid of them any more than he could explain why he couldn't get hard with Estelle trying every trick she knew.

But he couldn't get hard.

And he was afraid.

He didn't think it had anything to do with what had happened to his great-grandfather. He wasn't the kind of man who thought the past had anything to do with the present. He lived from one minute to the next, and that was the way he thought about things—you handled that minute's problems and then you moved on to the next one.

It wasn't because of any basic insecurity, either. He'd never had any problems along that line, having grown up bigger than most of the people he associated with and therefore having been accorded the kind of healthy respect that people give to those they're sure can beat the shit out of them without half trying.

And they were right.

Homer could do it, and he would if you gave him half a chance.

He'd had more than his share of fights in working his way through the public school system, partly because a lot of kids thought "Homer" was a sissy name and partly because there were always some people who just had to find out if he was as tough as he looked.

And of course partly because there always were some idiots who subscribed to the old notion that "the bigger they are, the harder they fall," which might very well have been true, but they forgot that to get someone to fall you had to knock him down first.

But no one could knock Homer down. Usually, if they even managed to lay a hand on him, they did it no more than once before being flattened themselves.

He'd had plenty of fights, all right, but he'd never lost a one. Never even come close to losing. Winning all the time was the

kind of thing that contributed to a fella's sense of well being
and security, and Homer had a sure sense of his capabilities.
He knew that the Harps were not as big as he was, though
they were plenty big, and he figured that he could take either
Absalom or Jonah, or both of them at once.

What he also figured, though, was that it wouldn't do him
any good, not unless he killed them. Just beating them to a pulp
wouldn't count for anything; they were the kind who'd just
keep on coming back.

Except he was pretty sure they would never come back
openly, not them.

They'd come back in the dark of night, when you were asleep,
when you were least expecting it. They might wait a month, or
they might wait a year; but for sure they would come back.

And they would get you.

They'd gotten Jeremiah West, hadn't they? And everyone
else involved in hanging Michael Harp had died, or at least the
three main ones had.

But that shouldn't make him afraid. He knew how to take
care of himself even when the people he was up against were
sneaks.

Keep a pistol by the bed, for one thing, which he already
did, just on general principles.

Keep a good dog in the yard, which he also did, a pit bull
that was meaner than a hippo with the hemorrhoids. He'd tear
anybody that came into the yard into pieces so little you'd have
to look for 'em with an electron microscope.

Keep a good security system in operation, which was
something Homer did anyway. You needed a good alarm these
days. Hell, everyone knew that the sheriff didn't *prevent* crime.
That just wasn't possible. He caught people after the crime had
been committed—if he was lucky. A good alarm, though, was
something that could at least help prevent crime, sort of like a
good pit bull, but louder.

So why was he afraid?

It was impossible to say.

But he was, Goddamnit.

Estelle was working him over with her tongue, and he could

see that dark muff of hers shaking in his face again. He raised his head half-heartedly and began applying himself to her. She moaned and twisted against him, almost swallowing him in the process; it was a wonder she didn't choke herself to death. The woman in *Deep Throat* had nothing on Estelle, however, and he could feel her working up and down on him.

Ordinarily, it would have been enough to get a rise out of him even if he'd been a dead man. He would have been shooting off like Mt. St. Helen's.

Tonight, it didn't do a damn thing for him. He sighed and lay back on the pillow.

Estelle didn't slow down, not for a long time, but it was just no good and she had to get out the vibrator to finish herself off.

Gus Morrow wasn't even trying to sleep.

After he and his wife had gone to bed and watched Johnny's monologue, he got back up and went into the living room. His wife asked sleepily what the matter was, and he told her that he wanted to do a little reading.

She went on to sleep, being tired, never stopping to wonder what it was that Gus could have found so interesting. As far as she knew, he hadn't read anything other than the weekly newspaper from the county seat in the last twenty years, except for an occasional article that she would point out to him in *The Reader's Digest*.

Gus went on into the living room, sat down in his recliner and pushed back. He tried to relax, but he couldn't. His mind was spinning as he thought of the Wests and what might happen to them.

It was O.K. to say he was going to warn them, but he knew that he and Stoney were just kidding themselves if they thought a warning would do any good.

It wouldn't. Those people weren't going to listen to something like Stoney had told him to say, and he couldn't make it any stronger.

Hell, what could he say, when you got right down to it?

Something like, "Move in down there, and you're gonna get murdered in your beds, sure as shootin'"?

That was ridiculous. He could say it, maybe, but they'd think he was some crazy old coot who ought to be locked up in the loony bin. And they might be right, that was the bad part.

Maybe he was crazy. Maybe that was it. He didn't have any real reason to think that the Harps were going to kill anybody. Like the sheriff said, there wasn't any proof they ever had.

It was just some crazy idea that had come into his mind the minute Ab Harp had come into his store, like the two things had happened at once and like there must be some connection between them.

There didn't have to be any connection. It was probably just something he'd dreamed up.

Sure, that was it.

He was just an old fool, thinking an old fool's thoughts. Time for him to get his old butt into the bed and go to sleep. He had to get up early and open the store so the fellas who worked in the county seat could come by and pick up the bologna and cheese and cold drinks they'd be needing for lunch that day.

He got out of the chair and went into the bedroom, where his wife was sleeping soundly. She didn't wake when he got into the bed.

He lay there, willing himself to sleep, telling his eyes to close.

It didn't work very well. Sometime after midnight he drifted off, but he woke with a start about every fifteen minutes or so.

By dawn, he had sweated through the sheets, though the air-conditioner was on and running full blast.

Stoney Thompson didn't sleep well, either.

He got to bed at his usual time, which was right after David Letterman gave out the top ten list, and went to sleep almost as soon as he got stretched out.

But he tossed and turned and twisted the covers and caught himself looking at the clock too often.

He got up and had himself a glass of ice water and a Snickers bar, but that didn't help things. He turned on a late movie for a minute or so, but that didn't help, either.

He finally went back to bed and told himself that he was

better off for minding his own business. What happened to a bunch of folks that moved into the neighborhood wasn't any concern of his.

He told himself that over and over, but he never really got himself to believe it.

The Harps were all sleeping peacefully.

Jonah and Absalom had shared a few joints with Cherry and Nita and then fucked them into insensibility. The fracas in Joshua's shack was forgiven and forgotten.

The kids slept quietly, dreaming whatever dreams their talk with Joshua had inspired in them. The dreams must not have been harrowing, for neither child stirred all night.

Joshua slept better than all the rest.

His dreams were of sweet revenge, of settling a debt that had been owed for a hundred years. The fact that Tobe Gregory and the others who had hung Old Michael Harp had died shortly after the hanging did Joshua no good at all. What he wanted was the death of more Wests.

Now he was going to have it, and he dreamed of all the ways it could happen to the man, the children, the woman.

Tomorrow he would begin training Matthew and Mary. He would teach them what it meant to be a Harp.

Those dreams were the sweetest of all.

CHAPTER TWENTY-FIVE

They started with a pig.

Jonah and Absalom stole it from some black man who lived off on the other side of the county. It wasn't a full-grown pig, but it was big enough, and stealing it presented a real transportation problem, since the Harps didn't have any transportation other than their own feet.

So they stole the black man's car, first. Hotwired it, drove it to the pig pen, and shoved the squealing shoat into the back seat. The owner of the pig and the car was either a very sound sleeper or else he was not at home; at any rate, the twins made their escape without arousing any opposition, even when the squeals of the offended pig reached ear-piercing levels of intensity.

They drove the pig to the highway as near to the shacks as they could get, and Jonah dragged it off into the woods. It struggled and squealed all the way, but that didn't bother Jonah. He knew what was going to happen to the pig. Let it holler. There wasn't anybody around to take any notice of it now.

Absalom drove the car back near the black man's house and parked it in a grove of trees. There was a tire iron under the seat, probably the man's security measure in case he was stopped by robbers or something, Absalom thought.

Had to be a real dumbass nigger to think a tire iron would help him, and Absalom couldn't stand dumbasses. Niggers, either. So he took the tire iron and jammed it into the little opening where you were supposed to insert cassette tapes and wiggled it around.

After that, he got out of the car and smashed out the windshield and all the windows. Then he unscrewed the valve stems on all four of the whitewall tires. Using the tire iron, he popped open the trunk and let the air out of the spare, too.

He opened the hood and ripped out all the spark plug wires he could reach. Goddamn new cars, he thought. You couldn't hardly get to the wiring anymore. He wondered how anybody could work on them. It was enough to make a man proud he didn't own one of the fuckers.

After he had pulled out the wires, he took off the air cleaner and clubbed the carburetor with the tire iron. He gave the air-conditioner compressor a couple of whacks, too, and gouged holes in all the hoses he could see.

When he got tired of that, he broke out the headlights.

He thought about pissing in the seat, but the pig had been pretty scared and had already taken care of that job for him.

He threw the tire iron into the bushes and started to walk back home, but when he turned back to look at the car one last time he saw that the radio antenna was still sticking up.

He went back and snapped off the antenna and threw it on the ground.

Then he left. He was whistling "Dixie" by the time he got back to the dirt road he had taken to the grove.

He took the back way home, sticking to the dirt roads and getting off into the trees if anyone passed him. It was late at night, and he didn't see many cars, not more than one or two the whole way.

It took him five hours to get back to the shacks and it was nearly sunup, but Absalom didn't mind having stayed up all night catching the pig and getting himself back home. The fun they were going to have that day would be worth it.

He was still whistling when he got to the shacks.

They took the pig to the graveyard. It seemed like the best place. Jonah and Absalom held it to the ground by its legs, Jonah taking the back ones, Absalom the front.

It was hot even in the shade under the trees, and the sun flecked the ground with bright spots of light. There wasn't much grass growing in the graveyard because there wasn't enough sun. The ground was mostly bare, except for dead limbs and leaves and some hardy weeds that didn't need the light. The gravestones stuck up out of the ground like randomly tossed boulders, so aged and discolored it was hard to tell what their original purpose had been. Whoever had begun the graveyard had no doubt liked the idea of the graves being sheltered by the trees, but the end result of the shelter had not been pretty.

Another thing about the graveyard these days was the fire ants. They had made large mounds, and if you so much as brushed one of them the ants would come seething out and swarm over anything within reach. Their sting could raise blisters on the hardiest of men, and it was often fatal to young animals. No one had yet invented an insecticide that could rid an area of the pests once they had established themselves.

The Harps were to one side of the stones, near the place where there were graves but no markers, where the bodies of murdered travelers had been buried more than once, and where the Wests themselves lay under the earth. They were well away from the ant mounds.

By now the pig was pretty well tired out and had stopped squealing. It wasn't struggling enough to satisfy Joshua. He wanted the kids to get more of a feeling for what it was like to kill something that could fight back.

"Pig needs a little touching up," he said.

"Sure," Jonah said. He got his knife from his boot and jabbed the pig in the rump, digging in the point of the blade and wiggling it around.

The pig lurched forward and got away from Jonah, breaking his grip now that he was holding to only one leg. It shoved head-on into Absalom, who fell over on his back, still keeping his hold on the front legs. It was squealing and rooting in Absalom's belly.

"Goddamnit!" Absalom yelled from under the pig. "Grab this fucker and get it off me!"

Jonah dived for the hind legs, but the pig was kicking so hard as it tried to get a purchase for its hooves that he had difficulty getting a grip on it.

"Shit!" Absalom said. "This thing's gonna kill me! If you don't get ahold of it, I'm letting it go!"

"Better not do that," Joshua said, from where he was watching. "You'd just have to catch it again."

Jonah grabbed one of the back legs and held on. Then he managed to get the other one, and after a brief struggle he and his brother had the pig stretched out again. It was still trying to escape, but it was no longer squealing.

Joshua was satisfied, but not Absalom. "Next time you touch it up," he said to his brother, "don't do such a damn good job.

The pig was pitching up and down, arching its back and thrashing its stomach on the ground, making grunting noises.

Matthew and Mary were standing a few feet away, staring at the pig. It had been funny when the pig got away, and it had even been funny when the pig got Absalom down on the ground and rooted on him.

It wasn't funny now, though.

The pig was desperate and wild, its eyes rolling. There was some kind of gummy slobber coming out the corner of its mouth, and it was rubbing its belly raw on the dirt.

It didn't know what was happening to it, and it was scared.

Matthew and Mary didn't remember the turtle being scared. Maybe it hadn't been very smart or known what was going to happen. That was probably it. Sure, it had tried to get away from them, but that was what turtles always did.

Pigs were different. Matthew couldn't have explained why he thought that, but he did. He didn't want to look at the pig anymore.

"Now's the time," Joshua said. He pulled a hunting knife from his belt and handed it to Matthew.

Matthew reached out and took it, though he didn't want to. He felt his hand close on the leather-wrapped handle. He couldn't reach all the way around it like Joshua could.

Matthew could feel Mary standing close beside him, and he looked around at her. She had her eyes closed.

Joshua noticed the same thing. "Open those eyes, Missy," he said. "I ain't making you do the killing, since you're a female, but I want you to watch it. You got to know what it's like."

"I don't want to look," Mary said.

"You look, like I told you to," Joshua said. He put his hand on Mary's head and turned it toward the pig. She opened her eyes.

The pig was still struggling to escape, but it was tiring. It wasn't able to arch its back any longer; it was just scraping its belly from side to side on the ground, making the grunting noise, though even that was getting weaker.

Matthew stood there looking at it. His feet felt like they weighed a thousand pounds. He couldn't will himself to take a step forward.

"Come on, kid. We ain't got all day," Absalom said.

Matthew felt Joshua's hand in the small of his back. It pushed him toward the pig, and he didn't resist.

"Get down here with us," Absalom said. "Kneel down and get ready."

Matthew dropped to his knees. He could smell the pig now, but it wasn't the sour smell of the pig pen that came to his nostrils. It was something else, something just as sour, but something different.

Matthew knew that it was fear, and at that instant he smelled himself, too.

He smelled just like the pig.

"Goddamn," Jonah said. "Either you kill this son-of-a-bitch pig or I'm gonna do it myself. And if I have to do it, I'm gonna skin your ass, boy, I'll tell you that."

Jonah's face was red with the strain of holding the pig, and he was sweating freely. He stank, too, but he did not smell like the pig smelled, or like Matthew smelled.

"You heard him, damnit," Absalom said. "Let's do it. Ready, Jonah?"

"Hell, yes, I'm ready."

"On three, then," Absalom said. "One … two … THREE!"

On the count of three they heaved the pig over on its back.

"Now," Joshua said. "Kill it."

Matthew knew what he was supposed to do. They had explained it all to him in detail before going down to the graveyard.

It was very simple.

He was supposed to cut the pig's throat.

"First you stick the knife in," Joshua had said. "Left corner's best, since you're right-handed. That way you can pull back to the right. Don't worry 'bout having to pull too hard. The knife you'll be using will slide through that pig like it was sliding through shit."

Joshua smiled, thinking how easy it would be for Matthew to do it.

"Then," he said, "you just pull all the way to the right. Take your time. The pig won't be going nowhere."

Absalom and Jonah laughed at that. Matthew didn't see what was so funny.

"And that's the end of the pig," Joshua said. "A man's the same way. Cut his throat from one ear to the other, and he won't be much trouble to you after that."

It had sounded simple, all right, when Joshua explained it to him, but it wasn't so simple now. It was easy enough to talk about things like stabbing the knife in, but doing it was something else.

Matthew thought about the turtle again.

All you had to do with a turtle was hit it with a few rocks, and that was it. Why couldn't he kill the pig the same way? The sunlight glinted off the knife blade and into Matthew's eyes.

"Listen, you little asshole," Absalom said. "I'm gonna count to three one more time. If you ain't killed this fucking pig by then, I'll take the knife and cut *your* throat."

"And I'd have to let him, boy," Joshua said. "You got this one chance to prove yourself. There won't never be another one."

Matthew didn't say anything. He leaned forward and looked at the pig, trying to avoid its beady black eyes. It was thrashing its head from side to side, almost as if it knew what was about to happen.

Matthew told himself not to let that bother him. He was there to do a job, and he had to do it. Otherwise, everyone would hate him and think he was a coward.

He didn't want that to happen.

He gripped the handle of the knife with both hands and

took aim at the throat of the pig. Then he closed his eyes and lunged forward.

He got lucky. Instead of stabbing Absalom, he managed to get the pig. He didn't exactly hit the left corner of the throat, but he was close enough. The knife went in with surprising ease, practically right up to the hilt; it was just as sharp as Joshua had promised.

The pig squealed.

It seemed to Matthew to be a sound louder than anything he had ever heard, louder than Cherry and Nita screamed in the night sometimes, louder than the thunder of the worst storms, louder even that the explosion that time when lightning had hit a tree at the edge of the woods.

The blood gushed out over Matthew's hands, making the knife handle slippery and hard to hold. The blood was hot and thick, and Matthew was so surprised that he opened his eyes.

He wasn't looking down at the pig. He was looking right at Absalom, whose lips were peeled back in a joyous grin.

"Way to go, kid," Absalom said. "Now just do the cutting."

The pig was thrashing around harder than ever, and the blood was spurting out where the knife was sticking. Blood covered Matthew's hands and ran up his arms.

He made himself look down. The blood looked thick and dark.

He could hardly see the knife or the pig's throat. He didn't know how he was supposed to cut what he couldn't see, but he began sawing the knife to the right.

"Don't saw like that," Joshua said. "Just let it slide through. It'll go easy. Take your time, now."

Matthew didn't want to take his time. He wanted to do it fast and get it over with. Then he wanted to jump up and run to the spring and stick his hands in and leave them there until all the hot blood was gone.

He couldn't do that, though. Everyone was watching him.

He pulled the knife slowly and carefully. It cut through skin and cartilage and kept on moving, just like Joshua had said it would.

Suddenly the pig stopped thrashing. It gave one gigantic

shudder and then lay still on the ground, but Matthew kept on cutting.

"You can stop now," Absalom said. He released his hold on the pig's front legs and leaned back on his heels. "The fucker's dead as he'll ever be."

"Yep. You did good," Jonah said. He too let go of the pig, which lay there stretched out, unmoving.

Matthew stared at it in fascination.

Its head was nearly separated from its body, and it was covered with blood. Blood had gotten on Jonah and Absalom, too, but mostly on Absalom, since he had been at the front. It was on his clothes and on his face and in his hair, but he didn't seem to mind it. There was blood soaking into the ground, staining the dirt a dark black.

Matthew could hardly believe there could have been that much blood in just one pig.

Suddenly he wasn't afraid anymore. He felt entirely different now, but not the same way he'd felt when he killed the turtle.

This pig had known what was going to happen to it, but Matthew had killed it anyhow.

It had been living and breathing and fighting for its life, but there wasn't anything it could do. Matthew Harp, with his knife and his bare hands, had stopped all of that, stopped the living and the breathing and the fighting all at once.

He looked at the bloody knife, his bloody hands.

"I did it," he said. "It was easy."

"I told you it would be easy," Joshua said. "You're a real Harp, boy. I knew you had it in you."

Joshua stepped up to the pig and reached down his hand, dipping it in the bloody throat. He reached and made a mark on Matthew's forehead. Then he dipped his hand in again and brought it to the boy's mouth.

Matthew knew what to do, almost without thinking about it. He stuck out his tongue and tasted the blood. It tasted hot and wild and faintly sweet. It tasted good.

"Are we gonna bury the pig?" Mary said. She wasn't scared anymore, either. Matthew had killed the pig, and everything was all right. It was like with the turtle and the dolls, only the pig had been bigger. It hadn't been bad at all after all the squealing and moving around had stopped.

She looked at Matthew. She could see that he didn't mind what he had done, that he didn't even mind the blood that was all over him. She smiled. She was glad that everything was all right.

The twins stood up and looked down at the carcass.

"Maybe we oughta cut us off a ham," Jonah said. "Hang it out to cure. We could build us a little smoke house and do that."

"Be a good way to celebrate," Absalom said. "Let's do it."

"All right," Joshua said. "Let me have that knife, boy."

Matthew handed back the knife. He didn't want to give it up.

"You'll have one of your own before long," Joshua promised. "You've showed you know how to use it."

"Yes," Matthew said. "I want one."

He didn't mind the blood on his arms now. It felt almost pleasant as it began to dry stickily on him. He no longer wanted to wash it off.

And he wanted a big knife of his own, a hunting knife.

He wanted that more than anything.

INTERVAL 2

"... and therefore it cannot be long before we lie down in darkness."

—Sir Thomas Browne, "Hydrotaphia, Urn-Burial"

CHAPTER
TWENTY-SIX

Things can change in a hundred years, or even in a single year. In the year after Riley West and his family moved to the House, many things changed, all of them, Riley believed, for the better.

His children started school in the county seat and adjusted quickly, making friends and doing well in their studies. Both had been fairly good students before, but now they seemed more interested in doing their homework and reading their assignments.

Riley thought it was because they had suddenly become interested in learning.

Sam thought it was because they no longer had as many thing to distract them. In short, she thought that there weren't as many things to do outside of school and so the kids had simply compensated in the best possible way. It didn't matter to her. The result was the same.

Riley's job worked out well, too. He was liked by his co-workers and his boss, did a good job, and was considered by some to be a prime candidate to manage the lumber yard one day.

Living expenses were not as great in Springville as they had been in Houston, so Sam did not have to take a job, which was just as well. She had enough to do at the House during the day while Riley was at the lumber yard. Cleaning up was such a big job that it was two months before she was ready to allow any work on the House to begin.

They were still living in the trailer, though it hadn't been easy getting it down the hill. Riley had put in the septic tank before they moved, and he had gotten the electricity run from the road, so they had all the conveniences.

Except for cable television, which might have been another reason for Dan and Tammie's increased interest in books and schoolwork.

The children were not allowed to go into the woods, but they liked exploring in the house after school and even helped with the cleaning. They had been especially interested in the old boxes in the attic, and the things lying scattered about up there.

"I don't know why this stuff is still here," Riley confessed when they were clearing it away. "I guess it's because the people around here are so honest."

Sam was of the opinion that the junk was still there because it was completely worthless. Old rusty farm equipment, rotten leather plowlines, nothing that anyone could possibly use.

Dan thought differently. "This is great stuff," he said, examining the plow lines that were practically crumbling in his hands. "Can we keep it, Dad?"

Riley guessed they could, though he didn't see what use they could make of it. "Maybe we could use it for decoration some way," he suggested.

"Maybe we could leave it here in the attic," Sam countered. There was nothing decorative about any of it that she could see.

"It's antiques," Tammie said. "Maybe somebody would buy it."

"There's a thought," Sam said, brushing her hair back out of her eyes and leaving a smear of dirt on her forehead. "You might have the makings of an entrepreneur, kid."

"What's that mean?" Tammie said.

"Businessperson," Riley told her.

"That's what I want to be," Tammie said. "An ontrop ... a businessperson. If we sell it, can I have the money?"

"We can't sell it," Dan said. "It's keepsakes."

"Dan's right," Riley said. "It's something of the family's. We'll keep it for a while, at least."

Tammie wasn't too happy with this decision, but she didn't argue.

"I'm glad nobody took it," Dan said.

"Me, too," Riley agreed.

It never occurred to any of them that no one had taken it for the simple reason that no one would dare to enter the House.

Even the Harps had stayed away.

Another good thing was the little community of Springville. It was almost like a town from another time.

There was no crime there, no noisy trucks ripping up and down the streets, no ambulances wailing at all hours, no police sirens screaming day and night. It was a place where you felt safe, where you didn't really even seem to need to lock your doors at night.

The people had seemed a little unfriendly at first, especially the storekeeper, Gus Morrow, and their nearest neighbor, Stoney Thompson, but after a while the two men had come to be very close to the Wests.

Riley never asked them why they had been so cold and distant at first, spending most of their first meetings telling him that the house was dangerous, a firetrap, likely to be flooded if the river rose, susceptible to all kinds of thieves and robbers.

It didn't seem to matter much after the first month or two. The men had relaxed and become quite friendly, almost as if they were trying to make up for their earlier behavior.

One thing Riley took to heart, however, was their warning about the Harps.

"They live over by the woods, not more'n a quarter mile from your place," Stoney said one day. "Bad folks, if you get my meaning."

Riley wasn't sure he got it.

"They've had a bad history," Stoney said. He wouldn't say any more, but Riley was beginning to catch on.

Gus Morrow was a bit more forthcoming. "Nobody ever proved nothing, but their family was suspected of murdering some of your kinfolks, way back when. You heard about that, I guess?" He watched Riley closely.

Riley admitted that he'd heard about it. "Nobody ever really told me much about what happened, though."

"I'm not saying much, either. Just thought you'd like to know." Morrow turned back to the shelves he was stocking.

Riley tried to get him to say more, but Gus wasn't talking.

Sam was worried when Riley told her, but he assured her that there would be no problem.

"There's lots of families like that still living all over the state in these rural counties," he said. "They live by their own rules, but they generally don't bother anybody as long as they're left alone. They just want to be free to live the way they want to. Probably don't pay any income tax, don't work at regular jobs, and more or less go their own way. They won't be any problem to us."

He really believed what he was saying. He left out the part about the past connection between the Harps and the Wests because it was only speculation, and because he didn't think it could possibly have any effect on his family now. He didn't want to worry Sam unnecessarily.

Stoney Thompson and Gus Morrow felt increasing relief as the months went by. They had been sure, the day the trailer was moved in, that the Wests were as good as dead.

They had done what they could to discourage them, dropping hints as best they could, but Riley West wasn't a man to be discouraged. He had it in his head that he was going to live in West House, and nothing they could say to him would change his mind.

Gus didn't go back to see Homer Gregory, but the Sheriff had driven out to the store a month after the Wests arrived.

He bought a Coke from Gus' machine and drank it in the store while he talked to Gus.

"Looks like you were a little over-anxious about those people who moved in here," he said, taking a swallow.

"Guess so," Gus said. He still wasn't convinced, but it looked as if the sheriff was right about it.

"Yeah," Gregory said. "You got me all stirred up, though, I have to give you that."

He wasn't kidding. It had been weeks before he could do Estelle any good, and she had almost taken up with a man who drove a bread truck in the meantime. Things were back to normal now, and Homer was eating raw eggs and oysters again. Estelle hadn't had to use the vibrator recently.

"I guess I misjudged those old boys," Gus said. He didn't want to say the name, not in the store. You never knew who might hear you.

"You sure did," Homer said. "I told you that they weren't as bad as you thought they were."

Gus still thought the Harps were as bad as they had ever been, and he was convinced that was pretty damn bad. But it wouldn't do any good to say so to Homer. The only good thing, as far as Gus could see, was that the Harps weren't interested in the Wests after all.

"Think I'll drive on down there and introduce myself to the Wests," Homer said. "Every vote counts."

"You do that," Gus said. "They're nice folks."

He watched the sheriff's car pull out onto the dirt road. He still felt a little uneasy, but if nothing had happened by now, nothing was likely to happen.

At least that was what he told himself.

Most of the time he was even able to make himself believe it.

For Stoney, believing it was easier than it was for Gus, since Stoney had gotten to know the Wests better than the storekeeper had.

Stoney, getting more and more bored with *Name that Tune* these days, would often walk down the hill and talk to Sam West after the school bus brought the kids home. He didn't go earlier, because people in Springville would have talked about him. He was a single man, after all.

He would help Sam and the kids clean up in the House, not even thinking that until she had moved there he wouldn't have dreamed of setting foot inside it. When they got tired and thirsty, they would go to the trailer and Sam would serve lemonade.

Stoney would drink his lemonade from a glass with the

Flintstones painted on it and tell the kids stories about fishing in the river and about hunting in the woods.

"Will you take us hunting sometime, Mr. Thompson?" Dan asked. He thought it would be fun to go into the woods, but his mother wouldn't let him. Maybe she would, if Mr. Thompson went with him.

Stoney was immediately sorry he'd brought it up. He didn't go in the woods anymore, not since the coon hunters had gotten into such a mess. Fishing, though, that was different. There were several well-cleared trails down to the river, and the catfish were sometimes fairly cooperative.

That sounded good to Dan, and when Riley came home he agreed to the idea. He thought it was good for a boy to go fishing, and he invited himself along for good measure. Tammie wanted to go, too, but Sam decided to skip it. She liked eating fish, not catching them.

The first trip led to others, and Stoney began giving Riley some help on restoring the house.

The only time Riley had to work was late in the afternoons, after his job at the lumber yard was over, and on Sundays. It was slow going, but there was tangible progress after the cleaning was finally done. After six months, the House was beginning to look habitable.

"When can we move in?" Dan asked.

It was a late December afternoon, nearly dark, and the weather had turned cold. There were fireplaces in the House, and Riley had cleared the chimneys of bird's nests and other obstructions; a fire was blazing in the downstairs living room.

Stoney was there with them, helping to patch a wall. "You've got a while to wait, I'd say. It's beginning to look good, but you wouldn't be comfortable here yet."

"He's right," Riley said. "It'll take a long time to get things the way we want them. But it'll be worth it to do them right."

Dan understood, but he was impatient. He liked the idea of moving into the House, because there was so much more room than in the trailer. He also liked the fact that he would be on the second floor, high off the ground.

"I'm not ready to move," Tammie said. She was sitting on

the floor in front of the fire. "I like the trailer."

She hadn't said anything like that recently, and Riley had hoped she was over her initial reaction to the House.

"We'll have the bathtubs in before we move," he said.

"It's not the bathtub," she said.

"This is going to be a real nice place," Stoney told her. "You'll like it a lot."

"No, I won't," Tammie said, shaking her head and looking into the fire.

Stoney began to worry again that night, but still nothing happened. He told himself that he was acting like an old man. Surely, nothing was going to happen now.

Nothing did.

The work on the House continued throughout the winter; even the cold weather did not slow things down. Riley got the plumbing taken care of, got the wiring done, sanded the floors, painted, papered, installed the appliances, and generally got the place in shape.

"It's really looking good," Sam said early in the spring. It was the truth, and she was a little surprised. She knew that Riley was capable of doing good work, but he had never really stuck to anything for very long. Now he had virtually transformed the shell of the House into something approaching a fully restored estate. The result far exceeded her expectations.

"We ought to be able to move in soon," he said. "It's nearly ready."

"We ought to have a little party when we do," Sam said. "We could invite Stoney and Gus. And Gus' wife."

"Good idea. Sort of a housewarming, but on a small scale." Riley wasn't comfortable with lavish parties. Besides, they didn't have enough money left in their account for anything grand.

"Maybe Dan and Tammie could invite some of the kids from school," Sam suggested.

That was all right, too. "As long as they don't invite too many," Riley said. Then he had a thought. "Why don't we try to move in a year to the day after we first came here?"

"Good idea. Think we can do it?"

"Sure. It's almost done now. We can make it. It'll be a big day."

Sam gave him a hug. Her own misgivings were almost forgotten. She was almost as eager as Dan to move in.

The Harps had watched the progress of the House with great interest.

There was one question in the minds of all of them, all of the except for Joshua, who knew the answer to their unspoken question: "When?"

If anyone had asked, he would have told them, "When the time is right."

And if anyone had asked when the time would be right, he really could not have said. He knew, however, that the right time had not yet come, and he was convinced that when it did come, he would know it.

Something would tell him, some sign would come.

He had gotten the knife for Matthew, a fine blade that he had honed to a keen edge before giving it to the boy. He often saw him taking it out of its leather scabbard and looking at it respectfully, turning it over in his hands and eyeing the smooth coldness of the blade, the whetted edge that could slide through flesh as if it were water.

There had been no need to find a victim to allow Matthew some practice with the new knife, however. Matthew was clearly ready for whatever he was asked to do.

Joshua had already decided what that was to be. Matthew could have the boy and the girl. Mary could help him. Joshua was sure she would, though he would not give her any special responsibility. She was only a girl, after all, and females couldn't be trusted to do things of that nature, not if Cheery and Nita were any indication. He didn't think either one of them would be up to it.

And if the girl wasn't, either, well, that didn't really make much difference. Matthew could handle the two West kids.

He would have plenty of help if he couldn't.

As for the man and woman, Jonah and Absalom would have no trouble at all. The only argument was going to be over who got first go at the woman, and Joshua had an answer for that one already worked out.

He was.

The twins didn't know it yet, but their old man wasn't so old that he didn't think about a woman now and then. Had him one, too, when he wanted, which wasn't very often and was mostly whores anyway. He didn't tell the boys about them.

Anyway, it was time he had something a little better, and the West woman was better, no question about it. He liked to watch her as she worked around the house, never suspecting that his old eyes were on her all the time.

It was going to be a real pleasure to look into her eyes as she twisted under him, just before he killed her.

Or, hell, maybe he would let the boys have a go at her before they slit her throat. They were good boys. They deserved it.

But he was going to be first, no question about it.

He was going to kill the man, too. That was the way it had to be. The man was the one, the real West, the one who carried the blood.

It was going to be fun killing him.

He was going to see his children die and his wife getting raped, and then he could die, too.

Then the bodies would be disposed of and no one the wiser. If the fat sheriff cam bothering around, they'd tell him they didn't know a thing. If someone had disappeared, that was too damn bad, but what did it have to do with the Harps?

The sheriff wouldn't do anything about it, either. Hell, who cared about some strangers that had moved into the area? Nobody, that's who. After a few weeks, nobody would miss them anymore.

Everything was going to be just fine.

All the Harps had to do was wait.

Until the time was right.

PART III

"When many that feared to die shall groan that they can die but once ..."

—Sir Thomas Browne, "Hydriotaphia, Urn-Burial"

CHAPTER
TWENTY-SEVEN

Matthew had thought a lot about killing the pig over the past months.

He had thought about the blood, the way it smelled, the way it felt on his hands and arms.

He had liked it.

He had been afraid at first, though he would never have admitted that, and he had even felt sorry for the struggling animal, but everything seemed different now.

When he remembered it, he could still see the pig flailing itself against the ground, could still hear its agonized squeals, but now he felt no sympathy or sorrow at all. There was no piercing pain of regret for what he had done.

There was instead almost a sense of elation. He thought of it often, and replayed each minute of the event in his mind: the way Absalom and Jonah had held the pig, the way his grandfather had gently urged him forward, the way the knife had gone into the pig's flesh so smoothly, so easily.

The way the blood had spurted out.

The way the pig had stopped its squeals and its thrashing.

The way the blood had tasted then.

The way the ham had tasted later.

"I swear," Jonah had said. "This is the best damn ham I believe we've ever had. You can't beat the real thing, hung out in the smoke and spiced right. Hell, that shit you get in the store's half water, and it's probably not even really ham."

Joshua had cooked the ham in the wood stove, cooking it

slowly, taking nearly all day. He had cooked sweet potatoes and corn to go with it. The Harps did not have a garden, but they were quick to take advantage of anyone who did.

"I got to say you're right," Absalom said, taking a huge piece of the ham and shoving it into his mouth. He followed it with a forkful of potatoes and was too busy chewing to say any more.

It made Matthew feel good to hear them say it. He was the one who had killed the pig, and he knew they were proud of him for doing it.

He wanted them to be even more proud of him. He wanted to show them that they could trust him to do whatever they wanted him to do.

Every day he got out his knife and polished the blade, being careful not to cut himself on its keen edge. And he did have to be careful. He had just touched the edge with his finger once, sort of to test it, and it had sliced him almost before he was aware of it, the bright blood springing out on the skin and running down his finger.

He tasted the blood, but it didn't taste like the pig's blood had tasted. There wasn't enough of it, and it was his own blood.

He was still alive; that made a difference, too. To taste the blood of something you had killed was …. something he could not explain.

He knew very little of old Michael Harp, other than his name, what he had done to the Wests so many years ago, and what had finally happened to him. All these things were part of his heritage, part of the stories Joshua had told him from birth.

He knew nothing of Michael's habit of killing the chickens in his front yard, holding them up, and letting the blood drip down on his tongue, but he would have understood perfectly if anyone had told him of it.

He no longer wanted to play in the graveyard with Mary. Fooling around with the dolls was no fun for him at all. It seemed silly and stupid to him now.

He did consider the possibility of killing another turtle, but even that did not appeal to him. Turtles were nothing; they had no fight in them. It would be too easy.

There were no more pigs to play with, however, and the

animals in the woods were too difficult to catch. He sometimes wished that Joshua would get him something else to kill, but he understood that he was being saved for something special.

Joshua had explained it to him. "Our family's waited a hundred years for this, boy, and we're the ones who get to do it. We're gonna wipe out the last of the Wests, and you're gonna help us."

Matthew wasn't sure about one thing. "The Wests aren't the ones who killed old Michael, are they?" he said.

Joshua shook his head pityingly. "You just don't understand, boy. They didn't do the hanging, if that's what you mean, but it was their fault it happened. Some of the ones that did the hanging, their families are still around. We could've killed 'em anytime we wanted to. But that was taken care of a long time ago."

He told Matthew the story of how the ancestors of Gus Morrow, Homer Thompson, and Stoney Thompson had died.

"But who killed them?" Matthew said. He didn't see how people could just die like that, for no reason.

"Nobody killed 'em," Joshua said. "The fuckers just died. Some people say you can die from a guilty conscience, but I always thought God struck 'em down, myself. Struck 'em down for murderin' a man that'd never done a thing to 'em."

Michael figured that was possible. "But why do we hate the Wests, then? They didn't do anything to us." He paused. "Or did they?"

"Boy, they caused the murder of a Harp, who was just doing what Harps were meant to do. And then they caused the murder of old Michael. He told his boys to remember that, and they did. We ain't ever forgot, and we ain't going to forget."

"And so now we're going to kill them all?"

"You're mighty right, we are. Ever' damn last one of 'em, and after that there won't be any more. We'll kill the man and the woman and the kids, and that'll be the end of it."

"And it'll be like killing the pig?"

Joshua looked at the boy. "No," he said. "It won't be like that."

"Oh," Matthew said, looking down at the knife he now wore on his belt.

"No," Joshua said again. "It won't be like that at all." He smiled at Matthew's disappointment. "It'll be better, boy. A whole lot better."

Then Matthew was smiling, too.

Homer Gregory was not smiling.

He had been able to get a solid hour of sleep in his office after lunch, but that didn't make it a good day. Hell, he didn't even need the sleep much anymore, not since Estelle had dumped him. She was going with the body man from the Ford place now, a slim, muscular young fella with tattoos on both arms and God knew where else. Homer had run his name through the computers, tried to get something on him, but there wasn't anything to get.

He should have known it was coming, anyhow. He just wasn't able to keep up with Estelle, and he'd bet the body man, Lloyd Haskins, that was his name, wouldn't be able to keep up with her for very long, either, even if he was fifteen years younger than Homer.

Homer knew that he actually ought to be relieved. It had gotten to the point that he was having to take massive doses of vitamin E, and even that, along with the raw eggs and oysters, wasn't doing him enough good. He walked around half the time like an old man, and he was tired *all* the time. He needed the rest.

And besides, he knew it wouldn't take him long to hook up with somebody else. It never did. When you were the sheriff, and single, you found the pickings pretty easy, especially if you wore a big gun, and Homer wore the biggest .44 magnum he could find. There was something about a gun that got certain women hot, real quick. They probably figured, "Big gun, big dick." In Homer's case they were right.

Homer had learned to spot them.

Trouble was, there just weren't many women like Estelle. Sure, she was about to kill him, but he couldn't think of a better way to go.

There was something else worrying Homer, too, but he couldn't put his finger on it. It was like a little itch that he couldn't quite locate and therefore couldn't quite get to in order to scratch it.

It wasn't crimes. Not much was going on in the county. They'd arrested a few drunk drivers, caught some school kids with dope, busted a little meth lab that wasn't much more than a mom and pop operation, and had a few break-ins and one convenience store hold up.

All that was just the normal stuff that happened, no sweat, no strain.

So what was it that was bothering him?

He sat in his office, his feet up on the desk and looked around. The walls were covered with Wanted notices and other scraps of paper that he'd stuck up to remind himself of one thing or another, and right in the middle of the wall opposite his desk was a big calendar.

He hung up one like it every year because the dates on it were big and easy to read from across the room. The guy at the tractor place sent it to him, not that Homer was ever going to buy a tractor. The guy probably thought it was good advertising to have his calendar up in the sheriff's office where it could be seen by the gentry.

Anyway, it was the calendar that caught Homer's attention. He ran his eye over the dates, not knowing why any of them should seem significant to him, and then he got it.

It had been just about a year since those Wests had moved their trailer down the hill in Springville, just about a year since Gus Morrow had come in the office going on about how bad things were going to happen.

Well, nothing had happened at all. Homer had even gone down there and met the family, who seemed like nice folks. The woman, Samantha, had seemed more than nice, and Jesus, didn't he wish that Estelle or any woman he had a chance with looked like that. Long hair, smooth skin, big tits—but he'd never get one like that. Not a chance. He shook his head sadly.

It would be a shame if anything happened to them, especially her, and Homer had worried about it for a while, as he recalled. Not for long. Hell, it was like Gus was hipped on the subject of the Harps, who were probably just as bad as

Gus thought they were, and in fact had probably supplied the dope to those kids that had been arrested the other day, but who were pretty discreet in their doings. He'd never caught them at a damn thing.

And if they were bad, at least they weren't crazy. It would take someone crazy to do what Gus thought was going to be done.

So why was Homer thinking about it now? Why had it been itching at the back of his head like that?

No reason, he thought. None at all. What he needed to do was to find himself a woman. He decided to do so that very night.

CHAPTER TWENTY-EIGHT

"We'll move in tomorrow," Riley said.

Dan cheered. He was more than ready. Sam hugged her husband and laughed. Only Tammie did not seem pleased, but she tried to smile and appear happy. She was old enough to know that there was nothing she could do to change things when the grown-ups had their minds set on them. But she still planned to slip out of the House the first chance she got and spend the night in the trailer.

Sam noticed the look on her daughter's face, but she did not say anything. Maybe she would talk to her later, but she didn't want to spoil Riley's happiness in the present moment.

The House was completely ready. It was wired, painted, roofed, and reconditioned. It had new furniture and a modern kitchen with all the conveniences. The bathrooms had been added. There were air-conditioners for the bedrooms, and the rest of the house was airy and cool, thanks to the many windows and the surrounding trees.

Riley was sure that it was going to be a fine place to live.

"I've asked for the day off," he said. "Gus and Stoney will help us with the furniture we're taking from here, and we'll make it into an all-day party. Some of the guys from the lumber yard will be coming by after work, too."

"I know it's going to be great," Sam said. She was excited. After a year of anticipation, she had lost most of her foreboding about the house, caught up in the project as her husband had been. Things had gone so well that she could not see a reason to worry.

That night, she and Riley made love for the last time in the
trailer. It was slow and sweet, but when they were done, Sam
could not go to sleep. She looked over at Riley as he lay there,
thinking what a good job he had done on the house, how well
he had fit in at his new job, and she wondered why he had not
thought of the House before last year.

It was probably because he was so caught up in the old
game of trying to make everyone happy except himself. He had
tried to conform to everyone's idea of what success was—or to
what he had thought that idea was—by getting regular jobs and
trying to make money and buy things.

As it turned out, he had never been very good at that. He had
the ability to make her happy to make her smile and laugh, he
loved her and the children, but that had never seemed enough
to him. The world demanded that he reach a certain standard,
and he had tried to reach it.

He'd never been happy at it, not really, not the way he was
happy now.

She reached out and touched his hair, noticing for the first
time that it was beginning to be colored very slightly with gray.
Neither Riley nor she was young any longer, she thought. It was
good that they had made the move to the House when they did.
If they had waited any longer, it might have seemed a foolish
dream, out of reach of two old folks.

She thought briefly of the look she had seen on Tammie's
face earlier that day. It was clear that Tammie still harbored
reservations about moving into the House, and Sam wondered
why.

When they had first moved to Springville, she had tried to
talk to Tammie about it once or twice, but the girl could give no
explanation other than saying she didn't "feel good" about the
place.

Sam had understood at first, but as her own misgivings had
melted away, she had thought the same thing would happen to
Tammie.

Obviously, it had not.

She remembered the night Tammie had awakened in the
throes of a nightmare. When had that been? Before they moved,

surely. Riley had gone in to comfort her, but she had never told why she had been disturbed. Had she been dreaming about the House?

Well, it didn't matter. Dreams had no power to tell the future or indicate one's fate.

Sam drifted off to sleep, thinking about the party.

It was a lot of fun, even Tammie had to admit that. She had never eaten real homemade ice cream before, but now she thought it was the best thing she had ever tasted, smooth and cold and sweet.

Mrs. Morrow, a fat, cheerful woman, had made it, and they had frozen it by putting it in a metal bucket that had then been put into a bigger wooden bucket. They had packed ice around the metal bucket and put a crank on the top.

Tammie had helped turn the crank, and after a while they had ice cream. It had peaches in it, and Tammie ate two big bowls.

She had fun at the party, as long as they stayed outside. She listened to the men talk to her father about the House, about what a good job he'd done and about how it was as nice as any house in the county—maybe nicer.

She had to admit that it was a pretty house. She had never seen one like it, made all of wood and so big that it looked like a castle, almost. She had lived all her life in a trailer, which didn't really have a lot of room in it.

She liked the way it looked, and if it had been someone else's house, she would have thought it was just as nice as the men said. But it was her house, and she was going to have to live there, going to have to sleep in that room.

She hadn't said any more about it, however. It wouldn't do any good. But she still didn't like it. When she went in there, she felt cold, not the cold from the air-conditioner, but a different kind of cold, a scary kind, a kind of cold she couldn't explain to anybody.

Dan didn't seem to mind the House at all, and after the ice cream she let herself be drawn off by him into an exploring game that led them under the House.

Dan regarded this as his secret place, and he liked to go there to think about things, such as whether he would rather work at NASA after he got out of college or become a professional baseball player. He suspected that ballplayers made a lot more money.

Tammie liked it under there, too. It didn't feel the same as being inside, and they could watch the adults through the latticework without anyone knowing that they were being observed.

Once they had settled themselves, Dan surprised her by asking about her room.

"You still going to be a sissy about it?"

"I'm not no sissy. I just don't like it."

"Why not?"

"Just don't." There was no need to try to explain it to him. She knew she couldn't.

"Well, I like this place. I'd like to sleep out here under the porch, even."

"You'd get dirty," Tammie pointed out. "Mom wouldn't like that."

"It'd be neat, though. You could see all kinds of stuff at night, I bet."

Tammie got an idea, one that was even better than the one she had about sneaking back to the trailer.

"You want to?" she said.

"Want to, what?"

"Sleep here tonight." If she could get him to do it one night, maybe the next one wouldn't be so bad. Or maybe they could always sleep there, and she would never have to go to the room.

"I'd get dirty, you said."

"We could bring an old quilt or something and sleep on that. We wouldn't get dirty that way."

"Wait a minute. I didn't say *you* could come. I said *I'd* like to sleep here. By myself."

"I'd tell, and then Mom wouldn't let you. But if you let me come with you, we could both see stuff. Stars, maybe." She really didn't know what kind of stuff Dan wanted to see, but she was ready for anything other than the room.

Dan thought about it for a minute.

Tammie was all right, for a sister. She had been fishing with him and Stoney and Dad, and she had not been afraid to put the chicken livers on the hooks. When she caught a fish, she wasn't afraid to touch it. She wasn't afraid to come under the House, where there might be spiders or snakes or something.

So obviously she wasn't a sissy, though he didn't regret calling her one. He wondered why she didn't want to sleep in her room, but he didn't care much about the answer. All he cared about was getting to sleep out under the porch, something that he was pretty sure his parents would never agree to if he asked them.

Therefore he would have to sneak out, and if Tammie told on him, he'd get caught and punished.

"O.K.," he said. "You can come, too. But we'll have to be real careful so we don't get caught."

"I'll be careful."

"You better. I'll get that old blanket that Dad wrapped around the ice cream freezer. I think they put it in the kitchen. When they're asleep, I'll come by your room and get you. If you aren't asleep yourself by then."

"I won't be asleep," Tammie said.

They sat under the porch for a while longer, looking out at the adults, listening to their droning voices. Then they crawled out and asked if they could go to the woods.

"No way," Riley said. "You never know what you might run into in the woods. That's strictly off limits unless a grown-up goes with you."

"Good idea," Rod Saylor chimed in. He was sitting under an elm tree in a folding chair that he had brought with him. He had a Pepsi in one hand and a bowl of ice cream in the other. "You might run into the Harps, for one thing. I hear they live around here."

"Who's the Harps?" Tammie said.

"Some folks you don't want to meet, honey," Saylor said. "Believe me."

"Why not?"

"Let's just say they're not the nicest people in the county,"

Saylor said. He could see the hard look Riley was giving him. "That's all."

"Let's go play in the attic, then," Dan said, and Tammie followed him up the porch steps and into the House. She didn't like it in there, but if Dan was with her, it would be all right.

Joshua Harp watched the party with satisfaction.

He had been waiting for a sign, and now he had it. It was as plain as if someone had spoken into his ear. He had not been meant to act until now, the day the Wests actually moved into the house. He went inside the shack and told his boys to get ready.

Matthew heard him.

"Get ready for what?" he asked.

Joshua looked at him and grinned. "I think you know what, boy. I think you know."

And Matthew did know.

His face felt hot, and he could almost feel his heart beating. His hand went to the handle of the knife on his belt and caressed it gently. He wanted to pull it from the scabbard, but he restrained himself.

"When?" he said.

"Tonight," Joshua said. "After they're all asleep."

Jonah got up from the makeshift couch. "What about the women?" he said.

"Where are they?" Joshua asked.

"They carried that damn TV over to the other place. They're in there watching it."

"Don't tell 'em about what we're gonna do. Get rid of 'em tonight."

"How in hell are we gonna do that?" Absalom said.

"You'll think of something," Joshua told him.

Looking in his father's eyes, Absalom knew that he would indeed think of something. He felt his dick twitch against his faded jeans, and he knew he was thinking of the West woman. No need to have Cherry and Nita around, that was for sure.

"I'll send 'em to town for a drink," he said. "That'll work."

"Good," Joshua said.

CHAPTER
TWENTY-NINE

The Harps liked knives best, but they weren't the kind to take chances. They had guns, too.

Joshua had a 12-gauge shotgun, and the twins had .38 revolvers. They had not, of course, bought the weapons legitimately, or any other way. They stolen them over the course of the years from houses that the twins had burgled. They actually had owned a whole assortment of weapons at one time or another, but having no real need for them, and certainly no attachment to them, they had eventually sold most of them, either at flea markets or to people they overheard mentioning wanting a gun. The Harps didn't care who bought their guns. They sold to anyone.

The men were cleaning the guns with rags and oil while Mary and Matthew watched. Matthew liked the smell of the oil, and he was hoping he might be allowed to shoot one of the guns, though he didn't really think he would. The guns were for emergency only, Joshua had explained.

"We want to keep it as quiet as we can," was the way he put it. "We don't want any noise if we can help it. The less noise, the less likely it is that anybody will bust in on things and bother us."

"How're we gonna get 'em out of the house?" Jonah wanted to know.

"We can use the guns for that. You usually don't have to shoot anybody if you just point a gun at 'em and look like you're ready to use it. They'll be easy to get out of the house."

"Then we'll take 'em to the graveyard?" Absalom said.

"That's where we'll take 'em. But if we have to kill 'em in the house, that's fine, too. I hate to leave the blood, but if we got to, we got to."

"Right," Absalom said, grinning at Jonah. "There might be something else we want to do in the house, too."

"No there ain't. You can do that in the woods just as well."

"But—"

"No buts. I don't care if the skeeters chew your ass off, we ain't staying in that house longer than we have to." Joshua still didn't mention that he would be the first to have the woman.

"All right, then," Absalom said grudgingly. "But I still think—"

"Don't think. You ain't much good at it. I'll do that."

Jonah laughed at his brother. "You afraid of a few chiggers? Seems to me it might be even more fun outdoors. Add a little thrill to things, scrunching around in the leaves and all."

"Sure it will," Absalom said.

Matthew listened to all this with half an ear. He wasn't interested in what they were planning. He was interested only in his part, which had already been explained to him.

He and Mary were to be sure the West kids didn't try to run away. If they did, Matthew was to stop them. Matthew would have felt more confident about things if he were allowed to have a gun. If the adults thought they might need one, what about him?

"You're bigger than the boy, and a lot tougher," Joshua said. "He won't give you any trouble. You won't need a gun. That knife of yours oughta be enough."

"What about Mary?"

"She can take care of the girl. Can't you, Missy?"

Mary shook her head, though she really didn't understand what Joshua was talking about. Was this going to be like a game?

"Yeah," Joshua said. "It's a lot like a game." He looked at Matthew again. "And you know why your part in it's the most important?"

"I think so," Matthew said.

"Tell me again."

"Because if the boy kid hadn't got away the first time, there wouldn't be any more Wests. If they'd killed him, there wouldn't be anybody living over there in that house right now."

Joshua smiled. The boy was a good pupil. "You're right. "If they'd killed him like they should've, we wouldn't have to be going over there now to finish a job that's been hanging fire for a hundred years. You be sure you get him, this time."

"I'll get him," Matthew said, his and drifting to the haft of the knife and brushing it gently. "I'll get him."

Cherry and Nita were angry.

It wasn't as if it were the first time Absalom and Jonah had asked them to take a hike—literally—but they still didn't like it. It was "business," they had been told, nothing more, and they understood that. They didn't really give much of a damn what the men did; they were well aware that practically everything they had, not that there was very damn much of it, was obtained by less than legal means.

Besides, the "business" this time seemed to involve getting them out of the way, which it never had before. Every other time, the men had just left without saying much of anything, leaving Cherry and Nita at home to watch TV or sleep, or do whatever they pleased.

What they especially didn't like was that the kids hadn't been sent away, too. If there was business to be done, what did it have to do with the kids?

"I bet they're gonna do something about those people moving in that big old house," Nita said as she trudged along. It was a hot evening, and she had her hair pinned up on her head. The tight knit dress she wore was already getting sweaty, and she knew her shoes would be a wreck by the time she and Cherry got to the Elbow Room, which was the club closest to them. Even at that, it was more than a mile and a half away, and they had to get to the highway first.

"Ain't none of our business," Cherry said. She had on a pair of jeans that looked as if they were about to burst at the seams and a pair of roping boots. "You shoulda worn more comfortable clothes."

"Listen, they tell me to go off and have a good time, I'm gonna do it. This dress is guaranteed to get me the best-looking fella in the place within five minutes, you wait and see. And when it does, I'm gonna let him take me home and fuck his brains out."

Cherry laughed. "You do and Absalom'll cut his dick off and feed it to him. Probably sew your snatch up with fishing twine, too."

Nita nodded. "Yeah, I'm probably just kidding myself. Nobody'll come close to us if they know who we are."

"That's the damn truth. Sometimes I wish ...."

"You wish what?"

"Never mind," Cherry said. "You think we can hitch a ride on the highway?"

"We can try," Nita said. "But I wouldn't bet on it."

They did catch a ride, however, almost as soon as they reached the highway.

Sheriff Homer Gregory pulled up beside them and stopped the white county car. "You girls oughta know that hitchhiking is mighty dangerous around these parts," he said, and he damn sure wasn't kidding. He knew these were the Harp women, and if anyone could write a book about the dangers of being out on the road alone in that area, it was the Harps. He didn't let on that he knew them, though.

Cherry looked at him. He wasn't so bad for a lawman. A little old maybe, but that didn't mean anything. "No law against hitching, is there?" she said, giving him her best smile, which could have been better. She had a fairly large chip out of one of her front teeth, from where Jonah had hit her one time.

She had a nice ass, though, and so did Nita. An idea began to form in Homer's mind.

"No," he said. "No law against hitching, not that I know of. 'Specially not if you hitch a ride with the high sheriff."

Nita giggled. "I didn't know the sheriff was allowed to get high."

Her ass wasn't so bad, either, in that tight dress. Homer felt a twinge of excitement. Hell, they were ready for it. He could have told it from a mile off. And they hadn't even looked at his gun yet.

But they were Harps. That could turn out to be a hell of a problem.

"He's allowed to have a little fun now and then, though," Homer said. "You girls want a ride or not?"

They weren't sure. They were as wary of the sheriff as he was of the Harps. They walked a couple of paces down the road to confer.

Gregory sat patiently in the car, keeping the motor running and the air-conditioner on. He waved casually to any cars that passed him by, unconcerned with what the drivers might think; if they thought anything at all, it would be that the sheriff was doing his job, checking on hitchhikers or maybe helping some ladies with car trouble.

It wasn't long, maybe two or three minutes, before Cherry came back to the car.

Homer rolled down his window. "You girls make up your minds?"

"Maybe," Cherry said. "Depends on where you're going."

"Wherever you want to go," Homer said.

"Somewhere that we can have a drink or two and a little fun," Nita said. She was carrying a worn leather purse. She opened it and took out a pack of Doublemint gum, extracted a stick of gum and slowly unwrapped it. She tossed the paper on the ground and slid the stick of gum slowly in and out of her mouth.

Homer decided not to arrest her for littering.

"Know what we mean?" Cherry said.

Homer knew what they meant. Goddamn, he was ready for it, too. Anybody that could handle Estelle could handle any other two women at the same time, no question. He'd had enough raw eggs and oysters to take on three women if he had to.

He got out and opened the back door. "Get in," he said.

Cherry and Nita slid in the back seat. Homer shut the door and got in the front.

"There ain't no door handles back here," Cherry said. She

was looking at Homer's eyes in the rearview mirror. "And what's this screen for?" she said, referring to the heavy wire mesh between the front and rear seats.

"It's to keep you from assaulting the driver," Homer said.

"I kinda thought you *wanted* to be assaulted," Cherry said. "Where're you taking us, anyhow?"

"Someplace quiet. Someplace where you can get plenty to drink and nobody will bother you."

"Maybe we want to be bothered," Nita said. She was holding the stick of gum by its tip. It was very damp now, and it folded in the middle.

"This damn thing's limped out on me," she said. "I hate it when you suck on something for just a little while and it limps out on you. Don't you just hate that, Cherry?"

"I sure do," Cherry said.

"Cherry," Homer said. "That's a nice name." He eyed Nita in the rearview. "What's your name, honey."

"Nita." She put out her tongue and laid the gum on it, then sucked in into her mouth. "You sure you know what you're doing, Sheriff?"

"Damn right," he said. "I always do."

"I hope you ain't on duty," Cherry said. "I'd hate to take a man away from his duty."

"Don't you worry about that," Homer said. He picked up his microphone and called the dispatcher. He told her that he was going off duty and that he had really had a rough day. He didn't want to be disturbed at home for anything less than an assassination attempt on the president of the United States, "and I happen to know he ain't in the county."

When he signed off, Cherry and Nita were giggling together in the back seat.

"Don't you want to know our last names?" Cherry said, still giggling.

Play dumb, Homer told himself. You're taking a hell of a risk, but it's damn sure gonna be worth it. Play dumb.

"No, ma'am, I don't," he said. "I never like to know too much about a woman. Takes the mystery out of things."

"You're cute," Nita said. "You got a gun?"

"Biggest damn gun *you* ever saw," Homer said, pulling his pistol and holding it up with his right hand while he steered with his left.

"I didn't say *pistol*," Nita told him. "I said *gun*." She and Cherry giggled again.

"I can't show you that right now," Homer said. "But you can bet I got one. It's even bigger than the pistol."

"Now, Sheriff," Nita said. "It's not nice to lie."

"It ain't a lie," Homer said. "You just wait."

While the two women whispered and giggled, Homer told himself, "You are gonna have some fun tonight, boy. You better just hope it don't get you killed."

CHAPTER THIRTY

It was very late, after midnight.

Riley and Sam had finally gotten everything cleaned up about ten and then had gotten the children to bed. Tammie had not wanted to go into her room, but after Sam had talked to her for a while, she had finally given in and gone.

Now the House was quiet.

Riley and Sam were sleeping soundly, tired from the long day, though it had taken Riley nearly an hour to wind down. He was wired on having at last moved into the House.

"It's great, isn't it," he said to Sam as they lay in their bed, just that day moved from the trailer. "Even better than you thought it would be, right?"

"Right," Sam admitted, and it was the truth. She had never thought he could really do it, but he had pulled it off. When he had begun talking about his plans, she had thought they would come to nothing, as they had so often in the past, but this time he had really done it.

She said so.

"Yeah," he said, shaking his head as if he still didn't quite believe it himself, "I did, didn't I?"

He was happier than he could ever remember being.

Sam, on the other hand, was apprehensive. She couldn't say why, but the feeling she had experienced when she first saw the House had returned. Not as strong as before, maybe, but it was there, nevertheless. She managed to fight it off, however, thanks to the exhausting day, and soon she was asleep.

Dan was not asleep.

It had not been easy to stay awake at first, but it got easier the longer he kept his eyes open. In fact, it seemed to him that the longer he stayed awake, the more wide-awake he became.

He lay in the bed, listening to the drone of the air-conditioner in one of his widows. He was glad he had it, because the day had been hot. He liked the stream of cool air that floated out into the room.

He didn't want to get too comfortable, though. He was afraid that if he did, he would go to sleep for sure.

After his parents had told him good night he stayed in the bed for what seemed like a long time. When he was certain that no one would be coming back to check on him, he got up and went to a window, one without the air-conditioner, and looked out.

The night was bright with moonlight, so bright that all the shadows under the trees looked even darker than they would have without the light to contrast with them. There was a slight breeze, and the tree limbs shifted slowly, causing the shadows to move as well.

Dan felt chilled and turned off his air-conditioner. The hum died away, but he was not any warmer.

He stood in the room, listening to the sounds of the house. Now and then there was a creaking noise, as if the wood beams were rubbing together somewhere in the walls. He could hear the trees moving, too, even though his windows were closed.

He suddenly wanted to get out of the room and get under the porch. There was no use waiting any longer.

He opened the door and looked into the dark hall. There was no one there, so he went to Tammie's room and went in.

She was sitting straight up in the bed waiting for him. He was surprised; he'd thought she would be asleep for sure.

"You ready?" he said.

She jumped out of the bed without a word and walked by him into the hall. He followed her.

She did not stop outside the door but went straight downstairs to the kitchen, making no noise at all. Dan joined her there and looked for the blanket. It was on the floor of the pantry. He got it out. It was still damp from being wrapped around the freezer, but it would do.

"We can sit on this," he said. "We won't get dirty if we're careful. It's a little wet, though."

Tammie still didn't say anything. She was ready to get out of the house.

"Let's go," Dan said.

They opened the kitchen door as quietly as they could. The hinges were well-lubricated and there was no noise. They closed the door behind them and went down the steps.

When they were under the porch, Dan spread out the blanket, disregarding the fact that he had already gotten dirt on his pajamas while crawling to the right spot. He and Tammie sat and looked through the latticework.

"Look," Dan said. "You can see a long way, all the way to the woods."

Tammie spoke for the first time. "Who's that?" she said, pointing.

Dan looked out across the field and saw the dark figures moving toward the House.

The Harps had waited until they were sure everyone was asleep.

"After midnight, that's always the best time," Joshua said. "People start sinking down in that deep sleep, and when you wake 'em up they're so foggy they don't know what the hell's happening to 'em. Makes it easier all around."

"I want that woman to be awake," Jonah said. "I sure as hell don't want her to just lay there like a dead fish."

"Yeah, we got wives for that," Absalom said, and laughed.

"She'll be awake," Joshua said. "By the time you get to her."

"What's that supposed to mean?" Jonah said.

"Never mind. You about ready?"

"Hell, yes."

"Get the kids, then."

Matthew and Mary had been allowed to go to sleep. Joshua thought it best that they be well-rested for the night's work.

Jonah went next door to wake them.

Absalom had one question about the whole affair. "Do you really think we're gonna get away with this?" he said, rubbing an imaginary spot off the barrel of his pistol with the ragged end of his shirt tail.

Joshua looked at him and decided to tell the truth. "Maybe not. I don't give a damn, long as we get those fucking Wests. Do you?"

"I guess not," Absalom said. He had been brought up on the story of the Wests and felt almost as much of an obligation as Joshua did. "I was just wondering if it was worth it, though."

"You know it is," Joshua said.

"They're liable to check out the graveyard," Absalom said. "New graves'll be easy to spot."

"We ain't dumping 'em in the river," Joshua said. "They belong in the graveyard."

"What about our kids? What'll happen to them if we get caught?"

"The law won't do anything to kids that age, 'cept maybe put 'em in a foster home. Besides, they ain't caught us yet. Ain't never caught us before, either."

That was true. When Absalom thought of some of the things they'd done and gotten away with, it seemed almost as if they were meant to do what they did.

It was almost like a law of nature. There were sheep and there were wolves, and the Harps sure as hell weren't sheep.

Jonah brought in Matthew and Mary.

"You kids ready?" Joshua said.

Matthew nodded. Mary still wasn't quite sure what was going on. She looked around the room and rubbed her eyes.

"Let's go," Joshua said.

The figures coming across the field looked like something out of a movie with knights and dwarfs, Dan thought. Three of them were big, and two were little.

"Are they coming here?" Tammie said.

"I don't know," Dan said.

"Isn't the party over?"

"Yes. They don't look like they're coming to a party, anyway."

"I don't like them," Tammie said. "They make me scared."

"We'll go wake up Dad and tell him," Dan said. "He'll know

what to do." He didn't want to leave his spot under the porch. The figures made him scared, too, though he would never have said so to Tammie, and he felt that he would be safe if he stayed where he was. At the same time, he felt a need to warn his parents.

"Are they robbers?" Tammie said.

"I don't know. Let's get Dad."

Tammie grabbed Dan's hand. "I don't want to go out there. I'm too scared."

"I'll go," Dan said. "You stay here."

"I can't stay by myself. I'm too scared. I need to go to the bathroom. Real bad."

"Then you'll have to come with me. You can't go to the bathroom here."

They started crawling out from under the porch.

"I thought I saw something moving up there," Absalom said. "Those people got a dog?"

"We've been watching them for a fucking year," Jonah said. "You ever see a dog there?"

"Nope, but I sure as hell saw something."

"Your eyes are just playing tricks," Joshua said. "They ain't got no dog. If they do, we'll kill the dog, too."

"I don't like killing dogs," Absalom said. "I ain't never killed any dogs."

"It's not a dog," Matthew said. His young eyes were keener than those of the adults. "It's kids."

"Son of a bitch," Joshua said. He started to run. "Come on. We got to get over there before it's too late."

The others scrambled after him. Mary's legs were too short and she could not keep up, but she made a good effort. The weeds were hitting her in the face.

"Wait," she said, nearly out of breath already. "Wait for me."

Matthew turned back to her just as she stepped in a small hole and fell forward. "Mary fell down!" he yelled.

"Goddamn!" Joshua roared. He came to a stop and Jonah nearly ran up his back.

The men turned to help the girl, who was being pulled to

her feet by Matthew. She was crying, tears running down her cheeks.

The men did not stop to check and see if she was hurt. Joshua simply grabbed her up under his left arm and took off running again, Mary jostling up and down under his arm, bumping into his side, her feet swinging wildly. She began to cry louder.

Joshua didn't bother telling her to hush. If Matthew was right, if he had seen the West kids, they were probably in the house already, warning their parents.

"Goddamn!" Joshua yelled again in frustration.

"Kill 'em all!" he yelled as he ran. "If you have to shoot 'em, shoot 'em. Just be sure you kill 'em all!"

CHAPTER THIRTY-ONE

In the graveyard the shadows danced.

The cool moonlight, pale and white, flecked the ground and the gravestones, looking like drops of water or silver coins, moving as the leaves moved.

On a stone that had once been white but was now dark and streaked with moss, a field mouse sat and worried something in its paws.

Far away, an owl hooted.

The mouse ran down off the stone and disappeared into the darkness of the shadows.

It might have been the hoot of the owl that frightened the mouse.

Or it might have been something else, something else that seemed to be dancing in the graveyard, dancing among the shadows and weaving in and out of the moonlight.

Or course, there was nothing else there, nothing at all.

The dancing, or whatever it was, could only have been a trick of the moonlight as it played among the leaves, a trick of the shadows as they swept across the stones.

It could have been nothing else, for nothing else was there.

CHAPTER THIRTY-TWO

Sheriff Homer Gregory thought he had died and gone to heaven.

He had sometimes dreamed of being the middle of a sandwich between two hot naked women with firm breasts and even firmer asses, but the reality of it was so much better than he had dreamed that he was practically ecstatic. He had shot his load so many times that he wasn't even sure he could stand up when it came time to get off the bed.

But that didn't matter much. He didn't intend to get try getting off the bed until the next day, and maybe not even then. As long as Cherry and Nita would stay there, he was willing to stay with them.

And if it killed him, then by God let it kill him. It was damn sure worth it.

They were lying on Homer's king-size bed, sweaty in spite of the air-conditioner. Homer was in the middle, looking a little like a beached whale with his white stomach sticking up in the air, the women resting on either side of him.

He was fondling Nita's tits with one hand and Cherry's ass with the other.

If only Estelle could see me now, he thought.

And then he thought, *She probably wouldn't give a damn. She might even want to jump right in the middle of us. Wouldn't that be something, though. Three of 'em!*

"Goddamn," he sighed. "I never felt anything like it, girls. I got to tell you. I never have."

Nita said, "You're all right, Sheriff. I wouldn't've thought a lawman could put out like you have. Damn! I thought Absalom and Jonah knew how to put it to a woman, but you take the cake."

Homer appreciated the compliment, but he wished she hadn't mentioned the names. He tried to change the subject.

"I'll say one thing," he told them. "If I had me a couple of gals like you, I'd sure never let you outta my sight."

"Those bastards we hang out with, they don't care about us," Cherry said. "They just kicked us out tonight like we were dogs. Didn't ask if we wanted to leave, just showed us the damn door."

She ran a hand down Homer's stomach. "I guess we showed them, huh?"

"Why'd they kick you out?" Homer said, and immediately regretted it. "Not that I mean to get into your business. Let's—"

"They said they had stuff to do," Nita said, rolling over on her back and sitting up. "Didn't want us around to mess it up. They think I don't know what they're up to, but I sure as hell do."

"Well, boys will be boys," Homer said. He laughed weakly. "Now, why don't we—"

"They think we don't know about that woman," Cherry said. "They're gonna fuck her sure as we're laying here, but they ain't fooling us one little bit."

Oh, shit, Homer thought.

"Probably do worse than that, too," Nita said. "You really oughta stop 'em, Sheriff."

"Well, now we don't really know that those boys—whoever they are—are gonna do anything like you're saying. Why don't we just—"

Cherry slapped Homer's hand off her breasts and scrambled off the bed. "Are you the sheriff, or not? It's your job to do something if we tell you that there's a crime, ain't it?"

Homer struggled to sit up. He didn't know what had happened to change the mood, but something sure as hell had.

"It's my job, all right," he said. "Now if you've got any proof—"

"Sheriff, we're talking about the Harps," Nita said. "We're telling you that they're gonna rape a woman and probably kill her and her whole family. Now what're you gonna do about it?"

Homer sighed. He didn't even have to ask who the woman and the family were, but he did it anyway.

"Their name's West," Nita said. "They live—"

"I know where they live," Homer said. "Are you sure about all this? You're not just making it up because you're mad at somebody?"

The women looked at one another.

"We're sure," Cherry said.

"Damn," Homer said. He rolled over and got off the bed. He found to his surprise that he could stand up, after all, so he started looking for his pants.

He had tried to shut the Harps out of his head, but they had been there all along. It looked like he wasn't going to be able to avoid them any longer. If he hadn't picked up the women .... He stopped that line of thought. He had picked them up and it had been a hell of a lot of fun. He didn't regret it.

But nothing that much fun was ever free. He should have known that. Sooner or later the bill always come due, and now he was just going to have to pay up.

Cherry and Nita were slipping into their own clothes, and Homer could hear them whispering to one another.

"I wish you could've kept your damn mouth shut," Cherry said, wiggling into her jeans. "We're in deep shit, now."

"Me!" Nita said, trying to get her hair back up and not doing a very good job. "It was you that started it. You said—"

"I didn't say anything!"

"Yes, you did. You said—"

"I don't matter now who said what," Cherry said, realizing that Nita was probably right. She decided to change the subject. "How much money you got with you?"

"I've got about sixty dollars. Why?"

"I've got fifty or so. You ever thought you might like to go down to Houston?"

"Houston?" Nita said. "What the hell?"

"It's a big place, lots of horny men. Couple of good looking women like us oughta do all right there, and we got money for the bus. I don't think I wanta go back home."

Nita looked thoughtful. "What about the kids?"

"They'll be all right unless Joshua gets 'em killed. He's got some crazy scheme or he wouldn't've sent us off an kept them there. No matter what happens, you ain't gonna have those kids again."

"Why not?" Nita demanded.

"You ain't that dumb," Cherry said. "Whatever happens there tonight, we're gonna get tied into it one way or the other. The court'll take the kids."

"You're probably right," Nita said.

"Hell, yes, I'm right."

Homer, now fully dressed, interrupted them. "You two about ready to go?"

"We're ready," Cherry said. "Does the bus still stop in this damn town?"

"Stops at the Chevron station out on the highway," Homer said. "If they put a sign out for it."

"You can give us a ride out there, then," Cherry said. "It's on the way."

"All right," Homer said. "Go get in the car. I got a couple of calls to make first."

He watched them twitch out of the bedroom. *Damn,* he thought, *I sure wish I'd never got into this.* Then he thought about what had just transpired in the bedroom and changed his mind again. No matter what happened later on, it was still worth it.

He went to the telephone table and picked up the phone. Time to call the jail.

Dan and Tammie burst through the front door and charged up the stairs. Their parents were awake before the kids came tumbling in through the bedroom door.

"Mom! Dad!" Dan yelled. "Someone's coming!"

"What?" Riley said. "Who?"

"Coming!" Tammie said, out of breath. "Coming!"

"Calm down," Sam said, getting out of bed. She opened her arms and Tammie ran to her. She hugged her daughter to her. "Riley go see what's going on."

"Look outside, Dad," Dan said. "Look outside."

Riley got out of bed and put on a pair of pants. He looked out the window. The moon silvered the field and he could see the running figures as they sprinted through the weeds.

"I don't understand," he said, watching them.

Sam came over, Tammie clinging to her legs, and joined him. "Maybe there's some kind of trouble, Riley. Go down and see what they want."

Riley didn't know what else to do. He left the room and went down the stairs. As soon as he set foot on the porch, Jonah and Absalom fired their pistols.

The bullets slapped into the wall just over Riley's head. For a split second, Riley did not know what had happened. Then he heard the slightly delayed cracks of the pistol shots.

By that time, the twins had fired again. Two more bullets slugged into the House.

Riley turned and ran back inside.

"Goddamn!" Joshua screamed. "You two couldn't hit the side of a fucking barn."

Mary was crying as she jostled along under his arm. She was confused and scared.

The twins didn't answer Joshua. They just kept running. It was about a hundred yards to the house, and nobody was that good a shot with a pistol. Besides, they were shooting on the run. It was a miracle that they'd even hit the house.

They knew they shouldn't have fired, however. It was just wasting ammunition. They'd have to get West when they arrived at the house, if he didn't make his getaway first.

Riley pounded up the stairs, his heart thudding.

"They're shooting at me!" he yelled.

"What?" Sam said.

"Shooting! They're shooting! We've got to get out of here."

Tammie began crying.

Sam looked around the room, searching for a place to hide. There wasn't anywhere.

Riley couldn't figure it out. Why was anyone shooting at him? There must be some kind of mistake, but it didn't look as if whoever was doing it was interested in listening to reason.

He was not interested in guns, didn't own one. There was no way he could defend himself and his family.

He could think of nothing to do but to run.

"We can go upstairs and hide in the attic, Dad," Dan said, tugging at Riley's hand.

Riley tried to push aside the panic, to think. Not the attic. They would be trapped in the attic. There was only one way in, and they could not escape through the windows. They had to get downstairs, get outside. If the shooters were interested in burglarizing the house, they could have it, as long as the family was safe.

"Everybody downstairs," he said. "Let's go."

He hustled them out of the room, wondering how far they would be able to go. No one had on any shoes. Sam was in her nightgown, and the kids were in pajamas.

It didn't matter.

They had to get out of the house.

When the Wests got to the porch, the Harps were only twenty yards away. Joshua dropped Mary to the ground and brought up the shotgun. The twins stopped and steadied their pistols, taking deep breaths to steady their ragged breathing. This time they were going to do things right.

Matthew, in his eagerness, charged on past the adults, his knife gripped tightly in his right hand.

Joshua saw him just in time and held his fire. The shotgun pellets might have spread and hit the boy.

Jonah and Absalom didn't have to worry about that, and they blasted away.

Matthew came to a dead stop as the bullets whizzed over his head.

Something seemed to pluck at the top of Riley's left shoulder and he was slammed against the wall.

"Run!" he screamed to his family as he fell. "You've got to get away from here! Run!"

CHAPTER THIRTY-THREE

Gus Morrow didn't like being waked up late at night by the telephone. He was always certain that if the phone rang at a time like that, it could only be bad news.

This time he was certainly right.

It was news of the worst kind.

"I think the Harps are after the Wests," Homer Gregory said after he identified himself. "I think you were right about them, after all."

"What made you change your mind?" Gus said.

"Never mind that. We got to try to stop 'em, I guess."

"*I* don't. You're the law, not me. Call out your deputies."

"I did. There's been a four-car wreck out on the highway, and everybody on duty's already there. It's a real mess. So I'm calling you. You know what I mean?"

Gus knew. It was almost as if there was something inevitable about it. What he had dreaded most was now coming true, and he was going to have to do something about it. He cursed himself for having said anything to Homer in the first place.

"You call Stoney," Homer said. "I'll be by in a little bit. I just hope we won't be too late."

Gus hoped so too.

Stoney heard the first shots while he was getting dressed. He didn't want to be involved in this, not in the least. He wanted to mind his own business and stay out of things.

But there were the kids. They'd gone fishing with him, treated him almost like a grandfather. He'd liked that.

And Riley and Sam were all right. Nice people.

Those Goddamn Harps.
He wished Homer would hurry.

Riley lay on the porch. He didn't feel any pain in his shoulder, but he was sure that would come later.

Sam was looking down at him, terror on her face. Dan and Tammie didn't seem to realize what had happened.

"Run," Riley told Sam through gritted teeth. "You've got to get away."

"I can't leave you," Sam said.

"Yes, you can. If you don't they'll kill you right here. Run."

Something in his voice convinced her.

"Come on, kids," she said, taking their hands. "Let's go."

They ran down the steps, into the yard, and around the corner of the house.

"Shit," Joshua said, seeing them leave the porch. "Matthew, you and me'll go after them. You boys take care of the man and then come on."

He started for the house, Matthew behind him.

Jonah and Absalom took their time. The man wasn't going anywhere. At the same time, they didn't dawdle. They didn't want to let the woman get too far ahead of them.

Mary didn't know what to do, so she trailed along after Matthew, still confused and tearful.

Riley dragged himself to the doorway and into the house. His shoulder was starting to burn, and so was he.

With anger.

He did not know what was going on, but he was suddenly mad as hell.

He had never done much that was right in his life. He had failed at one job after another, and it had always been more or less his own fault. He had begun to wonder if he was ever going to do anything that mattered to him, if he was ever going to accomplish something that had any meaning, that he could be proud of.

And now he had. He had moved his family into the House, and it was a wonderful place, in a fine location, a place where his family history had begun.

He had done it himself, with his own hands and with a little help. He had gotten a good job, and for the first time he felt good about himself and what he was doing.

And now these bastards with their guns were trying to take it all away from him. Trying to kill him and his family for some incredible reason.

He didn't even know who they were! They had to be crazy.

Well, they could try to kill him, but he wasn't going to make it easy for them. He wasn't just going to lie there on the porch and let them come up and kill him like some kind of stunned animal.

He stood up inside the door and walked unsteadily into the kitchen. His left arm hanging at his side. Rummaging around in a drawer under the cabinets with his right hand, he found what he was looking for—the butcher knife.

It was the only thing resembling a weapon in the whole house, and he didn't know how much good it would be up against guns, but it was better than nothing.

He heard the men stomping up the steps and across the porch and pressed himself against the wall by the kitchen door.

Let them come.

He was ready.

"Shit," Jonah said. "There's nobody here. Where'd he go?"

"There's blood on the wall," Absalom pointed out. It looked black in the moonlight. "He didn't get very far."

"Yeah, but what if he's got a gun?"

"He didn't shoot it at us, did he?"

"No."

"Then he ain't got one, you pussy. Let's go in and get him."

"Since you're so fucking sure of yourself, you go first," Jonah said. It was one thing to kill old ladies in their beds of to murder helpless tourists who were pissing their pants; it was something else again to go up against someone who was determined to fight back and who might have a weapon to do it with.

Absalom looked at his brother with contempt, then jumped inside the door, trying to do it like he'd seen Sonny Crockett do it on *Miami Vice*. He held his pistol firmly in his right fist, gripping his right wrist with his left hand and sweeping the gun around the room.

There was no one there, and Absalom went on in.

Jonah followed him. "I thought you said he didn't get very far."

"Hell, I know we winged him. He went down like a sack of shit. He's got to be here somewhere."

There were three doors to choose from, one to the right and two in the wall in front of them.

"Which one do you think?" Absalom said.

"You're the smart guy. Why don't you tell me."

"You take the one on the right, then. I'll take one of those in front of us."

Jonah didn't waste time talking. He went to the door on the right and stepped through it. He found himself in what had been the "sitting room" of the house in former times, a room which Riley had converted into a TV room. There were a small couch and two lounge chairs lined up in front of the TV stand. Jonah began looking around carefully, but he didn't see anyone or anything of interest.

Absalom took the door leading to the kitchen. He went through in a rush, once again doing his Sonny Crockett imitation.

Riley waited until he came to a stop, then stepped up behind him, the knife raised high. He brought it down fast and hard.

Absalom must have heard him at the last minute. He half turned, trying to get the pistol around for a shot, but the knife pierced his shoulder before he could make the turn.

The pistol went off, and the bullet buried itself in the wood floor. The sound of the shot was nearly deafening.

Riley tried to pull the knife out of Absalom. He had no idea where he had stabbed the man. His own arm was nearly numb from the earlier bullet wound and the force of the blow he had struck, and he twisted the knife awkwardly.

Absalom yelled with pain as he was falling down, and the knife came free. He hit the floor and twisted around, raising the pistol. Riley fell forward, plunging downward with the knife.

Absalom skittered to the side like a sick spider, and the knife stuck in the floor, jarring Riley further. He suppressed a yell and jumped up.

Absalom tried to get to a sitting position and fire the pistol.

Riley jumped aside just as Absalom fired, twice.

One bullet went wide, hitting the wall.

The other bullet struck Jonah, who was rushing through the door, his gun at the ready. A gout of flesh and blood was ripped from Jonah's side, and he screamed in fear and shock.

Jonah went back out the door much faster than he had come through it, flying a foot or two through the air and sliding for several more feet on his ass before he fell over.

Riley ducked down and jerked the knife from the floor.

Absalom kicked at him weakly but missed.

Riley kicked at Absalom, not so weakly, and connected with his jaw. Absalom's head hit the floor with the hollow sound of a melon, and Riley turned and got out of the kitchen.

Jonah was lying in the floor of the living room, his heels drumming on the wood. He seemed to be saying something like, "Help me, help me," but Riley wasn't interested.

He went on outside. He had to find Sam and the kids.

Sam was running as fast as she could, but she could see that it wasn't going to be nearly fast enough. The weeds were raking her legs, and her bare feet sank into the sandy earth, which tugged at her, not wanting to give up its hold.

Worse, the stickers were like knives cutting the soles of her feet off. The stickers were shredding the bottoms of Tammie and Dan's feet, too, but they were so scared that they kept on running in spite of the pain. Tears of fear and pain ran down their faces.

It was like some scene from a horrible dream, the woman and the children, their feet bloody, being pursued across the moonlit field by the shotgun wielding man and two other children with wild eyes, one of them waving a hunting knife in the air.

Sam put her foot into a salamander mound and fell headlong. The stickers plunged into the soft flesh of her arms and stomach as she hit the ground. They pierced her flimsy gown.

Dan and Tammie, running just beside her, did not even see her fall. They were staring their tears at the wall of trees ahead of them. They thought that if they could get to the trees they would be safe.

They kept running.

Joshua was on top of Sam almost as soon as she fell. He sat astraddle of her back, his knees in the sand.

Matthew and Mary came up to him, looking at him, wondering what they were to do.

"Get the boy!" Joshua said. "Goddamnit, don't let him get away!"

Matthew did not answer. He began running after the children.

Mary, after a moment's pause, followed him.

CHAPTER THIRTY-FOUR

Homer pulled the county car to a stop in the Wests' yard. He, Gus, and Stoney stared at the House, not giving any thought to the fields.

The House was quiet and dark.

"Maybe everything's all right," Gus said. "Maybe they're all asleep in there. What put this wild hair in your ass, anyhow, Homer?"

"Never mind what put it there. You heard Stoney. He said there were shots fired down here."

"Could've been a car backfiring, I guess," Stoney said.

"Yeah, well, if that's what it was, why's the front door wide open?" Homer said.

"Damn," Gus said. "I guess you better check it out, then, Sheriff."

Homer got out of the car. "You two come with me. If there's Harps in there, I might need a little help."

Gus and Stoney reluctantly got out of the car. They had armed themselves with shotguns, with which they had never shot anything bigger or more dangerous than quail. If there were Harps in there, neither Gus nor Stoney thought he would be of much help.

Homer mounted the steps. Gus and Stoney stayed by the car.

"Come on," Homer said, looking back at them over his shoulder. "You won't do me any damn good down there."

He stopped when he got to the door and saw the bloodstains on the wall. "Oh, shit," he said.

Stoney and Gus didn't say anything. They watched him go into the House.

"It's all right," he said in a minute. "There's nobody here."

They went in. Homer was standing in the kitchen door.

"Somebody was here earlier, though," he said, motioning for Stoney and Gus to come on. They went over to the doorway and Homer pointed out the bloodstains on the floor.

"Oh, Jesus," Gus said. "They've killed them."

There was a trail of blood leading to the back door.

"Maybe not," Homer said. "Anyway, we've got to find out for sure." He followed the trail of blood.

Gus and Stoney looked at one another.

The look said that they didn't want to go after Homer, that they wanted to be at home minding their own business, that the Harps were too much for them, or for anybody.

But they went, their hands sweaty on the stocks of their shotguns.

Absalom was hobbling along, half dragging Jonah across the field. They were both bleeding, but they were both very much alive. If they didn't bleed to death, they would easily recover. Absalom's bullet had torn out a big hunk of Jonah's side, but it had not hit anything vital; Riley had stabbed Absalom in the shoulder muscle, and while Absalom was having a little trouble with his arm, he was not badly hurt.

As they made their way across the field, they could see Riley running just ahead of them, and they could even make out the small figures of the children as they entered the woods.

They couldn't see Joshua and Sam because of the weeds, and they had no idea where their father and the woman were.

All they wanted to do was get one more shot at the man.

This time, they would not miss.

Riley was panting as he ran. His shoulder was hurting now, throbbing with every beat of his heart, but it didn't seem to be bleeding.

His main concern was Sam. He could see the children, being pursued by two other children. Surely whoever the other children were, they were harmless. What could children do?

That wasn't a good question.

Ten minutes before—or five, it hadn't been long at all—he would have said that he could never have stabbed a man, or kicked him, any more than a child could. Yet he had just done both, and he felt good about doing it. There was still hot anger in his veins, burning through him.

How dare those men come into his House and try to kill him? Who did they think they were? Who did they think *he* was? He had never felt a rage like this one, and he knew that if he had to stab someone else, he could do it, with pleasure.

It was easier than he would ever have dreamed.

Joshua was still on top of Sam, mashing her face into the sand with his left hand as he pulled on the zipper of his pants with the other. He had worked her gown up over her waist and been gratified to discover that she was not wearing any underwear.

He had laid the shotgun aside and he was ready to punish her the way the wife of a West should be punished—by showing her what a real man, a Harp, could do for her.

She was struggling mightily under him, trying to free herself, trying to throw him off, trying anything to get away from him, but he was too strong. He kept his knees clamped tightly around her, kept her face pressed so hard into the sand that she could hardly breathe.

Then she felt his hot breath on the back of her neck, felt his hardness pressing against her, and she tried to scream.

Her mouth filled with sand.

"There they go," Homer said when he got outside. He pointed across the field.

Absalom and Jonah were limping along, making good progress considering their respective conditions. Riley ran in front of them.

"That's just three people," Stoney said. "Where's the rest?"

"They're headed back toward the shacks, looks like," Gus said. "You think it's just Harps?"

"There's one way to find out," Homer said. He started across the field.

Gus and Stoney looked at one another again, but they followed him.

Dan and Tammie passed by the shacks without noticing them. They were too afraid to notice.

Then they entered the trees.

Dan stopped, and Tammie nearly bumped into him. Neither one could speak. They were out of breath, and Tammie was crying.

It was dark in the woods, the trees cutting off much of the moonlight.

The children looked around in panic. For the first time they realized that Sam was no longer running beside them.

Tammie began crying harder, sobbing in ragged gulps.

Dan tried to tell her that it was all right, that everything would be fine, but he couldn't say it.

Because it would be a lie.

Everything wasn't all right. Their father was lying on the porch, probably shot. Their mother was lost somewhere. And they were in the dark woods, being chased by—

—Matthew Harp, who burst into the trees brandishing his knife, his wild red eyes like animal eyes in the night. A flicker of moonlight flashed off the blade of the knife.

Tammie stopped sobbing and screamed.

Dan grabbed her arm and started to run, pulling her along as fast as he could. He was afraid that it would not be fast enough to get away, and he had no idea where he was going. All he knew was that he had to keep running, that he could not let the wild-eyed kid with the knife catch them.

Absalom stopped and looked back.

"Shit," he said. "We got company."

Jonah didn't feel like looking around, but then he didn't feel like going forward, either. He just stopped, his head hanging. He kept one hand pressed to his side.

"It's that Goddamn fat sheriff," Absalom said. "What the fuck's he doing here?"

Jonah didn't answer, but he was at least curious enough to look around.

"I don't know," he said then. "Let's just kill the fucker." He saw that there were two other men with Gregory. "Let's just kill all three of 'em."

Absalom didn't see that there was anything else they could do. They had made a mess and now they were caught fair and square. It was either go to the pen or have the guts to try shooting their way out of it.

He triggered off a couple of shots. One of the men flipped backward, obviously wounded or dead. The other two hit the dirt as well, but Absalom could tell they weren't hit, just getting out of the line of fire.

Jonah fired three rounds, causing the sand in front of the men to geyser into the air, but he didn't hit them.

Then the men started firing back.

The shots surprised the hell out of Joshua, who looked around just as Riley cannoned into him.

The sight of the old man straddling his wife and about to penetrate her from behind had almost maddened Riley. He was going to beat the bastard to a pulp, and then he was going to cut him into tiny pieces with the butcher knife, pieces so small that they'd be able to bury him with a teaspoon, one piece at a time.

The blood was pounding so hard in Riley's head that he did not even hear the shots.

His impact with Joshua carried them several yards away from Sam and from the shotgun.

It also caused Riley to drop the knife.

He felt around in the sand for it, but Joshua was fighting like a wild man, clawing at Riley's eyes, kicking at Riley's groin, and pounding like a sledgehammer on Riley's wounded shoulder.

Riley collapsed on the ground, groaning. His shoulder felt as if someone had jammed a red-hot iron rod into it.

"Bastard!" Joshua said, getting to his feet and kicking Riley's arm. "Fucking son-of-a-bitch West bastard!" He kicked again and again, kicking Riley's arm, his ribs, his chest, his face.

Riley felt something crack, *heard* it crack in his chest. Pain shot through him. He lost consciousness.

Joshua was so infuriated that he was almost unable to stop

kicking Riley even when he saw that his kicking was no longer effective. He did not think of the shots he had heard behind him.

He was not interested in that anymore. He wanted the woman.

He looked around.

Sam had recovered enough to see what was happening. She had also seen the shotgun lying beside her and picked it up.

She had never fired a gun in her life, was barely aware even of how to hold one. She gripped it awkwardly, the stock sticking beneath her armpit rather that resting against her shoulder as she took aim at Joshua. She wasn't at all sure that she could shoot the gun, much less shoot it at another human being.

Joshua roared and charged at her.

Sam was suddenly sure that he did not qualify as a human being, not considering what he had tried to do to her and what he would no doubt try to do again.

She pulled the trigger.

CHAPTER THIRTY-FIVE

"The dirty fuckers killed Gus," Homer said.

All he could think of was how pissed Gus' wife was going to be. She hadn't wanted Gus to go along, and she followed him all the way to Homer's car, haranguing him about staying at home and how dangerous it was to go off at night looking for crazy people.

Gus had told her not to worry, that he'd be back in a little while and that everything would be all right, and now here he was, flat on his back in the field, the pale moon shining in his face.

"He's not dead," Stoney said. "Not yet, anyway. Quarter inch lower, and he would've been, though." He was kneeling beside Gus, looking at the wound, which was a very shallow groove running right across the top of Gus' head.

Homer felt a little better about things. "You sure?"

"He's knocked out, but his breathing's still regular. He must be alive."

"Good," Homer said, feeling relieved. "Now let's see if we can do something about those damn Harps."

Homer peered across the field. The two men who had shot at them—probably Absalom and Jonah, he thought—had knelt down, and it was hard to see them in among all the weeds. There was something else happening over there, too, but Homer couldn't quite make out what it was. Looked like a scuffle of some kind.

A shotgun roared.

Homer flopped down before he realized that no one was shooting at him. There was another fight going on, all right.

"This is beginning to sound like a war," Stoney said. "You got any kind of a plan, Sheriff?"

"Hell, no," Homer said. "I didn't think things were going to get this bad."

Stoney resisted the temptation to say that Gus had tried to warn Homer. If the sheriff had acted then, none of this would have happened.

"I guess we might try a few shots over at where we think the Harps are laid up," Homer said. "Maybe we'll scare 'em out of their cover."

Stoney didn't know about that. His shotgun was useless at that range. "Give it a try," he said, not being able to think of anything better.

Homer got up on his knees and snapped off a shot in the general direction of Jonah and Absalom. There was no reaction, though he could see some thrashing around where the shotgun blast had come from, and then someone jumped up and ran for the woods.

Homer, not knowing who the fleeing figure was, didn't fire at it. He fired off another round in the direction of the spot where he thought the twins had gone to ground.

There was no reaction this time, either.

"Shit," Homer said.

"What do we do now?" Stoney said.

"You think Gus'll be all right if we leave him here?"

"He won't be any worse off than if we stayed here with him," Stoney said. "I'm not any doctor, and neither are you."

"Then let's see if we can stir something up by heading on over there," Homer said, gesturing with his pistol barrel. He stood up and started walking toward the Harps.

Joshua was lucky in two ways.

For one thing, Sam, not knowing anything about guns, didn't blow him in two. She didn't even manage to kill him, because she had shot far to the right of him.

The shot pattern spread out before reaching him, though it was impossible for all the pellets to miss him at that range.

Some of the shot buried itself in his arm, some in his thigh. That was painful enough.

What was worse was the pellet that punched into his left

eye, mashing it to useless jelly.

The other lucky thing was that Joshua was half-turned from Sam when she fired, so the pellet didn't go very far. It stopped short of burying itself in Joshua's brain.

It hurt like hell, nevertheless.

Joshua fell to his knees, his hands clutching his face, howling with rage and frustration. And pain.

Sam threw the gun aside and started toward Riley.

Joshua reached out and grabbed her ankle as she passed him, pulling her down beside him. She fell heavily, and he tried to get on top of her, his hands fumbling at the shreds of her gown. He got his knee into her belly to hold her down.

She looked up in horror at the face that hung over her, a mask of madness, blood running from the socket of one ruined eye.

Joshua's knee slid off her, and she felt something hot and hard push against her stomach. It was almost impossible to believe under the circumstances, simply incredible, but the madman was erect and trying once again to rape her.

Joshua was beyond pain now, beyond fear, beyond anything but his urge to fuck the woman, the woman that West had brought there, the woman that had borne yet another male West to carry on the hated name for another generation. He was going to plunge into her, rip her womb to shreds with the one weapon he had left, the best weapon of all.

Sam clawed at his face, scratching wildly, sinking her index finger in the already damaged eye socket.

She shoved it in hard.

Joshua felt as if someone had jabbed a screwdriver into his brain. He jumped back and up, as quickly as if he had been struck with a thousand volts of electricity, making a noise like a wounded or dying animal.

This time Sam got past him and to Riley's side. "Riley," she said. "Riley."

He did not look good. His face was bruised from the kicking and his shoulder looked like a raw steak that dogs had torn in a fight. But his eyelids flickered and opened.

"Sam?"

Sam, who had not cried before, cried now.

Joshua's head was so full of pain that it felt as if it might explode and shower fragments of his skull all over the field. He could not see, not even out of his good eye. Still howling, he staggered off toward the woods. He cupped his head in his hands, shaking it from side to side.

"Here the dumb fucker comes," Absalom said as Homer approached them. "Looks like he wants to be a hero."

"Well, we better let him get damn close before we shoot," Jonah said. "The way we been going, we'll just miss."

"I got one of 'em," Absalom protested.

"Take your time anyway," Jonah told him. "I'll go for the sheriff; you take the other guy."

"Right," Absalom said.

They were lying prone in the weeds and didn't have a very good view; on the other hand, they were fairly well concealed. They didn't think the sheriff could see them.

Jonah wasn't feeling so hot. He'd lost a lot of blood, not to mention a hunk of flesh. He could almost feel the maggots getting into him and chewing away.

He was tired of lying there in the dirt. He wanted to get back to the shack and have a drink, maybe five or six drinks, and get a bandage on his side.

He was in such a hurry that he disregarded his own advice and started shooting a little too soon. He managed to hit Homer, but not to kill him.

Homer fell like a pole-axed buffalo and lay there twitching.

Stoney dropped beside him and loosed off three rounds from the shotgun right at ground level. The pellets mowed down quite a few weeds and sheared the top off a salamander mound but otherwise had no effect.

"Let's get our ass outta here," Absalom said.

Jonah didn't argue. He had a hard time getting up, but he made it, and the twins limped off in the direction of the shacks.

"You all right, Homer?" Stoney said, the sound of the shotgun blast still ringing in his ears.

"Hell, no, I'm not all right," Homer said. "The sons of bitches shot me."

Stoney could see that. There was a dark stain spreading on Homer's uniform pants, on the inside of his right thigh.

"Goddamn," Stoney said. "A little higher up and—"

"Don't even say it," Homer said. "I don't even want to think about it."

"But, Jesus, Homer. A quarter inch lower on Gus, six inches higher on you—"

"Six inches higher, my ass. Three inches, if that. You don't know what I've got down there."

"Uh, I guess not."

"Don't matter. Help me get up."

Stoney stood and put down a hand. Homer took it and pulled himself awkwardly to his feet. It wasn't easy. He was so big that he nearly pulled Stoney over instead of rising.

"Think you can walk?" Stoney said.

"If I take it easy," Homer answered. "Look, Stoney, this is getting to be a hell of a lot more dangerous than I thought it would. You and Gus don't have any part in it. Those boys are headed for the shacks. I'm going on down there and get 'em. You go back and see what you can do for Gus."

"But—"

"No buts about it. I got you-all into this, but I'm not gonna let you get killed. Now you go see about Gus. If he's not hurt too bad, try to get him back to the car and take him to the hospital. Then call the jail and get the deputies out here. I don't give a damn what else they're working on. Get 'em out here."

Stoney thought about it for a second. "All right. If you're sure."

"I'm sure. You go on."

Stoney turned to go. "You want the shotgun?"

"You keep it. If I can't stop 'em with this .38, I can't stop 'em at all."

Stoney walked back toward where Gus was lying.

Homer watched him for a second, just to make sure that he was really going and not hanging around to play hero.

How the hell did I get into this? Homer wondered. He'd made it for years by just being a good old boy and treating people right. How had he let himself get caught up in something like this, something dangerous?

He thought about the story of how old Michael Harp had killed most of the Wests on the day they moved into the House for the first time.

It was almost like history was repeating itself, except that this time there was a chance that the Wests might come out of it alive. He wondered where the hell they were.

Maybe some of them were in that scuffle.

He looked again and saw someone running for the woods. It looked like it could be Joshua, but Homer didn't have time to find out. Absalom and Jonah had already made it home, and he was going after them.

This time, he was going to be more careful.

This time, he told himself, they were going to be the ones who got shot.

Sam helped Riley to his feet. She had stopped crying.

It was hard for him to stand because of the pain. He knew that he must have a broken rib, or maybe two. Hell, maybe more. And it, or they, must be about to puncture his lungs.

He couldn't worry about himself, though.

"Where're the kids?" he said.

"Oh, God," Sam said. "They were with me. They were running right beside me."

Riley tried to keep the pain and fear out of his voice. "Where are they now?"

"I don't know," Sam said. She began crying again.

Riley took her face in his hands. "You've got to think," he said. "Where did they go?"

"They … they might not have seen me fall. If they kept on running, they might have gone in the woods. That's … where we were headed."

Riley looked around. "The man that was on top of you—"

"He ran away. He—"

"To the woods?" Riley said.

"Yes, God, yes, he must have."

"I'm going after him," Riley said. He started walking, each step sending a new thrill of pain shooting through him.

"Wait," Sam said. She wiped the tears off her face with the back of her hand.

Riley stopped. "Wait for what?"

"I'm coming with you," Sam said. "After I find the shotgun."

Chapter Thirty-Six

D an and Tammie stumbled into the graveyard.

They didn't know what it was, but they knew that it was as far as they could go.

Above them, the tree branches moved in the slight breeze. The leaves rasped against one another.

Dan alone might have been able to go a little farther, but Tammie could not. She was too tired, and Dan had been almost dragging her for several minutes. She could hardly get her breath even when they stopped; they had to stand still while she took in great gasping gulps of air.

They looked around them at the tumbled gravestones flecked with moonlight and wondered where they were.

"I want Mom," Tammie said when she got her breath. "And I need to go to the bathroom."

Dan wasn't worried about the bathroom. He was worried about his mother and father, and he was even more worried about the boy who had been chasing him and Tammie, the one with the knife.

What had happened to him? Had they lost him, or was he still after them?

There was a rustling sound in the woods behind them, and then Matthew and Mary walked into the graveyard.

They were much more used to the outdoors than Dan and Tammie, much more accustomed to running in the fields. They were hardly winded.

Matthew still clutched the knife. Both he and Mary glared at the other two children. Then Matthew smiled. It was a smile that made him look a lot like Jonah and Absalom, a Harp smile.

"What are they gonna do?" Tammie said, looking up at Dan. "Make them stop looking at us like that."

"You leave us alone," Dan said to Matthew. He tried to sound brave, but he was scared and his voice shook.

Matthew laughed. "We're gonna get you, West. You can't get away from us now."

Mary, who still wasn't sure what was going on, echoed him. "Yeah. You can't get away from us now."

"How'd you know our names?" Dan said, his curiosity stronger than his fear. "We don't know you."

Matthew advanced on Dan and Tammie, slashing the air in front of him with the knife.

"You know us," he said. "And we're gonna get you."

"Yeah," Mary said. "We're gonna get you."

Dan backed away, keeping himself between Tammie and the boy with the knife. "Why?" he said. He didn't even know what was going on.

"Because you're a West. And we have to kill you."

Tammie was crying again. She bumped into a headstone and came to a stop. Dan stopped too. He could not back up any more. He could feel Tammie trembling behind him.

"Now I got you, West," Matthew said. He ran forward, swinging the knife.

Homer Gregory reached the shacks and looked around. *Best damn camouflage job I ever saw*, he thought. And it didn't even look like the Harps had done it on purpose.

If you hadn't known the shacks were there, they would have been easy to miss. They were so much a part of the woods by now that it was as if they were growing right out of the ground.

He wondered where the hell Absalom and Jonah were. He couldn't very well go knocking on the door, even if he could find the damn thing, which he probably couldn't, what with all the vines and shit. He didn't want to go peeking in any windows, either. That was a good way to get your fool head shot off.

He tried to be as quiet as he could, but he wasn't much of a woodsman. It wasn't easy for someone as big as he was to move without making at least a little noise, especially when he'd been shot in the thigh, even if it was just an in-and-out wound. He was afraid that Absalom and Jonah would know he was coming.

He was right.

He looked around a corner of the first shack and saw nothing. He went around it slowly.

"Looking for us, Sheriff?" Absalom said from the trees.

Homer turned, but it was too late. The twins were already firing.

Homer went down, falling heavily against the wall of the shack, but not in time to avoid the bullets. He was hit at least twice. One of them was just in his arm, but the other one was somewhere in his chest.

Homer couldn't tell where, but he could tell it was bad.

He'd dropped his gun, too, and though he scratched around with his hand in the sand, he couldn't find it.

He sat there, propped against the wall, looking at the trees.

Absalom and Jonah stepped out, their pistols leveled on Homer. Absalom was holding onto Jonah, and he was laughing. "Well, now, Mr. Sheriff. Nice of you to pay us a visit. Too bad you won't be staying long."

"Shut up and shoot him," Jonah said. "I need a drink."

But Absalom thought of something even funnier to say. "Tell the truth, you'll be staying a damn long time. I bet they ain't never gonna find you, not even by the next election."

"Fuck you," Homer said. It wasn't very original, but it was the best he could do under the circumstances.

He had been about to say, "You'll never get away with it," but he'd decided that was even worse. Besides, they probably *would* get away with it. Fucking Harps. He should've listened to Gus. Hell, he should've done something about them years ago, before Gus ever came to talk to him about the Wests.

He sighed and took a deep breath. It hurt him to breathe.

"We gonna put him in the graveyard or the river?" Absalom said.

"I don't give a shit if we leave him right there," Jonah said. "Either you kill him, or I will. I want a drink right now."

"Shit," Absalom said. "If you feel that way about it, go ahead. *You* shoot the fucker."

"All right," Jonah said. "I will."

He aimed the pistol at the middle of Homer's head and pulled back the hammer.

Matthew slammed into Dan. The knife cut a slice from Dan's arm as Matthew bore him to the ground.

Dan kicked and scratched, but Matthew struggled to a sitting position atop him.

"You leave my brother alone!" Tammie said. She leaned down and grabbed a handful of Matthew's hair and pulled it as hard as she could, pulling his head up so that his red eyes stared into hers.

Matthew swung upward with the knife and sliced open the front of Tammie's gown, cutting a bright red streak that ran right up her belly and chest.

Tammie screamed and jumped back. She looked down in horror at the blood that welled out of the cut. Mary ran over and grabbed her from behind, putting her arm around Tammie's neck and pulling her to the ground. They rolled in the leaves, Tammie screaming and Mary pummeling her with her small fists.

Dan was not much good at fighting. He had not had a lot of practice, but he was desperate. He reached up and grabbed Matthew's knife arm, but Matthew was stronger and wrenched it away. Dan swung his fists, hitting at Matthew's face. He felt the other boy's lip smash against his teeth.

Matthew threw his knife aside and tried to grab Dan's arms. He wanted to pin them to Dan's side. Dan didn't want that to happen, and he windmilled his arms rapidly, trying to hit Matthew's mouth again, or his eyes, or his nose.

It was a good try, but Matthew was on top, and he got control of Dan's arms without sustaining any more damage. He forced them to Dan's sides and trapped them there with his knees.

To the side, Mary had done the same thing to Tammie, though she had Tammie turned face down.

"Get off me! Get off me!" Tammie yelled, kicking her feet futilely against the ground.

Matthew leaned over and reached for the knife. His hand closed on the haft.

He looked down into Dan's staring eyes, eyes that were following each movement of the knife.

"It's going to be just like the pig, now, West," Matthew panted.

He brought the edge of the knife down against Dan's throat.

"Wha-what pig?" Dan managed to say.

"You'll find out," Matthew said, and laughed.

"Which way?" Sam said when they entered the trees. She wished that Riley could go faster, but she knew that he could not.

"I don't know," he said, looking around helplessly. "I don't know."

"That way, then," Sam said, pointing ahead and slightly to the right. There was a limb hanging at an odd angle, as if it had been broken.

"All right," Riley said.

They moved into the woods, and they had not gone far when they heard the sound of Joshua's moans in the distance. They knew that they must be going in the right direction.

They did not know that they were headed for the graveyard, and Joshua did not know that he was leading them there. He was so crazed with pain and with disgust at his failure to rape the woman that he was no longer fully aware of what he was doing or where he was going.

It was as if he was following some instinct that led him not to his shack but deeper into the trees, to the graveyard.

Somewhere buried in his mind there was still the desire to kill the Wests, to rid the world of the ones he had been taught to hate almost from his birth, but he knew that he had lost the means to do it. He did not even know where his shotgun was.

So he crashed through the trees, holding one hand in front of his injured eye as if to protect it from the flailing branches of the trees, damning the Wests for their existence and blaming them for all that had happened to him.

So this is it, Homer thought. *Shot like a damn dog by the fucking Harps.*

It was damned embarrassing, he had to admit it. He'd always thought he'd die in bed, not from any illness but from a heart attack brought on by strenuous fucking.

He almost laughed to think that in a way he had been right.

It wasn't a heart attack, but it had been brought on by fucking, sure enough. Too bad he couldn't have let those bitches walk right on to wherever it was they had been headed and minded his own business. It was all Estelle's fault. If she hadn't thrown him over for the damn body man, it would never have ended like this.

He heard the hammer click back on Jonah's pistol and opened his eyes. Damn if he was gonna die with his eyes closed. Let the bastards know that he was looking at them when they pulled the trigger.

"So long, Sheriff," Jonah said.

There was a loud explosion and Homer sagged to the ground.

CHAPTER THIRTY-SEVEN

Riley wondered what someone who saw him and Sam would make of the sight: Two people walking in the woods, a woman in a tattered gown, a man who looked like he'd just survived a terrible auto crash.

And the woman was carrying a shotgun.

They were both near exhaustion, and both of them were having difficulty walking, Riley because of his injuries and Sam because of the way her feet and legs had been lacerated by stickers and thorns.

It would have been pathetic if it hadn't been so frightening.

There was some kind of a maniac there in the woods with them, and their children were probably in there somewhere, too, lost and afraid. At least Riley hoped they were in there.

The alternatives were even worse.

Riley thought for a minute about the men he had left back at the house. He was pretty sure that they weren't dead, but he didn't really care, as long as they were so disabled that they couldn't come after him. He didn't think the one he'd stabbed was hurt badly, but the one who was shot could be in pretty bad shape.

He had never looked back to see if they were following him, and he'd been unconscious when they fired on the sheriff and the others. He did not even know that the sheriff had come to help him and his family.

Sam was vaguely aware of other shots besides the one she had fired from the shotgun, but she had not thought about their significance. Her mind was otherwise occupied. She was worried about her children.

They both heard the blast from the shacks, however, even though it was muffled by the trees.

They stopped and looked at one another.

"What was that?" Sam said.

"Someone shooting," Riley said.

There were several more shots, then silence.

"Do you think Dan and Tammie … ?" Sam said.

"No, they must have gone this way," Riley said, though he could no longer hear the sounds that Joshua had been making.

"Are you sure?"

"I know they're around here somewhere," Riley said. He could not tell her why he was sure that the children were nearby, but he was. "We've got to keep looking."

"But those shots—"

"They don't have anything to do with us. Let's go." Riley pushed tree branches aside and moved slowly forward.

Sam followed.

Homer found it hard to believe that he was alive.

He found it even harder to believe that Jonah Harp was no longer standing in front of him about to shoot him with a pistol.

Instead, Jonah was slowly folding his knees, the pistol dropping from his limp hand. His chest was practically shot away, nothing left of it except raw flesh and muscle and sinew. There was a hole in him big enough to see the woods through, or at least it looked that big to Homer. He couldn't really see anything through it, however.

Absalom was shooting at someone who was standing just at the corner of the house, flame spitting from the end of his pistol barrel.

A shotgun boomed again, ripping the limb off a tree beside him, and he turned and ran into the woods.

Stoney Thompson knelt down beside Homer. "Good thing I didn't go after any deputies," he said. "They wouldn't've been able to do you much good by the time they got here."

"You're sure as hell right about that," Homer said. "What the hell did you shoot him with?"

"Full choke twelve-gauge," Stoney said.

"I bet it's hell on birds."

"I just use it for duck hunting. They're usually so far away it don't tear 'em up too bad."

"Sure. Where's Gus."

"Right here," Gus said.

"How you feeling, Gus?" Homer said.

"Not so hot," Stoney answered for him. "Probably got a little concussion. At least he could see how many fingers I was holding up. But he's probably better off than you are."

"Yeah," Homer agreed, wondering just how bad he was hurt. "But considering how much worse I might've been if you hadn't come along, I guess I can't complain."

"What're we gonna do about the other one?" Stoney said, referring to Absalom.

"I don't think I can go after him," Homer said. "And I sure ain't gonna tell you to do it."

"Yeah. But somebody's got to. We don't know where Joshua went, either."

"You volunteering?" Homer said.

Stoney thought about it. "I guess I am," he said. "What about you, Gus. Can you go with me?"

Gus didn't want to go. His head was hurting like a bastard. But he'd come this far.

"Yeah," he said. "I can go. You gonna be all right, Homer?"

"Don't know," Homer said. "Not that it makes much difference. You boys be careful, you hear?"

"We will," Stoney said. "You can count on that."

They went into the woods where they had last seen Absalom.

Homer watched them go. When they had disappeared into the trees, he slumped back against the house. He guessed it would be all right to close his eyes now, and so he did.

When Matthew touched Dan's neck with the keen edge of the knife, bright blood sprang out. Matthew knew that the knife would slide right through, just the way it had gone through the pig.

Dan stared up into the boy's crazed Harp eyes, trying not to cry.

Mary, crouched atop Tammie, watched Matthew, her eyes round.

"What're you gonna do, Matthew?" she said, staring at the blood with fascination.

"Do him like the pig," Matthew said. "You know." His head was filled with visions of blood, the way it had spurted onto his hands, into his face, hot and sweet. He had been afraid then; he was not afraid now.

"No!" Mary said. "You can't! He's not a pig; he's a boy!"

Matthew thought about killing the turtle. That had been nothing, not compared to the pig.

And the pig would be nothing compared to the boy.

It was going to be wonderful.

"Better than the pig, then," he said.

Mary jumped off Tammie and ran over to Matthew. "No, Matthew, he's a boy, not a pig!"

Matthew held the knife to Dan's throat and looked at Mary.

"He's a West. I have to kill him. I *want* to kill him."

Tammie was getting up, trying to see what was happening. She saw the boy on top of her brother. She saw the knife.

"Don't you remember the turtle?" Mary said. "How it smelled? We *ate* the pig. What're you gonna do with a boy?"

Matthew was confused now. Mary was right. The boy was different. Did he really want to kill a boy?

"Kill him," Joshua said, stepping out of the trees. His face was covered with blood and sweat. There was blood on his shirt and pants. His hair was matted and wild.

Matthew jumped up, surprised and a little frightened at the terrible sight.

Dan squirmed from under him and got up.

"Stop him!" Joshua said. "Don't let him get away!" He flung himself across the graveyard, leaping over the stones, and grabbed Dan by the pajama collar.

Dan twisted around and kicked him in the shin. Joshua loosened his grip, and Dan broke away.

Matthew jumped on Dan's back, but Tammie ran over to them and began beating on Matthew with her balled fists, screaming and yelling incoherently as she struck at him.

Joshua grabbed her and threw her aside. Her head struck a gravestone and her cries stopped abruptly.

"Tammie!" Dan said.

Joshua got hold of him again. This time, he had a good grip. He turned him to face Matthew.

"Now," Joshua said. "Now you kill him."

The fuckers killed Jonah! Absalom thought as he ran awkwardly through the trees.

He couldn't believe that his brother was dead, but he had seen it happen. There wasn't much doubt about it, not considering the size of the hole in Jonah's chest. Joshua would blame Absalom for letting it happen, naturally, but there hadn't been anything he could do, not a damn thing. He'd tried a couple of shots, but he didn't know if they'd hit anybody. Probably not. But he couldn't stick around and let himself get blown away like Jonah, could he?

He knew they were probably coming after him. He had to get to a place where there was some cover, where he could hide and pull off an ambush.

There was only one place like that anywhere close.

He headed for the graveyard.

Riley could see it all happening through the tree branches; it was almost as if it were in slow motion.

Tammie was lying on the ground, not moving. There was a bright red line of blood running up her stomach and chest.

The crazy man, the one who had been on top of Sam, was standing there holding Dan, his big hands on either side of Dan's head, holding it steady, keeping Dan motionless. There was blood on Dan's neck, running down onto his chest.

A little girl was standing there, watching them.

There was a boy with a knife. He was walking toward Dan, pointing the knife at Dan's throat.

The man was saying, "Kill him."

"No!" Sam said, stepping around Riley, pointing the shotgun at the boy with the knife. "Put down the knife."

"Don't be afraid," Joshua said, somehow not surprised to

see the woman. "She won't shoot. You're too close to her kid. If she shoots you, she'll kill him, too."

"Yeah, don't worry about her," Absalom said, stepping out of the trees behind Sam. "I got plans for her."

He rammed his pistol hard into her back. "Gimme the fucking gun."

Sam turned, trying to hit Absalom with the gun barrel as she did, but he stepped aside and she missed.

Riley was already running toward them, and he collided with Absalom. They both went down, Absalom on bottom.

They landed on a fire ant mound. Thousands, maybe millions, of the tiny creatures thronged out, furiously ready to defend their home. They swarmed over Absalom stinging him in a righteous frenzy as Riley rolled away.

Fire ants can move so quickly that it is nearly incredible. In an instant they were inside Absalom's clothing, on his face, in his hair, in his eyes, in the stab wound that he had received.

Absalom was screaming and bucking up and down, swatting at his body, at his face. Blisters were already appearing on his skin, each one many times bigger than the ant who had caused it.

There were only a few ants on Riley, and he did not even try to brush them off. He watched in horror as Absalom thrashed and kicked.

But he did not try to help him.

Sam had the shotgun leveled on Matthew again. She was not interested in helping Absalom any more than Riley was.

Since there appeared to be a stand-off, Riley knelt down by Tammie to see if she was all right. She was breathing quietly.

"She's going to be all right," Riley said, standing up. He hoped he was right.

Absalom had gotten up, too, and he was dancing a jerky dance. There was some doubt as to whether he could see any longer. The ants had probably destroyed his eyes. And still they swarmed over him, stinging and injecting their poison.

Absalom ran screaming into the trees. He fell when he ran headlong into a hackberry, and then he got up and tried to run again.

There was the boom of a shotgun, and Absalom stopped screaming. He fell face forward to the ground.

"Had to put him out of his misery," Stoney Thompson said, walking up. "Only humane thing to do."

Gus was with him. "What we got here?" Gus said, looking around the graveyard.

Joshua was now more dangerous than ever. When he had entered the graveyard moments before, he had been a madman.

Now, he was a frustrated madman.

One of his eyes was gone, and Matthew hadn't been able to kill the West boy.

They'd killed Absalom right in front of him.

They were going to ruin everything.

It was all the Wests' fault, of course. The fucking Wests had ruined everything again, the way the Wests always did. It was just the way it had always been, the way it had been a hundred years before. It was no wonder that old Michael had warned the family, had instructed them to pass it along through the generations.

Now Joshua had failed just as the others had. He had been the one with the opportunity to wipe out a hundred years of disgrace, the one who could have finally avenged old Michael's death and put an end to the hold the Wests had kept on the Harps for all that time.

Or maybe he hadn't failed. Not yet.

He still had the kid. They couldn't shoot Joshua without hitting the kid, couldn't shoot Matthew, either.

So there was still a chance.

They were all looking at him, and he smiled. It wasn't a smile of failure. Hell, let 'em shoot. Let them kill the kid for him. That would be just as good as anything.

And if they wouldn't do it, Matthew would.

"Kill him," Joshua said again.

CHAPTER THIRTY-EIGHT

Dan felt the old man's calloused hands mashing his ears. No matter how hard he tried to turn his head, he could not do it. But even with the hands over his ears, he could still hear, and what he heard was Joshua's command to Matthew.

For some reason, the fact that the boy was supposed to kill him no longer frightened Dan.

The boy had tried to kill him once already, but he had gotten away. He could still feel the sting of the knife on his neck, but even that did not scare him. They could try to kill him again, but he was not going to let them.

Not without fighting.

If he could not move his head, he could still move his legs, but he knew that he could not do much damage to the man with them. The man was behind him, and he had on boots. Dan was barefoot.

There was a chance, however, that he could do some damage to the boy, who was going to have to come closer if he really intended to kill Dan. He watched Matthew's advance very carefully.

Matthew was looking intently at Dan's throat, fascinated by the thin track of blood.

It was as if everyone in the graveyard was holding his breath. No one dared to shoot for fear of hitting Dan. They were too far away to get to Matthew, who could easily plunge the knife into Dan's body before they reached him.

Even if Riley had dared to move, he knew that he was much too slow because of the beating he had received. His chest ached from the cracked ribs.

Everyone waited to see what Matthew would do. Even Mary did not try to stop him this time. Joshua had spoken, and she knew better than to contradict him.

The only one who had a plan was Dan. He waited until Matthew was quite close and then kicked him hard. In the crotch. Just like he'd seen the guy do it in a movie about Butch Cassidy he'd watched on TV. Dan had never been kicked there, but it had sure seemed to work well for Butch.

It worked for Dan, too.

Matthew screamed a high-pitched scream, threw the knife into the air, and crumbled to the ground, clutching himself and moaning. The knife landed by Dan.

Dan was yelling, too. He had felt his big toe crack when it connected.

Joshua let Dan go and dived for the knife.

He was lucky again. Dan was still in the way long enough for Joshua to get the knife and roll behind a gravestone.

As soon as Dan scrambled away, both Gus and Stoney fired their shotguns. The pellets screamed off the gravestones and sunk into the tree trunks.

Dan jumped on Matthew and began hitting him as hard as he could. He didn't like the idea of being killed, and he was taking out his resentment on Matthew.

Sam put down her shotgun and went to Tammie, while Riley went to pull Dan off Matthew. Sam was thinking that she would never mistrust her daughter's intuition again. Or her own.

Gus and Stoney triggered off shot after shot at Joshua as the maddened old man dashed from gravestone to gravestone. They may have managed to lodge a pellet or two in his feet or calves, but they did not do enough damage to slow him down.

And when they realized what he was up to, it was too late.

He was after the shotgun that Sam had dropped.

He scooped it up, dived behind another stone, came to his feet, and ran into the woods.

"Damn," Stoney said as the trees closed around Joshua. "I'm not going in there after him. He'd pick me off easy."

"We've got to go back to the shacks for Homer," Gus said.

"What if Joshua's waiting in the woods for us?"

It was not a pleasant thought. Stoney shook his head. "Maybe he's long gone. He'd be a fool to stick around here. Not even Homer can ignore all that's happened tonight. If they catch any Harps, they'll put 'em in jail forever."

Gus agreed. They went to see how Dan and Tammie were.

Tammie was beginning to regain consciousness, and Dan was struggling furiously with Riley. He wanted to get back to beating Matthew.

"Calm down," Riley said. "Let's check on your sister. And you're hurting my ribs."

Dan stopped struggling. He'd forgotten about Tammie. He ran over to his sister.

She opened her eyes completely as he bent over her. "Dan?"

"Yeah. It's all right, Tammie. Dad and Mom are here."

Stoney leaned over, thrusting three fingers in Tammie's face. "How many fingers am I holding up?" he said.

"You tried that on me already," Gus said.

"It's supposed to be a good test," Stoney said. "How many, Tammie?"

"Three," Tammie said. "I need to use the bathroom."

"She'll be all right," Stoney said.

"What about that kid Dan kicked?" Gus said. "Seems like he might be the one that needs help."

They looked around, but Matthew and Mary were gone.

The Harp children had taken advantage of everyone's interest in Tammie to get out of the graveyard. Matthew had not been able to move very fast, but he had managed to get up and limp away, with Mary's help.

He and Mary were looking for Joshua, but they could not find him anywhere.

"Why did he run away?" Mary said.

Matthew had difficulty talking. "I ... don't know. We'll find him."

But they didn't.

They went all the way back to the shacks, passing by the body of Jonah at the edge of the trees.

"They killed him," Mary said. "Those men with the guns killed him."

Matthew looked at the body. It was a mess, not nice and clean, the way it would have been if the men had used a knife. It was almost as bad as the turtle. He did not know for sure who the men were, but he hated them.

"Look," Mary said.

She pointed toward the shacks, where Homer was leaning against the side. They looked at him from the trees.

"You think he's dead?" Mary said.

"I don't know," Matthew said. "He *looks* dead. I hope he is."

But they decided not to chance going to the shacks. Obviously Joshua was not there.

"He didn't care about us," Mary said. "He left us there. If those people catch us, they'll put us in jail."

"Maybe they won't," Matthew said.

"They will so. You were going to kill that boy. You were going to cut him up like the pig."

Matthew thought about how it would have been. He did not remember ever having cried, but tears popped into his eyes now.

"I wish I'd done it," he said, hitting his fists against his thighs. "They killed Absalom and Jonah. I wish I'd done it."

Now, however, he would never get the chance. His knife was gone. Joshua had run away and left him and Mary alone. Absalom and Jonah were dead, and he had no idea where Nita and Cherry were.

"What are we gonna do?" Mary said.

"I don't know," Matthew told her.

Stoney took Dan piggy-back and Gus carried Tammie. Riley and Sam took the shotguns.

"The sheriff's back there a way, hurt pretty bad," Stoney said. "We got to get him to a hospital. Wouldn't hurt the rest of you to get checked over, either."

Riley knew that Stoney was right. "Good idea," he said. "I don't know if we can even make it back to the House."

"I'll get Homer's car and drive down to the shacks for you," Stoney said. "You can wait there."

Riley didn't know for sure where any shacks were, but he was willing to wait there as long as there was a chance of getting a ride. His feet were cut, his face was throbbing, and his chest felt as if it might be on fire.

"Let's go," he said.

"You're not goin' anywhere," Joshua said, stepping from the trees. His face was a mask of blood and sweat.

He pumped the shotgun.

"No!" Riley said, raising his own gun and stepping in front of the others to take the first load of buckshot if he had to and give Sam a chance to fire.

Riley did not have a chance, not in the ordinary way of things.

But something extraordinary happened.

Joshua faltered.

It was as if something brushed by him, something unseen by anyone who was there watching, something that probably did not even exist.

He seemed to take a half step back, and his eyes jerked to the side, looking for whatever it was that had touched him.

There was nothing, of course, except maybe a spider web carried by a vagrant breeze.

What else could it have been?

Whatever it was, however, it gave Riley the split second's advantage that he needed.

He pulled the trigger and the shotgun boomed.

Joshua Harp's head came apart, hit straight on by the full choke blast of Stoney's gun. There was a red rain in the graveyard for some distance around Joshua's trunk, which stood there for a minute, still holding the shotgun that Joshua had intended to kill the others with.

Then it fell backward, the trigger finger tensing and firing a shot into the tree tops.

The trunk bounced slightly when it hit. It was lying in an unusual part of the graveyard, in that there were no gravestones there. No one noticed that fact at the time, though, or even chanced to wonder if there might be someone buried there, after all.

It never occurred to them that there would be anyone buried in an unmarked grave, someone the Harps might not have wished anyone to know about, and it certainly never occurred to them to think that the Wests from a hundred years ago might be resting there, though not resting very comfortable until that very moment.

Sam turned away from the gory sight, and so did Dan from his perch on Stoney's back. Riley looked at it with horrified fascination for a moment; then he too turned away.

"Don't worry about it, Riley," Stoney said. "It'll never even come to the grand jury."

"That's not what he's thinking about, idjit," Gus said.

"Yeah," Stoney said. "I guess not."

Homer was glad to see them.

"I wasn't sure how many of you were gonna make it back," he said. "If anybody did. What about the Harps?"

"Let's just say you won't be having to worry about them any more," Stoney said. "How're you doing?"

"Not so damn good. If you'd left me here much longer, I mighta had to walk to the hospital by myself."

Stoney put Dan down. "I'll go get the car," he said.

CHAPTER THIRTY-NINE

The bus station in Houston was on Main Street, near downtown. Not the best place to be arriving late at night, but Nita and Cherry didn't know that. They had never been to Houston before.

They stepped off the air-conditioned bus into the humid Houston night.

"Jesus," Cherry said. "And I thought it was hot back in Springville. I never felt anything like this."

"Let's go inside," Nita said. "Maybe we can get a sandwich or something."

They went inside the terminal and looked around. The place was bathed in a seedy fluorescent glow.

There were not many people around, just those who had gotten off the bus and several others who were waiting to leave, along with a few who were obviously there just to get out of the heat and one or two unsavory characters whose purposes were not so easily determined.

"I got to pee before we get anything," Nita said.

Cherry followed her to the restroom.

A man watched them go. He was thin as a hoe handle and dressed in faded jeans and snakeskin boots, with a western-cut sports jacket and a straw cowboy hat. He was smoking a non-filtered cigarette, and he blew a thin stream of smoke out his nostrils.

When they came back out of the restroom, the man was still watching. He threw his cigarette butt on the floor and mashed it with the toe of his right boot. Then he walked over to Cherry and Nita.

"You two new in town?" he said. He had a raspy smoker's voice.

Cherry gave him a quick once over. "We might be. Who wants to know?"

"Name's Larkin. Most folks call me Lark. What's your names?"

They told him.

"Mighty pretty names. Mighty pretty gals, too. Gals like you could earn a pretty penny in this town if you knew the right folks."

Cherry glanced at Nita to see if she was getting the message. She was. "And you do, I guess. Know the right folks, I mean."

Lark gave a good-old-boy grin and pushed his hat up on his forehead. "I surely do. And I could introduce you, if you wanted me to."

Are we lucky, or what? Cherry thought. "You got a car?" she said.

"Cadillac," Lark said.

"Let's go," Nita said, hooking her arm through Lark's. Cherry took the other arm and the three of them left the bus station.

It turned out that Lark's Cadillac was two years old, but that didn't bother Cherry and Nita. They figured that they'd have their own Caddy in a year or two if they worked hard at what they were best at.

And it would be brand new.

The emergency room was not crowded; it seldom was in a place the size of the county seat.

Homer was seriously wounded and had passed out by the time they got him to town, but the doctor assured everyone that he would be fine.

Gus and Tammie were in even better shape; they had slight concussions, but there was no need for them to stay in the hospital overnight.

Riley had to have his ribs taped. Two were cracked, but there was no danger that they would puncture his lungs as he had thought. He would be sore for a long time, but he would recover easily enough as long as he didn't strain himself. His other contusions and abrasions were minor.

The cut on Dan's throat was not deep; it did not even require stitches. His feet were swollen from the stickers, some of which were difficult to remove, and they hurt worse than his throat.

Sam and Tammie had the same problem with their feet, as did Riley. It was going to be difficult for them to walk for several days, but the damage was minor, considering what might have happened to them.

"I just can't understand it," Riley said to Stoney as they drove back to the House. "What was wrong with those people? Why were they doing those things?"

"It goes back a long way," Stoney said. "The Harps have always had it in for your family. Me and Gus, we tried to warn you."

"I don't remember any warning," Sam said.

Stoney and Gus were embarrassed. "We didn't try hard enough," Stoney said. "Gus, he went to the sheriff, but Homer didn't think there was anything to worry about. We all should've done better."

"Let's get back to why they hate my family," Riley said. "Tell me about that."

"It's hard to explain," Gus said. "You know about Jeremiah West and what happened, I guess."

Riley said that he knew, though he really didn't know much.

"The Harps killed him and his family, all except one boy, right in that house of yours," Gus said. "Nobody knows what happened to the bodies, but they know the Harps did the killing. So our great-granddaddies—Homer's, Stoney's, and mine—they hung one of the Harps for punishment. It all goes back to that."

"I don't see how they could hate us for something that happened that long ago," Riley said.

"It's just the Harps," Stoney told him. "It's the way their minds work."

"I'm just glad it's over," Sam said, and then she thought about the *way* it had ended. She had never dreamed of such violence. "What will be done about the ... bodies?" she asked.

"I expect the county will take care of that," Stoney said. "I talked to the Sheriff's Department, and someone's probably called an undertaker to go after them by now."

"I hope so," Sam said. "And what about those children?"

"They'll turn up," Gus said. "Don't you worry about that. When they get hungry enough, they'll probably show up at my store, asking if they can have an R. C. and a Snickers."

He hoped he was right about that, but Sam didn't question him any further, so he let the subject drop.

The undertaker had indeed been called.

When the hearse arrived at the shacks, the attendants found the body of Jonah without too much trouble. Stoney had told them how to get to the graveyard, and they found the body of Absalom there.

But they did not find Joshua.

"I thought he said there was another guy here, with his fucking head blown off," one of the men said. "You see any guy with his head blown off lying around?"

"Nope," the other man said. "I don't see a damn thing."

They looked around the graveyard, shining their powerful flashlights all over. It did not take them long to find the place where Joshua had died. There was still considerable red residue in evidence.

"What the hell," the first man said. "You think an animal got him?"

"There's not any animals bigger than a wolf in these woods. And he damn sure didn't walk away."

"What're we gonna do, then?"

"We're gonna get the two we can find and haul ass. I'm not going looking for any corpse that can walk around without its head. You can, though, if you want to."

"Fuck that. Let's get the other two. If the sheriff wants the one that's missing, let him come after him."

It was cool in the bedrooms of the House. Everyone had bathed and put on fresh night clothes and gone to bed, though Dan and Tammie had insisted on sleeping in their parents' room even if they had to sleep on the floor. Riley and Sam had agreed. They didn't particularly blame the kids.

It was a long time before anyone got to sleep, but sometime just before dawn everyone wound down and the room was filled with the sound of quiet breathing.

Outside, the moon had gone down. The night was at its darkest, and every vestige of a breeze had vanished. Two small figures crouched at the edge of the woods and stared at the black bulk of the house massed against the night sky.

"What're we gonna do with granddaddy?" Mary said. It had been hard work dragging him into the woods and hiding him, and she still didn't see why Matthew had wanted to do it.

"We're gonna bury him in the graveyard," Matthew said. "That's where he'd want to be."

"What're we gonna bury him with?" Mary said. He was a lot bigger than the dolls they had played with, a lot bigger than the turtle.

"We'll get a shovel at the house," Matthew said. "We can do it."

He seemed to know what he was talking about, so Mary took his word for it. But she had other questions.

"What're we gonna do with ourselves? Can we go back home?"

"Not for a while," Matthew said. "They'll be looking for us."

"Where can we stay, then?"

"We can stay in the woods. It's not cold or anything. We'll be all right."

"But we gotta eat. We don't have anything to eat."

Matthew caressed the handle of the knife. That was the main reason he had gone back to the graveyard, to get the knife. He had thought of taking Joshua's body only after he had retrieved his knife.

"I can get us food," he said. "We can eat turtles if we have to."

"Yuck," Mary said.

"It's better than nothing," Matthew told her.

"Why are we looking at that house?" Mary said. "I'm tired."

Matthew gripped the knife in his right hand. He thought about the blade, about how sharp it was, about how it had felt when he had pressed it to the boy's neck, about how the blood had popped out along its finely honed edge.

"Wests live there," was all he said.

About the Author

B ILL CRIDER, the author of more than fifty published novels and numerous short stories., passed away in 2018 He won the Anthony Award for best first mystery novel in 1987 for *Too Late to Die* and was nominated for the Shamus Award for best first private-eye novel for *Dead on the Island*. He won the Golden Duck award for "best juvenile science fiction novel" for *Mike Gonzo and the UFO Terror*. He and his wife, Judy, won the best short story Anthony in 2002 for their story "Chocolate Moose." His story "Cranked" from *Damn Near Dead* (Busted Flush Press) was nominated for the Edgar Award for best short story.

Curious about other Crossroad Press books?
Stop by our site:
http://store.crossroadpress.com
We offer quality writing
in digital, audio, and print formats.